URBAN AFFAIR

Also by
TONY LINDSAY

Chasin' It
Street Possession

URBAN AFFAIR

Tony Lindsay

www.urbanbooks.net

Urban Affair

Urban Books
74 Andrews Avenue
Wheatley Heights, NY 11798

ISBN 1-893196-27-5

First Printing December 2005
Printed in the United States of America

10 9 8 7 6 5 4 3 2 1

Submit Wholesale Orders to:
Kensington Publishing Corp.
C/O Penguin Group (USA) Inc.
Attention: Order Processing
405 Murray Hill Parkway
East Rutherford, NJ 07073-2316
Phone: 1-800-526-0275
Fax: 1-800-227-9604

To my wife,

Thanks for the support, Heather. Love always.

Acknowledgements

First I would like to acknowledge my publisher Carl Weber for his foresight and strong interest in good urban fiction. Next would have to be the Black bookstore owners who have never turned me down when I requested signings, Books Ink, African American Images, Afrocentric, Black Images, all the Shrines of the Black Madonna, Readers Choice, Cultural Connection, Jokae's,Nubian, Medu, HUB, the Karibu's, Cush City, Basic Black Books and Ligoriuos just to name a few. No acknowledgment list would be complete without the bookclubs who have shown me much love: The Sistah Circle Book, GRITS online, You Go Girl, Go on Girl and Brown Eyed Intellect, these clubs and others have been my support. To the individual readers who have supported me since timbooktu.com and One Dead Preacher; much, much love and I hope to never let you down.

Tony

Chapter One

When she was thirteen years old, she swore she would never eat again. At fourteen, she swore she would never kiss a boy again. She was fifteen when she swore never to socialize with the other black girls at her school, and it was at her sixteenth birthday party when she swore never to speak to her father again. Life had taught her that swearing "to never" was useless, but here she is at twenty-five, swearing to never date another broke-ass brother.

None of the white boys she dated were broke, but financially strapped brothers seem to find their way to her twenty-third floor condominium with regularity. Ninety-eight percent of them said the same thing when they entered: "This is a nice place, and look, you can see the lake," as if she hadn't seen her own view. When these words were uttered, Patrice predicted the relationship would have a lifespan of about two weeks. Her recent broke-ass brother, Raymond, has lasted four weeks, but his time is ending tonight.

The evening had gone well: an uplifting play at the ETA Theater, which she paid for, dinner at The Fire House restaurant, where his credit card was not approved, so she paid again, and back to her place for drinks. He did buy the beer and Margarita mix.

The night had been romantic—albeit costly. Raymond is a gentleman. He opened doors, pulled back chairs and helped her off with her wrap. He met her at the theater with his car washed and grocery store carnations in hand, and he sang Luther Vandross songs to her during the drive home. He reminds her of Luther a lot, when he was heavy. If not for Raymond's light complexion, he and Luther could pass for twins.

Once they get to her place, he massages her shoulders and rubs her feet, but the intimate mood is instantly destroyed for Patrice when he requests that she "give him some head."

They are in her bed, lounging. She is wearing only her Betty Boop sleeping shirt and he is in his jeans and no shirt with shoes and socks off. They are looking out at the lake when he asks, "Why don't you give me some head, baby? I bet them thick lips of yours will feel good on me right about now."

Patrice sits up prone in the bed.

Words have always had such power in her life. The way people have said things to her has caused her to fight and love.

"What did you say, Raymond?"

"A little head, baby, you know? You ain't done that for me since we been together."

At the age of twenty-five, fellatio is not new to her. She has read articles, books and watched videos on the subject. In fact, she feels quite knowledgeable of the practice and considers herself skilled in this particular area of sex; but there is a way to request such pampering, and *give me some head, girl,* isn't it.

He has upset her, so she gets out of her king-sized bed and walks to her floor-length window and takes hold of the thin cord, and pulls back the blinds. Don't people know the power of words? Don't they know that *how* they say things matter? Is she the only person that feels the power of spoken words? Looking out at the lake, she can't distinguish the dark sky from the water.

Patrice was actually planning on displaying her fellatio skills for him this evening. If only he could have been patient and said it differently. Throwing his fat butt out immediately is on her mind until she thinks about the pill she bought from Amy. Last Thursday night, the pill perked him up for almost two hours of lovemaking. He had stayed hard and ready.

Patrice did as Amy advised, ground it up and served the pill in his beer, unbeknownst to him. Raymond was good without the Viagra, but with the little blue pill, he proved exceptional. Last Thursday, night she experienced three, deep-inside-her climaxes, and those weren't everyday events in her life. And since he had already drunk the beer with the pill mixed in it, what good could come from running him immediately out the door?

No, she won't give him some head, but he isn't about to leave without giving her a repeat performance of last Thursday. She turns from the blackness of the window and walks back to the bed, leaving the blinds open.

"I thought you loved me enough to do that for me." He rolls away from the edge of the bed, making room for her. "I did it for you. I showed you I love you."

"Love me?" She pulls her Betty Boop gown over her head, revealing her nakedness.

"Yeah, I love you, and I know you love me. You scream every time we do it. And besides, your actions show me how you feel."

"My actions?" She positions herself in the center of the bed.

"Patrice, why would a woman as successful as you be bothered with a brother like me—a fat brother with nothing? Only love could make a woman like you see me. See the real me. Sometimes a person's body makes them confess what is in their heart." He places his head on her thigh. "When we're doing it and you scream, that's your body telling your mind to catch up."

"Raymond, I don't love you." She strokes the top of his head pulling his dark brown, curly hair straight.

"Yes, you do. You just don't know it yet. And don't worry about giving me some head. I want a taste of you." He spreads her thick thighs.

*****

The sun isn't up, but he is. From Chance's twenty-third floor view, the dark lake looks motionless. Many mornings he has stood before the glass wall of his bedroom, knowing things are not as they seem. The lake moves, and he really isn't the man who he pretends to be.

It wasn't him last night dining at the same restaurant as R. Kelly and Jessie Jackson Jr. No, he is a man that should be eating a meal standing at a counter. A meal that came out of a brown paper bag served with french fries, but he hasn't done that in years.

He and Michael Jordan use the same tailor. The salesman that sold him his BMW sold Kanye West and Twista theirs. He and Herb Kent use the same maid service. He is a success. His lake view condominium tells him that. His bank statement tells him that. His plasma television tells him, and the month-long trip to London told him that. He is doing okay for a kid who was once a ward of the state.

Last night while dining with a woman more beautiful than any he'd ever dated, his thoughts were on eating a polish sausage from the street stand on Ninety-fifth and the Dan Ryan. The particular time he remembered was when he was seventeen years old and he was providing a meal for himself and his girlfriend, Patrice. Neither of them had eaten the day before. He was happy buying that meal. He was not happy buying the beautiful woman sitting across from him a two-hundred-dollar meal which she was picking over.

The dark morning gives way to first light. He tells himself he can't afford to be melancholy. Today a plan comes together. Chance is to meet with the biggest prospective client of his career thus far. He has to be on point, bright and informative.

A cold shower, a hot espresso, a five-stack of blueberry pancakes with maple syrup, a tumbler filled with orange juice along with the pretty smile of Nadine, the waitress who serves him breakfast, should chase away the melancholy.

There was a time when it would have been Patrice's smile that brightened his attitude. She would fill his ears with encouraging, motivating words. Tell him that he could do any thing in the world that he wanted and there was nothing to fear but fear itself.

When he met Patrice, he was thuggin' and knew no fear. Nothing in his thug world scared him, because he was ready to die. Then she came into his world and made him think past a day; made him believe that there was a future for him too, and he didn't have to live from hand to mouth.

He didn't fear anything in his thug world. Fear came when he turned his back on the streets and went into her society. Planning for a future he hadn't cared about was foreign to his thinking. He hustled for the day, got meals for a day, rented a room for a night, sold enough weed to re-cop the next day. No long-term plans until Patrice gave them to him.

Patrice looked at life differently than he did. She *did* things to life. Life *didn't* do things to her. People reacted to what she did. From his perspective, life responded to her. As far as Chance was concerned, life was beating him down. Making it through a day was all he expected during his thuggin' days.

And in his heart, he didn't expect to make it through a day. He took from people who were as poor as he was. He knew it was only a matter of time before someone killed him, and most days he was disappointed that no one did. He hated living poor, and he hated the thieving and drug selling he had to do to survive.

He'd been placed in foster homes where people didn't live poor, didn't live from day to day. He knew of and had lived a better life, but those were foster homes, not his home. Not how he could live on his own. On his own, he lived from day to day.

Early in life he became aware that if he followed the rules and went to school, the state system would take care of him. He had to follow the rules or at least act like he was following them, but he was part of a group of kids who didn't follow the rules. This group of kids only went to school when they were caught and forced to go. They knew how to make money on the streets and how to live outside of the foster care system, and he was part of them.

It wasn't a choice he could remember making. He was always one of them, one of the bad kids; the kids who got punished the most, the kids who could fight, the kids who ran away from every foster home placement, the kids with juvenile police records, the kids who were forced to go to bad boy schools. It was these kids he kept seeing all his life, and these kids and how they lived were his reality, not the cleaner, stable life of some foster homes.

The life that he lived was day to day survival. He knew a better life existed, but it wasn't for him or the kids he knew. They lived a lesser life, made better by a little fast money and getting high. He knew early on that street life was lesser than that of the foster homes. On the streets, he had less food, fewer clean clothes, less television, fewer baths and no school. But on the streets, he was with his friends, kids who talked like him, fought like him, stole like him. He got in where he fit in, and he accepted the life that fit.

6

He could have followed the rules and gone to school, but he didn't, because going to school meant he had to change and do stuff. He would have to change the way he talked and he would have to learn his multiplication tables and how to read better. He read well enough to survive on the street, and adding and subtracting was all that was needed to count money. Going through all that stuff for school didn't seem worth it. How he lived was how it was. Day to day survival was all he knew. Then Patrice came into his life and changed his perspective.

A man provides not only for himself. A man, Patrice told him, takes care of others. A man provides for more than just a day. He helps secure the future for those he loves. Chance had been told love was for marks and suckers, and he believed that until he laid eyes on Patrice.

She did something to his insides the first time he saw her. He got all hot from the inside out, and he found it hard to breathe. When he met her, he was supposed to be jacking her car, but upon seeing her, he helped her get away, turning his back on his boy from childhood. From the start, she pulled him away from the streets.

At this moment, he misses getting her perspective. He misses her big, full breasts, wide hips and soft hair too, but what he misses most is talking to her and being around her. He misses their friendship and her companionship. What he misses the least is her father. Patrice and her father are a package deal, so there will be no Patrice in his life. The warm smile of the waitress with the short hairdo will have to do this morning.

*****

Raymond didn't disappoint her in the bed. However, the difficult part will be getting him out of her place before the alarm clock goes off. She wants him out and informed never to call her back, before the reality of her workday sets in. She has a professional agenda to deal with, and hearing her alarm will summon it. Raymond is not a professional issue.

It would have been easier to kick him out last night, but she passed out after her fourth climax. She hadn't planned on falling asleep on his large, hairless chest, and as pleasant as it is to wake up on a man's chest, Raymond will have to be banished. Friday morning of a working weekend is here. She springs from the bed, taking the cover sheet with her.

"Raymond! Wake up, dude! It's time to hit it!" She is at the foot of the bed, shaking his feet.

"What?" He answers sleepily with his eyes closed.

"You got to go. My husband is coming back today!"

Wiping the sleep from his opened eyes, he says, "Huh, husband?"

It has worked in the past, telling men that she's married.

"Yes, my husband. I'm sorry I didn't tell you, but he wasn't supposed to come back for another three weeks. I thought we would have had more time together. I wanted to tell you in a better way than this, but we don't have the time. He works for the FBI and travels for months, but his assignment got shortened and he's on his way home. You got to move it, man!"

She goes to her bureau and starts pulling out framed pictures of Chance. Over their eight-year relationship, she has pictures from different stages of his life. The ones she is placing on the bedside table and on the dresser are from the last two years. The one she hangs from the wall outside the bathroom was taken the day after he asked her to marry him.

"I saw the picture hook in the wall and wondered where the picture was." Raymond stands from the bed. "I knew this was too good to be real. Every time I open up to a woman, shit happens. "

8

The clincher is her grandmother's wedding ring, which she gets from the jewelry box and slides on her ring finger. This convinces most men.

Seeing her put the ring on adds speed to Raymond's dressing.

"You said he's with the FBI." Raymond points to the picture on the dresser.

"Yes, he's a field agent."

"Ain't you scared of cheating on him, knowing how FBI people find out things?"

"He trusts me and has no reason to suspect or look for anything."

"Damn. I trusted you too, and I thought you loved me."

Patrice sees his eyes watering and bites her lip to keep from laughing. *Who is he trying to fool?* she thinks.

"I'm sorry, Raymond, but you have to leave now."

"So, when will we see each other again?"

"We can't, baby. And Raymond, please, please don't come by or call."

"But . . ."

"He'll be here soon. Raymond. You have to leave now."

"I spent my last money on the drinks. I don't have gas money."

Escorting him out the door, she grabs her purse from the kitchen counter, retrieves a ten-dollar bill and hands it to him.

"If you see my husband on the elevator or in the lobby, please, please don't say anything to him!" She closes the door quietly but securely. She hears Raymond's rapid steps across the stone tiles in the hall. He's gone for good. Of that, she is certain.

*****

URBAN AFFAIR

His hand-sewn, one hundred percent cotton, monogrammed white oxford shirt is starched to perfection. He bought the shirt yesterday and had it starched and pressed at the dry cleaner in his building. Chance frequents the cleaner's because of their next-day shirt service. No matter what time of day he drops a shirt off, it will be ready the next morning. He has developed into a man who appreciates guarantees.

In his business, where image is predominant, a crisp white shirt, a well tailored suit, a clean shaven face, pearly white teeth, persistence and creativity have opened more doors for him than the company name he works for. A lot of salesmen depend on the corporate name to get them in to see a prospect. Not Chance. He depends on his image and determination.

The sales presentation he is currently engaged in took him three months to set up. The first month, Mr. Sidney Sharp, the owner of East Lake Bakeries, wouldn't even take his calls. He would have his secretary tell Chance that they were totally satisfied with their present supplier of butter and butter flavoring.

Chance suspected that the largest bakery in the Midwest had to need more than one supplier of butter and butter flavoring. When he asked the secretary who their suppliers were, she gave him only one name: Better Butter out of Michigan City, Indiana.

Chance rented a Chevy, slid on a pair Levis and one of his college sweatshirts and drove out to Michigan City, Indiana. He played the part of a graduate student from Chicago State University. However, being a graduate from the university with a bachelor's degree in marketing, it wasn't much of a stretch for him. He knew who to talk to and what questions to ask.

He discovered that the relationship between East Lake Bakeries and Better Butter went back over twenty-five years. The only large client Better Butter supplied was East Lake Bakeries. However, they were not a subsidiary of the bakery, which, to Chance, meant the relationship was not etched in stone.

While driving back from Michigan City that afternoon on Interstate 94, Chance noticed a Better Butter truck. He followed the truck all the way into Chicago to the East Lake plant, where he learned that Better Butter delivered every day but Sundays, and was scheduled to arrive at three-thirty in the morning.

That afternoon's shipment was an extra run due to an increase in production. Chance wanted to tip the guard who gave him the information, but it would have been out of character for a student. He thanked him profusely and drove to his high-rise Marine Drive condominium with a big smile on his face.

During the second month, Chance continued to call Mr. Sharp, who continued not to accept or return his calls. This didn't worry Chance, because he was armed with a powerful tool—information. East Lake Bakeries was totally dependent on one supplier—a supplier whose delivery schedule was known by Chance.

The first manipulation of the schedule was the most dangerous. It was a slippery, rainy morning and at 2 a.m., there was little traffic on the dark highway. Chance followed behind the gray Better Butter cargo truck in his black five-series BMW. His goal was to stop the truck from making the delivery.

His plan was to call the police from his cell phone and report that the driver was operating the vehicle hazardously, but after four calls and following behind the truck for over twenty miles in the heavy rain, he began to think the police weren't going to stop the truck. He sped ahead of the truck a couple of miles and pulled off to the shoulder. He retrieved his .9mm from the glove compartment. He hadn't fired the gun in over four years. He'd told Patrice he'd thrown it away once he was released from the county jail, but he couldn't. He'd tried, but the gun had been part of his life for so long that he couldn't part with it. He could only make so many changes for her.

If the police weren't going to stop the truck, he would have to. He wasn't a great shot, but he figured if he fired enough rounds, he could shoot out one or two of the tires, and hopefully the driver would pull to the side of the road without causing an accident. Chance wanted to stop the truck, not kill the driver.

Out in the rain, standing on the passenger side of his BMW, he readied in a marksman stance, supporting the weapon on the roof of the car. He focused on an approaching truck. Seventeen shots should hit something, he thought. Once the truck was upon him, he saw it was a white truck with FEDEX printed on the side. He relaxed the pistol. A Greyhound bus passed him, three other trucks and over twenty cars. No Better Butter truck.

He got back into his BMW, rain-soaked and frustrated. While looking into his rearview mirror, he saw a large group of blue lights flashing. In the center of the flashing blue and white strobes he made out the truck's lights. A satisfied grin showed on his wet face.

The second manipulation was better planned. When the truck exited the interstate in Chicago, Chance staged Operation Damsels in Distress. He hired five strippers to stand around a red mini-van with a flat tire. The women were dressed revealingly enough to stop a blind preacher. When the driver got out of the truck to assist the ladies, Chance immediately climbed in and drove it to the South side of Chicago, where he set it ablaze.

The third manipulation proved more effective than Chance imagined. He'd followed a Better Butter truck to a food stop. The cargo door was closed but not padlocked. Chance quickly got aboard and let loose fifty caged lab mice. His thinking was that when the truck got to East Lake, the shipping and receiving personnel would see the mice and refuse the shipment.

That's not what happened. Somehow, the mice got into the butter. The butter tested contaminated at East Lake, Indiana state health officials began inspecting the Better Butter plant, and Mr. Sharp returned Chance's call.

The office in the East Lake plant is small and muggy. Chance sees drops of sweat rolling down the brow of his prospective client's nose. The armpits of Mr. Sharp's thin cotton-blend shirt are beginning to moisten with perspiration.

Chance seldom sweats. He perspires so little that Patrice, who was worried about the dry condition, had him get his glands checked. The doctor told him that his lack of perspiration was hereditary. Chance doesn't care about heredity. Where he came from isn't important. Where he's going is all that matters, is what he tells himself.

Mr. Sharp scratches at the unseen stubble on his fat jaw. "Mr. Bates, your company has been trying to get us to do business with them for years. Did you know that?" He is a tall, heavy man. The crown of his head is bald, and a section of his lower lip has been removed. Chance suspects lip cancer from cigars.

"Sir, honestly, I did not." Of course he knew. Securing this account would lock him into the number one salesman position for the year. Landing East Lake Bakeries has been the goal of every salesman in the region.

"I have only been with the company a year and only recently assigned to this territory. I am aware, sir, that East Lake is the largest bakery in the Midwest and the quality of your products has kept the company in the lead position. In my mind, Mr. Sharp, the number one bakery should be supplied by the number one butter producer."

"We were, until some disastrous things started happening to Better Butter." He looks hard at Chance when he says disastrous. He picks up an unlit cigar from the small ashtray on his desk, puts it in his mouth and allows it to rest on what is left of his bottom lip.

"How long have you been in sales, Mr. Bates?"

"A little over a year, sir. Since I graduated."

"From college?"

"Yes, sir. I have a degree in marketing from Chicago State University."

"So, you are what, twenty-two, twenty-three?"

"I'm twenty-six." Chance sees no reason to tell Mr. Sharp that he got kicked out of high school as a freshman and got his GED while locked up in the county jail. Nor does he see a need to tell him that he spent his high school-age years living on the streets, selling weed and jacking cars. No, he didn't go to high school for four years then straight to college. It took him five years of night classes at Chicago State University to get a bachelor's, but he got it, thanks to Patrice and her father.

"And for some reason, Mr. Bates, I get the feeling that you are either the top producer or darn close to being number one."

"You flatter me, sir. But it's the product, not I. We produce the largest line of butter and butter flavoring in the country. Our selection and quality cannot be matched."

"Your product is shit!" Mr. Sharp snatches the cigar from his mouth and places it back in the ashtray. "It always has been. Sure, you guys have the largest selection, but it's all weak. The quality, the flavor doesn't last."

"Sir, our customer satisfaction is high. We have brand loyalty."

Mr. Sharp dismisses Chance's recourse with a wave of his hand. "From retail consumers, maybe. People buy what's cheapest. My wife buys your butter all the time, but she has no idea what quality butter is. They use butter to put in something else. We use butter for the potent flavor. Your product breaks down the minute it hits the vat—no flavor left."

"Sir . . ."

"Young man, I know what I'm talking about. I been in this business for thirty years, and there is not a darn thing you can tell me about bakery goods. Now, I am going to order some flavoring from you, quite a bit actually, but the butter you can keep."

His desk phone buzzes. "Hold on a second, Mr. Bates... Okay. Send them in." He puts the phone back in the cradle. "People are going to join us for this meeting. A private detective hired by Better Butter and some other people. You do have a minute more, don't you?"

Mr. Sharp's face becomes expressionless as he looks directly at Chance. It's a poker player's 'no-tell face' that Chance sees across the cluttered desk.

Before Chance can answer, in walk three of the five strippers he hired to play damsels in distress and a short, round man in a very well tailored suit.

Chapter Two

It was called The Hole in the Wall because it was little more than that. The entrance to The Hole was on Madison Street, between Elmo's Refrigerator Repair Service and Stacey's Second Hand Goods. There were no address numbers on the club's door. Either a person knew where it was or they didn't. Stacey's and Elmo's had plate glass fronts to their businesses. The Hole had only the badly hung, worn and frayed thin pine door.

The patrons of The Hole didn't arrive until past three in the morning, after the legitimate nightclubs and bars closed. This particular hole in the wall was an after-hours joint frequented by whores, pimps, tricks and dope dealers. Not the type of place which prompted love, but this was where a young Sharon Bates fell for Dennis "Cherry Picker" Turner, "Cherry" for short.

It was a cold night, and the harsh wind blew up the mini-skirts on Madison Street like a saved and sanctified grandmother checking for intact hymens. Whores were chilled to the bone, and the tricks were few and far between. When fat, knock-kneed Linda walked up on Sharon and suggested calling it a night and going to The Hole to warm up, Sharon didn't hesitate to follow.

Both girls were renegades: whores with no pimps. Linda wanted no pimp; Sharon hadn't met one she felt was fine enough or had enough. Most of the ones she met she feared. That's why she tried to work in close proximity to Linda, who had shot more than one pimp or robber who tried to take from her.

The girls grew up in the same housing project building on Western Avenue, and had been friends since grammar school. Linda hit the stroll first, after she dropped out of high school in her second year. Her father told her to get out or go to school. She got out and went to the place she'd seen women make a fast dollar all her life.

On her own, she got a place in the projects, a phone, a television, a leather-look couch and easy chair. She had a maple bedroom set, a glass coffee table, a polar bear rug and six thousand dollars in the bank, which was quite a nest egg for 1979.

Sharon also dropped out of high school in her second year. She too turned to the stroll and sought her education from the streets instead of the classroom, because of what she viewed as Linda's success and her mother's example. Her mother, who worked full-time as a hotel maid, also worked the stroll from time to time. Of her eight siblings, Sharon took pride in the fact that she was the only one who was helping her mother with money.

She wasn't in a hurry to move away from her family, despite what the voices said. She tried not to talk back to the voices when other people were around, but sometimes she couldn't help herself because they were so persistent.

While walking through the cold, harsh wind to the club, the voices were telling her to pick up a brick and bust Linda upside the head, take her money and her apartment keys and move into her place. She screamed out "No!" The wind forced her words behind her, and Linda never heard the outburst.

Parked in front of The Hole was a four-door gold Buick Electra 225. Even in the bitter wind, the presence of the car caused the girls to pause and admire it.

"California license plates." Linda noticed.

"It's pretty. And look at the gold strip in the tires. It matches the color of the car."

When they walked into The Hole, the place was crowded but not packed. They easily found space at the bar. Neither minor expected to be asked for identification, and they weren't. Eighteen-year-old Linda ordered a shot of rum, and seventeen-year-old Sharon ordered a shot of Martell with a water back. Each girl drank the first drink quickly to knock the chill from her bones. The second, they ordered to sip and talk over.

Sharon didn't notice when Cherry walked up behind them. What she and Linda did notice were his manicured nails, the diamond rings on each finger, the gold watch wrapped around his wrist and the hundred-dollar bill in his hand when he paid for their drinks.

"You hoes look like y'all mighta been working hard out there in that cold. The least a California pimp like me can do is help knock some of the chill out of them tender thighs. I respect hard-workin' hoes. I hope y'all pimp respect how true y'all is to the game." He gathered his change from the bartender and said, "You hoes take care," and walked away.

Sharon lingered in the orange scent that he left. He smelled fresh, like the produce section in a supermarket. Later she would learn that he used orange extract as cologne, and the only thing fresh about him was his lies.

That night, however, when she turned around on her bar stool and saw him sitting at a table with four women she recognized as hoes, three black and one white, she saw that his perm hung down to his shoulders and his skin was both darker and smoother than hers. The voices told her that he was her pimp, and when he smiled at her and she saw three gold teeth, he had to do little more than what he did to get her to leave with him. He beckoned her to the table with his index and middle finger.

She got to ride in the front seat while the other four women were in the back. Cherry didn't make any introductions in the bar or once they got in the car. He directed his conversation at Sharon.

"I'm glad you choose to ride with a winner, instead of staying in that dump with a fat ho. You gonna see, my little young bitch, you made the right choice."

Sharon really didn't make the choice. He was so fine she *had* to leave with him, and plus the voices told her to leave with them just like they were telling her not to comment on him calling her a little young bitch. Part of her wanted to tell him, like Linda would, that his mama was the only bitch she knew.

"First thing we gonna do is get you out of that fake fur jacket. I got a little rabbit jacket at home that should fit that short, slim frame of yours, and then we got to get something done to your hair. Ain't no greasy-headed hoes in my stable. I don't play that Jheri curl shit."

Sharon heard snickers from the women in the back. She didn't know what they were laughing at. Her curl looked good. She'd just got her hair done that morning.

"You don't like my hair?"

"It ain't about what I like, ho, and it sho' in the hell ain't about what you like. It's about what motherfuckin' trade likes. And the level of tricks I'm about to put you up on ain't about that curl shit. You got to get relaxed and shiny. I got a high class clientele: doctors and lawyers and shit. You have hit the big-time, bitch. Now, sit back and shut the fuck up. I'm tired of talking."

She was already sitting back. She turned her head and quickly glanced at the women in the back. All of them had long, straight, shiny hair. She looked back at Cherry. His hair was shiny too, but he had curls. Curls for the girls. Pimpin' curls. She wondered which of the hoes rolled his hair for him before he went to sleep. Well, whoever did it was about to lose her job because Sharon was going to roll his hair up from now on. When she looked out the window, she saw the lake. They were on Lake Shore Drive heading south.

The woman's voice, her fifth grade teacher who died of a heart attack while she was teaching class, told her to ask where they were going.

The man's voice, the mailman who was killed the day after he raped her when she was eleven years old, told her to do as Cherry said and shut up.

The little girl's voice, the girl who had been raped, beaten and then set on fire by the same mailman, said nothing. She was crying like she was when Sharon and Linda found her smoldering in the stairwell of their building.

Sharon did like the mailman told her and said nothing.

They got off the drive by the Museum of Science and Industry. Cherry drove past the museum to a school. He turned around in the school parking lot and parked the Buick by Jackson Park. They all got out of the car and walked to a big building that looked like a hotel.

A doorman opened the door for them. They walked down a carpeted hall with windows for walls, into the foyer of the building. There, the desk attendant buzzed them past two huge wooden doors. When the brass door of the elevator opened, the operator, who had been sitting on a stool, stood and held the door open for them. They rode to the fifteenth floor. She followed them to the apartment numbered 1516. Cherry opened the door and allowed them all to walk in first.

The place was so white Sharon had to blink her eyes. White walls, white carpet, white sofas, white armchairs, glass tables with white legs and a white vase with white silk roses. Sharon noticed they were all taking off their shoes, boots and coats at the door. She did the same. The women all went to the glass coffee table in the middle of the room and sat on the carpet around it. Cherry walked into a room to the left and quickly came out with a triangle mirror and a razor blade. He placed the mirror, the blade and five little white packages with blue horses on them on the table.

Sharon sat on the couch and watched as the white girl opened the packages and dumped the powered contents into a pile on the mirror. One of the black girls took the razor and began chopping the pile. The voice of the little burned girl told Sharon to hack up some mucus and spit on the pile, to wipe the pile off the mirror onto the carpet and hike up her red mini-skirt and pee on it.

Sharon sat still. She knew it was cocaine and she knew cocaine was expensive. She did snicker, however, when the little burned girl told her to pee on the pile, because she imagined the women's shocked response if she had done it.

"What you laughing at? I know you ain't laughing at us," one of the black women snapped. She had huge titties, and Sharon could see them through the thin lace top she wore. They were big and they weren't sagging. Sharon's breasts didn't sag either, but they were in no way as large as the woman's. Sharon wondered how she managed to keep them up like that. She didn't see a bra or anything else to support them. She didn't answer the woman's question. Instead, she put her attention on Cherry, who hadn't sat at the table. He was standing, looking at her.

"You get high, little one?"

"No."

"Good. Come with me."

She stood and followed him into the room he just left. Sharon, being four feet eleven inches tall, barely came up to Cherry's shoulder blades. He was more than a foot taller than she was, but just as thin. His waist was probably a twenty-six or twenty-eight. Hers was a twenty-six. She liked his blue-and-black striped pants and his baby blue nylon shirt, but it was the bright blue alligator shoes that made the outfit, in her opinion.

The room they entered was a bedroom. He pointed to the big bed and she sat on the corner of it. There was no place else to sit. All that was in the room was the big bed. Sharon doubted that anything else could fit in the room. The spread that covered the bed had the same leopard pattern as the wallpaper, and the white carpet of the living room ran through this room as well.

When Sharon left The Hole, Linda asked is she was sure she wanted to leave with him. When Sharon told her yes, Linda told her to be careful because not much was known about Cherry, the pimp from California. Then she secretly passed her a straight razor, which Sharon took without any hesitation. In her skirt pocket, her small thumb was stroking the ivory casing of the razor as Cherry sat next to her on the leopard bed.

"So, where are you staying now?"

"I stay with my family; my mother, brothers and sisters."

"Your mama work the strip, don't she?"

"How you know that?"

"I know you, girl. What you think, I'll just bring any ho up to my place? I didn't just pop up at that dump. I been watching and asking about you for a while. Shit, you part of the reason I was at that place. My hoes hardly ever work Madison Street. I take hoes off of Madison and then put them up on class trade."

"I see those hoes on the strip all the time."

He poked her hard in the neck with his index finger. "Bitch, don't you ever contradict me." He wasn't yelling. His tone remained calm and smooth. "Ain't nobody there all the time. Yeah, they work the strip when my telephone clientele is down. You ain't seen them out there this week, have you?"

"No." She was rubbing the spot on her neck where he poked her.

"Like I was saying . . . I have been watching you for a while and you need direction. You going about this thing ass backwards." He put his arm around her shoulders and hugged her tight. The hug felt good to her. The voice of the little burned girl told her to lean on him, and she did.

"You a fresh little thing, and you out there selling your goods with the tired, old, fat hoes and getting paid what they get paid. Shit, you a young, tender thing. You supposed to get top dollar. But it ain't your fault, my baby ho. You just didn't know any better. It ain't never to be a day when you make less than five hundred dollars." He lightly stroked her cheek as he spoke.

The little burned girl told her to kiss him. She didn't.

"You got the number one commodity in this game: youth. And you're throwing it away for ten and fifteen dollars a pop. Your pussy's worth way more than that, and I'm the California pimp that's going to get you what you're worth. Are you hearing me, ho?"

"I ain't never had a pimp."

"I know, baby ho, and I know how hard it's been out there for you." He held her tighter and kissed her on the forehead. For the first time that night, she felt warm.

"You didn't see my hoes working out there in all that cold weather, did you? That's because we don't work to survive. We work to live well, and when you living well, you ain't out there selling your little pussy for ten dollars in zero-degree weather. No, my baby ho, that's ass backwards, and Cherry don't do shit ass backwards. Working to survive is for marks and lames. Smart people work to live well." His hand glided down her cheek, her neck and to her white turtleneck sweater. His finger circled her nipple.

23

"Right now, my baby ho, you working to survive. Probably giving your mama money and hardly able to buy yourself a little something. What's going to happen when the police catch up with you? Who is going to come and get you? Your mama, can she afford your bail? I bet you don't have two hundred dollars saved. Direction, my baby ho, you need direction and management. You chose the right pimp." He slid his hand under her sweater and cupped her breast.

He smelled so fresh, his touch was so gentle, his lips were so soft, and she was getting so wet.

"Call your mama and tell her you are going to be with me. I don't want her to put a missing persons report out on you." He kissed her lips gently. "You part of my family now."

"My mama don't have a phone."

"Both of y'all hoeing and no phone. Damn. All right, we will go see her later on." He stood from the bed.

The voice of the old woman schoolteacher told her to pull him back onto the bed.

The mailman told her to pull out the straight razor and slash him across the face.

The little burned girl told her to hug him again.

"Go in the bathroom right through that door and freshen up. It's time for me to see what you know how to do and what you got to learn."

The only voice she always heard while she was having sex was the little burned girl crying. She heard the little burned girl while Cherry was inside of her, but she wasn't crying. She was singing a happy, made-up song about Cherry and love. *Cherry loves us, yes he does, yes he does. He going to keep us safe and happy, safe and happy. Cherry loves us, yes he does, yes he does.*

Sharon had had big men inside her before, but never had she felt one touching her far inside places like Cherry touched them. He rubbed her insides. Her period was five days away, and what she knew about the rhythm method told her this was not the time to let a man climax inside her, but Cherry felt so good in there, she never wanted him to pull out. He was all up inside her, pushing against something that felt like it was going to burst open. He was twisting around so that all she could do was twist with him, until that thing he was hitting burst open, and all she could do was scream, "Cherry!"

Chapter Three

The man in the framed photos no longer exists in Patrice's life, even though he lives in the condominium next door. For years, it was he and she against the world. They were about to announce their engagement publicly when her father did something Chance wouldn't do for the years she'd known him: Look into his past and find out where he was born and who his biological parents were.

Had she known that finding out about his past would help end their engagement and friendship, she would have pleaded with her father not to do it. But what's supposed to happen, happens, and now she and Chance pass each other silently, as they do this morning in the hall of the building they live in. Patrice summons the elevators at the first bank. Chance walks to the end of the hall and calls upon those not facing in her direction.

Once she is on the carpeted elevator and flips open her Palm Pilot, Chance leaves her mind. She is scheduled for a 7:30 a.m. meeting with the mayor and his wife. The mayor's office wants to reach out to the large Black churches on the south and west sides of the city. Her firm is one of four public relations firms from which they are accepting presentations.

She was told by her father that she has the contract and should relax, but she can't relax. Her father is not a well loved man among church leaders. She will have to put her best foot forward in case some leaders express concern when they hear her last name.

TONY LINDSAY

She called the mayor's office on Monday morning and arranged to have the early meeting catered at her expense. The breakfast will include salmon, ham, hand rolled sausages, fresh baked rolls and bagels, farm fresh eggs and produce. Patrice is in the mood for grits, gravy and biscuits, but neither will be served. The centerpiece of the table will hold a card which will read: MAHOGANY PUBLIC RELATIONS WELCOMES YOU.

*****

Chance is sitting in Mr. Sharp's hot, stuffy little office, which isn't designed to hold six people. It is tight space, made for a working foreman who spends time out in the shop, not in an office.

There is a small PC on Mr. Sharp's cluttered desk and the walls are lined with gray metal file cabinets. When Chance first walked in the office, he wondered why the owner of the largest bakery in the Midwest didn't have corporate offices, but after meeting the gruff, overweight, cheaply dressed Mr. Sharp, he suspects Mr. Sharp is a hands-on type of guy who doesn't care about the image he projects.

There is not enough space in the tight room for the strippers or the detective Mr. Sharp calls into the room to sit. Chance stands and offers his seat to the stripper closest to him. She rolls her eyes and refuses the seat. The detective takes it.

"Ladies," the detective begins, "is this the man that hired you to distract the truck driver?"

Chance takes one look at the three platinum blondes and it's obvious to him that their loyalties lie with whomever is currently throwing money in their direction. The three look at Chance and answer "yes" in unison.

"You may all leave. The limo driver will take you back to the club. Send in the two guys waiting outside."

The first guy to walk through the door Chance recognizes as the gate guard who gave him the schedule information. He feels a heavy beating behind his temples, but he fights the impulse to rub them. He's trying hard to keep a calm, steady look on his face.

The detective asks, "Is this the guy who questioned you about the delivery schedules?"

"Yes," the guard answers without even looking at Chance.

At this point, Chance knows he's caught. He is wondering if any of this is incriminating enough to get him any prison time. No one actually saw him do anything, as far as he knows.

The next guy to walk into the office is just as short and round as the detective. He is dressed in a khaki uniform. "Mr. Bates," the detective addresses Chance, "this is my younger brother Frederick. He drives the route between Better Butter and East Lake. He is the only driver on the route, so everything you did affected him directly. They fired him after tens years of service. He's mute, has a young wife and three babies. You had fucked up his life until I got involved.

"In the beginning, I couldn't believe a person would do all of this to make a sale, until I found out what you had to gain in making the sale. And after I found out about your background, I was no longer surprised. You are a thug in a suit, a hoodlum with a degree."

The round man slaps a folder on Mr. Sharp's small desk. "Here is the background information you requested. You will be billed for this. Everything else goes in trade for getting my brother his job back. If it wasn't for Mr. Sharp," he says to Chance, "I would have the police outside waiting for you. You're a criminal—plain and simple."

The round detective, his brother, and the guard leave the small office. Chance's first impulse is to leave behind them.

Rocking back in his office chair, Mr. Sharp says, "Well, Mr. Bates, you don't look at all surprised, or more importantly, remorseful. If I didn't know better by the look on your face, I would think you are ready to finish your presentation as if nothing was said."

It sounds like a good idea to Chance. What do they really have? Why not go on as if nothing has happened? He takes the seat left open by the detective.

"Exactly as I was saying, Mr. Sharp. The best bakery should be supplied with the best butter and butter flavoring. I understand the doubts you have concerning our butter. With that in mind, I would like to offer you a sample shipment at no charge. Earlier, you said you would be ordering flavoring. We sell that by the barrel only. I can have at least five of them to you this afternoon and more in the morning. Does this fit into your plans?"

"Oh . . . you are a little shit, aren't you?" Mr. Sharp says, again scratching at his face.

Chance, weighing 143 pounds and standing five feet six inches, doesn't like being refereed to as a little anything. He adjusts his forest green, tailor-made light wool suit jacket and looks Mr. Sharp square on.

"Sir, did you agree to see me to do business or discuss sales techniques? If it's sales techniques . . . as you can see, my methods aren't textbook sound, but they did get me in to see you . . . and I have very little else to say in regards to them."

"Is that right? Mr. Sharp puts the unlit cigar back in his mouth. "Mr. Bates, I lied to you earlier when I said I'd be ordering flavoring from you. I got you here to see you squirm once the detective hit you with his facts. You didn't squirm, and I hoped you wouldn't. You see, a squirming type of fellow wouldn't be ideal for the position you'll be taking."

"Excuse me?"

"You got a new job, son. You're heading up the sales department for Better Butter. I bought the company yesterday."

"Congratulations, sir. I'm sure the company will do well under your direction, but I am perfectly happy with my present position."

What is really going on here? is Chance's thought. He surveys the small office again. His glance stops on the door. Are the police behind it?

"I didn't ask if you were happy with your present position. Pay attention, son."

Chance's eyes are back on Mr. Sharp.

"I got you by the short hairs. I can send you to jail if I decide to. In my opinion, that warrants your serious consideration. Now, listen to what I'm telling you." Mr. Sharp pauses, takes a deep breath and wipes the sweat from his forehead and nose. He puts the cigar back in the small ashtray.

"Son, in this situation, I have the power, and you are going to do what I say, or you're going to jail. The detective only gave you a peep at the cards I'm holding. If you call me on them by refusing to do what I tell you to do, I'll have you arrested and then you'll get to see all the cards I'm holding."

Neither man speaks as seconds tick loudly off the white wall-mounted clock above Mr. Sharp. He smiles. "Understand me, son?"

Chance is having a hard time believing that Mr. Sharp is trying to force him to take a job. If he really has evidence incriminating enough to send him to jail, why would he want him to work for him unless there was more to the bakery than baked goods? He decides to act interested to get more information, and move things along.

"Did you say head the sales team?"

"Yeah, you're running it. Keep the old staff, hire new, it's all up to you. But I want things in place and operating in a week. You're going to be selling the Chicagoland market. I have offices west of Lincoln Park that are available. I hope that area is not too yuppie for you. Me, myself, I can't stand it up there."

"No, I don't think the area will be a problem."

"Good. The offices were rehabbed last year to be my corporate headquarters, but as you can see, I am imbedded here. It's hard to move an old dog. My daughter and her marketing people use some of the area for work they do for East Lake. The rest of the space is all yours.

"My offer is this: a hundred-fifty K the first year, with a bonus, depending on quotas I'll establish after the first quarter."

Chance is relieved to hear that the mandatory position comes with a salary, a better one than what he's making now. A great deal better. If this is on the up and up, things are about to improve substantially in his life.

"Ten percent override on the team I put together."

"No. Five percent until after your first quarter."

"Done."

"You start tomorrow. My secretary has drawn up a letter of resignation for your company, explaining why you have to leave now. I think you will approve. You will update me daily. Maxine, my secretary, also has a cell phone for you. Welcome aboard, Mr. Bates. Oh, and, Chance, this is something I tell my salesmen: Sell or burn in hell. My secretary has everything you need. Good day."

*****

Patrice, who is dressed and ready for the presentation with the mayor, has to stand still inside the revolving door of her condominium building. Paramedics are lifting her date, Raymond, into the back of the ambulance. She walks backwards, staying inside the revolving door.

Derrick, one of the building's maintenance men, has walked from outside into the lobby. "They say he had a heart attack. A young fella, too. Lucky thing he had his nitrogen pills with him."

"Nitrogen pills?"

"Yeah. The young man has a heart condition."

"Did he say who he was visiting?"

"No, he wouldn't say. I asked him twice before the paramedics came. I don't think he has family in the building."

"Probably not." Even though the ambulance is making its way down the driveway, Patrice doesn't want to take the chance of Raymond calling out to her. "Derrick, I think I will drive to work today. Has the underground garage door been fixed?"

"Yes, ma'am. We fixed it last week."

On the elevator going down to the garage, Patrice remembers Amy telling her to make sure the men she gave the Viagra to weren't on nitrates, but she never thought a man as young Raymond would need nitrates. After all, he is only twenty years old.

Patrice looks at her reflection in the bronze mirrors of the elevator. She could still pass for a twenty-year-old, with her cream-colored complexion and long, jet-black hair. Her mother warns that her weight may age her if she doesn't work on it soon. Well, being heavy didn't stop Oprah, so it certainly isn't going to stop her.

*****

Having just left the Better Butter offices and Mr. Sharp, Chance is sitting parked behind the wheel of his five-series BMW. He is flooded with emotions, so much so that he can't start the car. His hands are trembling too much to hold the key steady. He thought for sure he was on his way to prison or at least jail. He drops the keys in the passenger seat and lets his seat all the way back. He lies back and breathes. The car is hot and stuffy. He opens his door for air and reaches for the key to start the car. He cuts the air conditioner on max and closes his door.

He has never earned a salary as high as $150,000. Nor has he ever been forced to take a job. He signed the employment papers Maxine, Mr. Sharp's secretary, handed him without reading a word. She told him full benefits start from the date of employment, which means his pension is vested as well. He could only halfway listen to her, because he was expecting the police to walk through door at any second.

He began to think that his being hired was a delay tactic for the police. Once he walked out onto the East Lake Bakery lot, he expected to be arrested. He wasn't.

Lying back in the BMW, the late July sun encompasses his dark face through the sunroof. This situation is an opportunity, he tells himself, and Chance Bates rises to opportunity. He always has. His mind drifts back to when he first learned to rise, when he first learned that if he didn't stand up for himself, he wouldn't stand at all.

Five boys out of the 200 that lived at the foster care child center were picked to spend two weeks out of the summer on a farm. He was one of the five. When the population was asked for volunteers to go to the farm, only twenty boys out of the 200 responded.

Two weeks on a country farm didn't appeal to the majority of the urban sons, but Chance, who had just finished reading *Sounder,* wanted to see a farm. Besides, the summer and school being out led to more fights at the center. And although he could and did fight, he was getting tired of it. The farm would be a much-needed break from the center.

The twenty boys who responded were all summoned one at a time the next morning to the director's office. Each boy's academic record was reviewed, and each was asked why they wanted to go the farm. Chance's school record at the time consisted of C's, D's and F's. When he was told that they were going to pick the students with the best grades, he protested.

"Did a person have to have good grades to be a sharecropper?" he asked. "In the book *Sounder* none of those people had good grades. I want to go on a farm and see how black people in the country live."

His protest got him selected.

It wasn't black people that owned the farm the five boys visited. Matter of fact, the only thing black on the Indiana farm were the cows. This surprised Chance because he thought cows were brown-and-white, and he would have bet anyone anything that pigs were pink and friendly. The mean, gray pigs scared him, along with the always angry, ground-pecking chickens and the big, white rats the farmer called possums.

Chance had seen flies in the city, but he'd never seen any that were as big as bees and that bit. Mary, one of the friendly workers who worked nights at the center, had a favorite saying: "Sleep tight, and don't let the bed bug bites." With Mary keeping their area of the center as clean as she did, Chance didn't think there were such things as bed bugs until his first night on the farm.

The boys weren't allowed to sleep in the main house of the farm. They were housed in a smaller building with migrant workers. They were told to go to sleep at seven that first night. But the boys, being away from the center and the social workers who enforced the rules, stayed up and chatted and played until the wee hours of the morning. The boys laughed at the migrant workers who did go to sleep at seven and slept in their clothes.

The boys were expecting to get up in the morning and go horseback riding or maybe swimming in some creek, which is how the center director said their days would be. They were awakened the next morning at dawn, not by the farmer, but by tick bites. The boys woke up from their bare bunks screaming, crying and trying to pick off ticks.

It was the migrant workers' turn to laugh, but they did show the boys to the showers. The farmer covered them in a tick-killing shampoo and suggested that they too sleep in their clothes. At this point, Chance was ready to return to the center, but the others boys held back complaints and hoped that what the farm director told them about was ahead. It wasn't.

It became obvious to the boys that they were at the farm to work. After an entire day of picking tomatoes, swatting away biting flies, finger and leg cramps, pricked fingers, snakes, dragonflies and the hot sun of the field, the urban sons were ready to leave. That night, no one had to tell them to go to sleep at seven. They went straight to sleep as soon as they lay on the bare bunks.

In the morning, after picking off the blood-sucking bed bugs, the boys elected ten-year-old Chance to go to the farmer and tell him that they were ready to go back to the center. Since the boys hadn't reported to the field for work, the farmer was on his way to the bunkhouse for them. The boys and he met right in front of the large, foul-smelling pigpen.

"We want to go home," Chance said.

"Naw, the bus ain't coming for y'all for another week and some days," the farmer answered. "Get on out in the field now."

"Man, we ain't going back out there. We came here to have fun on a farm."

"You little darkies gonna do what I tell ya." The aged, humped-back farmer was taking off his raggedy leather belt as he spoke. "Now, walk on up yonder there and get to work befo' I put this leather on your behinds."

Without a word being said, the boys moved in around Chance. They became one. Chance said, "You need to be puttin' dat belt on yo' fat-ass mama's ass, you honky motherfucka."

They knew when to fight and how to fight. While the farmer thought about what to do or say next, the boys were in motion. They were on him before he could blink. They had him down and in the dirt. The farmer was trying to crawl away, but the only opening they allowed led to the pigpen. He took it.

The bus that was a week and some days away came within three hours, and the boys were on their way back to the city.

There is a tap on Chance's car door window. Startled, he turns and sees the slender, coffee-colored face of Maxine. Chance guesses that she's about fifty and probably a heavy smoker because of her raspy voice. He rolls down the window.

"Mr. Bates, you left the resignation letter and your company cell phone. Believe me, young man, you're going to need the phone. Mr. Sharp keeps in touch with his employees." She hands him the phone and the letter with a smile. "Welcome aboard."

"Thank you so much, Maxine." He takes the items. "I look forward to working with you."

She nods her head. "Yes. Me too. Goodbye, and take care, son." She turns around and walks back to the building.

Son.

Hearing Maxine refer to him in this way gives him a comfortable feeling. Life, as far as he is aware, has never allowed him to be a son or even feel like one. He'd planned on having a son with Patrice, hoping the boy would get her size and skin color. Life is easier for bigger men: fewer fights, less proving of one's self.

He has a lot to pass on to a son. Every boy needs someone to teach him how to be a man, how to fight, how to survive when the odds are against him, how not to give up. There was no one man in Chance's life that guided him down the path of manhood. He took small bits from different men. And, truth be told, he is still gathering information on what a man is.

Chapter Four

The six months Sharon lived with Cherry and the other women, she never had a menstrual period. She worked almost every day of those six months. Cherry did take her from time to time to see her mother, but he never went upstairs to meet her mother or the rest of her family. He did, however, give Sharon two to three hundred dollars to give her mother whenever she visited.

Sharon never got to "date" the doctors and lawyers Cherry spoke of when they met, but he did hold her to the five-hundred-dollar-a-night quota and took her off of Madison Street. She worked Rush Street, North Clark, North Avenue and Broadway. What she charged ten for on Madison, she sold for fifty on Rush. And she met most of the tricks in bars instead of standing on a corner. Sharon supposed some of them could have been doctors and lawyers.

Two weeks after she joined Cherry's stable, the Buick Electra 225 was traded for a black Mercedes four-door sedan. Cherry was the only black pimp in the city driving a new Benz in 1979, and wherever they went, people gathered around. Five fine women getting out of a beautiful, long black car caught all the tricks' eyes. And if they wanted to get with the pretty women in the fine car, they knew they had to pay top price.

Sharon was only sick in the mornings and for only two weeks. She was able to hide it from everyone in the apartment. For a while, she thought it was just an upset stomach, until the voices told her she was pregnant.

The old lady schoolteacher told her she was going to birth a pimp's son. The mailman told her it was going to be another black bastard. The little burned girl told her she was going to have a love child that would be more special than any child ever born.

Sharon wanted to tell Cherry so many things. She wanted to tell him about the voices, about the baby and how much she loved him, but they hardly ever spent time alone after that first night. She always had to share him with one or two of the other women in the big leopard bed. And it was in that bed that the voices put an end to her life with Cherry.

Her flat stomach had only expanded slightly over the six months. It wasn't her stomach size that got the attention of Janet, the woman with the huge breasts. It was her lack of a period. That Sunday morning, the three of them, Sharon, Janet and Cherry, were in the big leopard bed together.

Janet, who was lying next to Cherry and Sharon, was angry because all Cherry allowed her to do was give him head. Once he was hard, his erection went to Sharon. This pleased Sharon. She was happy to have Cherry inside her. She was lying on her back with her knees pulled up and thighs wide open, letting him go as deep as he desired.

"Why you giving it to her? I got it hard," Janet whined to Cherry.

Cherry huffed. "You got on them raggedy-ass red drawers for a reason, and you know damn well I ain't getting in no mess."

His words caused Sharon to giggle. Cherry wanted her, not the big-bosomed Janet.

"These red drawers never stopped you before." She pulled at Cherry's arm. "This is the time I need you the most, Cherry. You know it stops my cramps. Come on, baby, slide it to me just a couple of strokes." She pulled at him harder.

Cherry shrugged his arm free and said, "You better grab that rubber dick and leave me alone, bitch. I told you last month I wasn't going in no more mess."

"But, Cherry, you fuck her damn near every night. You had to have been in her mess."

"No, I ain't. She ain't never brought no mess to this bed. It's only your nasty ass bringing that shit in here."

"I wasn't nasty before she got here."

Cherry increased the speed of his strokes into Sharon. To Janet he said, "Bitch, I'm into this, so shut the fuck up and rub my back while I'm doing this here."

"No."

"Then get your stankin' ass out the bed and send in my white ho."

"Cherry, don't you wonder why this bitch ain't never bleeding? The ho work every day."

"Hell naw, I don't wonder about no shit like that. What I wonder is how come you cain't do it. Now, I'm not going to tell you to shut the fuck up again."

"I bet she's pregnant, Cherry."

"Bitch, what the fuck is you talkin' about?"

"She's pregnant, Cherry. She has to be. She ain't had a period since she's been here. Your young girl ain't got sense enough not to get knocked up. That's what the fuck I'm talking about. Doing all that bragging on that young, tiny bitch, and she's about to drop a load on your ass."

Cherry stopped stroking. He looked down at Sharon and asked, "Is you?"

The little burned girl's voice told her to tell him yes. She told her to scream yes in his face and hug him tight and get him back to stroking.

Sharon heard the mailman laughing. He was telling her the shit was about to hit the fan.

The old lady schoolteacher told her not to answer, to just wrap her legs around his waist and get back to humping.

"I'm talkin' to you, ho. Is you pregnant?"

"Yes," she whispered, reaching up to his shoulders. She pulled him down to her. "Yes, I am. Yes, we are."

"*We?* Ho, is you crazy?"

"I told you, Cherry. She's stupid. You been putting that dumb ho ahead of us, and look what she did now. She's pregnant."

It was more a reflex than thought. With Cherry still atop her, Sharon balled up her dainty fist and extended her arm hard and banged into Janet's face. She got in three good blows before Janet rolled out of her reach.

"Bitch, I'll kill your ass!" Janet screamed, jumped out of the bed and ran out of the room.

Cherry rolled off of her, leaving her empty. He was standing—hard and erect—on the side of the bed. The little burned girl told her he still wanted her and she should reach for him.

Sharon grabbed a hold of Cherry's hardness and said, "It's our baby, Cherry. You gave it to me."

Cherry moaned from her touch and was about to climb back in the bed when Janet returned to the room wielding a butcher knife. Cherry and Sharon moved to avoid the strikes. The knife ended up stuck in the mattress. Cherry slapped Janet to the floor, and all three of the voices told Sharon to get the knife. She got it and held it behind her back.

Cherry kneeled down to Janet and began to beat her. "Bitch, you come up in my room with a motherfuckin' butcher knife tryin' to kill us." He slapped and punched her repeatedly.

"Get her, Cherry. Get her good!" Sharon cheered.

"You shut up, ho, with your pregnant ass. I'ma beat that baby out of your ass as soon as I finish beating this bitch's ass."

Hell naw, he ain't. This is our baby, the little burned girl yelled to Sharon. *Kill his ass. He ain't doing shit to this baby.*

I told you to kill him a long time ago, the mailman said.

Get him now before he gets you and the baby. Now! the old lady schoolteacher commanded.

It was Sharon's turn to wield the knife. She stabbed arms, legs, titties, necks, butts, faces, hands, knees, elbows and dick. When she left the leopard bedroom, only her limbs were moving.

When she walked out into the apartment with bloody butcher knife in hand, the other women stood motionless in the living room.

"He said he was going to beat my baby out of me. No. Ain't nobody hurting my baby. I'ma stab anybody that tries to hurt my baby!"

"Put the knife down," the white girl said.

"Why?"

"Because we can't help you with it in your hand."

"The only help I need is a coat." That she took from the chair by the door. "Shoes." That she ordered the white girl to kick from her feet to her. "And some money." That she grabbed from the cocktail table.

"That's the money for the coke man," one of the black women protested. Sharon pointed the bloody knife and the protest stopped.

Go stab them, the mailman said to her.

No, leave, the old lady schoolteacher directed.

Leave and go over Linda's, the little burned girl told her.

She left, leaving the apartment door open. No one followed her.

Chapter Five

After seeing Raymond being put in the ambulance in her driveway, Patrice chooses to drive to the breakfast presentation with the mayor. Driving is the right decision because slicing through the early morning traffic gives her a needed edge. She feels powerful behind the wheel of the big Bentley. She doesn't pass one car that is equal to hers in value. This attitude of superiority is what she needed before meeting with the mayor and his people.

Being behind the wheel of the Bentley reminds her of where she comes from and who she is. She has always been a rich girl from rich people. No need to be nervous in the mayor's presence. Her daddy is richer than he is and more powerful, let him tell it. "The mayor is an elected official, baby. He has to answer to a constituency. I answer to no man."

She is Malcolm Trent's daughter. Being nervous is foolish . . . but . . . the preachers will be there, and being a Trent may prove to be a problem.

When she pulls up into the driveway of the Swiss Hotel, a young, black parking attendant comes to her door. He looks cute in his red jacket, white shirt and tight black pants, she thinks.

"All day, ma'am?" he asks. He has black curly hair, ham-hock-colored skin and speaks with a French accent.

"No, just for the morning." She smiles and walks through the glass doors of the Swiss Hotel's lobby.

If her mother has taught her anything, she has taught her how to dress. "A girl, particularly a hefty girl, should always be feminine, dear."

Although she is dressed in a navy blue tailored business suit, it is a suit with a skirt, her large, collared blouse is a soft pink made of chiffon, and around her neck is a strand of the whitest pearls she ever received: a gift from Chance. Her attaché case and her shoes are made by Prada, her gold non-prescription eyeglasses are by Gucci, and when she checks the time, it is a Rolex face that she sees: 7:30 a.m.

Her competition, the other public relation firm owners, will have arrived by now. She wants to enter the room after them, giving them a chance to note that Mahogany provided the breakfast. She confirms the conference room with the desk clerk. A young, small, blond lady who Patrice is certain can't weigh ninety-five pounds bloated.

Skinny women perplex her. Why would one starve oneself for the trivial pay-off of admiration? Patrice would rather eat. She smiles at her own thought and strolls across the lobby to the elevator.

As she hoped, the other firm owners are in attendance. She spots them before she enters the well-lit conference room. They are sitting next to the mayor's table on the far side of the room. The mayor and his guest are sitting in front of the stage. On the stage is a podium and microphone.

The room is filled with people sitting at round, white linen-covered tables, eating and socializing. It looks more like two in the afternoon than seven-thirty in the morning. Overhead, Patrice notices eight crystal chandeliers lighting up the room. The area is buzzing and Patrice loves it. Standing in the entryway, she counts five rows of four tables. There is enough space between tables and rows for her to walk and mingle without toppling over chairs.

In the middle of the room is the plentiful breakfast buffet. It looks better than Patrice expected, trimmed in huge, green leaves, melons, bananas, coconuts, and papayas. The aroma of the breakfast fills the room. In the center of the buffet is a large, dark brown card with gold letters reading: MAHOGANY PUBLIC RELATIONS WELCOMES YOU. The card is larger and more prominent than she imagined. Thing are going well.

When she enters the square conference room, she gives smiles and waves to everyone, but her attention goes to the preachers who have had problems with her father in the past.

Bishop Latham and his guest are at the table closest to the door. The stout, graying bishop is standing, talking to one of the mayor's assistants. His suit is like one Chance would wear: a gray, single-breasted pinstripe. She pauses, allowing the mayor's assistant to leave. She approaches the bishop before he can sit. She greets him with a handshake followed by a quick hug.

"How have you been, Bishop Latham? I saw your telecast last Thursday. Your choir can truly bring the spirit." It's obvious to Patrice that he doesn't recognize her, but he accepts the compliment with good cheer.

"Bless you, child. That's a kind thing to say. I am proud of the choir. My son directs it. My wife used to have it, but she turned it over to the boy after she got started with our married couple's ministry. You have to come by for service one Sunday. We have a sunrise and mid-day. I'm sure one of them can fit into your busy schedule."

He now knows who she is. Her father's construction company was building the bishop's church when the union workers went on strike. Instead of dealing with the union, her father's attorney found a loophole in the contract, which allowed him to pull out of the deal and keep the money. The bishop's church didn't get constructed until five years later. Her father brags that he made enough money on the deal to pay for her college education.

She tuned into the bishop's telecast last Thursday because Raymond said his sister sang in the choir and he wanted to watch it before they got busy. During the telecast, her time was spent pulling Raymond's attention away from the television. Not being raised in a church, and accepting her father's belief at a young age that there is no God, she had no idea what a good choir sounded like. She had heard Raymond say that the bishop's choir could "bring the spirit."

"Perhaps the mid-day service would be possible one Sunday, sir."

"I hope to see you soon, baby. And be sure to extend the invitation to your father." The Bishop gives her a wink and a hug goodbye.

Patrice continues to smile, says goodbye to all at the table and heads over to Pastor Angston's group. Approaching, she notices Pastor Angston's eyes are on the slight cleavage she's showing. He's definitely going to get a hug.

The embrace she initiates after the handshake is tighter and longer than she intended, and after he releases her, Pastor Angston keeps his hand on the small of her back. The tall, slender preacher smells like Chance. He must wear the same cologne. Black by Kenneth Cole is Chance's fragrance. Pastor Angston's pink suit is only a shade or two darker than Patrice's pink chiffon blouse.

"Girl, I haven't seen you in my church since your cousin got married there three years ago." That was the only time Patrice had set foot in his church. "You know the Lord's doors are always open to you."

"Why, thank you so much, Pastor Angston. I heard you folks are breaking ground right next door."

Her father owned the lot next door to Pastor Angston's church and had charged him twice the market value for the land. The uninformed Pastor Angston didn't complain once. After the deal was done, her father made a mockery of Pastor Angston in one of his lectures, saying, "Anyone that spends other people's hard-earned money foolishly and uninformed should not be a leader." Patrice doubts that Pastor Angston or any of his flock went to her father's lectures, but she's going to be friendly just in case.

"Yes, yes, the Lord has been good." He raises his voice a notch or two to let the tables close to him hear the announcement. "We are building a new building!" He pulls Patrice in for another embrace. "You don't have to wait until it's finished to come visit us now."

"No, I won't wait until then, Pastor Angston. I'll try to get there before that."

"I'm going to hold you to that." He releases her and pats her at the small of her back so close to her butt that she jumps a little.

Patrice notices that all of Pastor Angston's guests are women. She's heard he has a deaconess board as opposed to a deacon board. She smiles and nods to the women as she makes it to the next preacher's table.

The next table is that of the Reverend Doctor Talbert. He is the man who speaks out the loudest against her father's book and his wealth-building lectures.

"Dr. Talbert, how are you doing?" He too is a stout man, but not graying. His thinning, wavy hair is holding its red color. He is a man in his late fifties, Patrice guesses. His red hair is a stark contrast to his navy blue double-breasted suit.

When he looks up, Patrice sees surprise and suspicion in his green eyes. He immediately looks behind her. She suspects he's looking for her father.

He stands and extends his hand. "How are you, young lady? Is your father coming?" His eyes are stern.

Patrice smiles and says, "No, this event is sponsored by Mahogany Public Relations. My father has nothing to do with this."

"Young lady, your father has something to with everything that happens in the black community. Don't you know that?"

Of course she knows that it is her father who enabled her to provide the bountiful breakfast at cost.

Still smiling, Patrice says, "Not everything, Dr. Talbert, although he is a very busy man."

"Yes," he says dryly. "A very busy man, and please send him my regards." No hug is exchanged. Dr. Talbert sits and Patrice leaves, making it to the mayor's table. Well, Dr. Talbert will be a vote against her if it comes to that. No time to dwell on the negative, she tells herself. She has a service to sell, and the plan is to wow the people buying the service. Dr. Talbert can be dealt with later. Now is the time to wow the money. When she approaches the mayor's table, the mayor, his wife and his chief assistant greet her with big smiles.

"Ms. Trent, everything is wonderful. I had no idea this many church leaders would attend. I hoped, but I had no idea, and this breakfast is scrumptious. I can't remember the last time my husband and I sat down for breakfast together. Thank you."

The mayor's brunette wife, who is dressed in a two-piece yellow suit with a white blouse styled the same as Patrice's pink one, is giving her credit for getting the churches out. She had nothing to do with that, but when one sees the centerpiece, it does look like her event.

"I had little to do with the church leaders coming out," she says to all at the table.

"Modesty is a good quality," the short, burly, cheap brown suit-wearing mayor says with a quick grin. "We thank you for your efforts." Turning to his overweight assistant he says, "Charles, isn't it time we start?"

"Yes, your honor, it is."

Patrice makes her way to the table with the other public relations firm owners. She greets them with cheerful hellos. Murmurs and grunts are returned. Patrice planned on the breakfast impressing them and intimidating them a little. She didn't think it would stop them from working the room. If they choose to feed their faces instead of working the room, that is an added advantage for her. They should be up meeting and greeting. *Player haters,* she thinks and sits.

*****

Resigning from the company where he'd worked for the past year was something Chance had never thought of. Financially, the company had been good to him. After Patrice's father fired him, none of the people he'd done business with in the past would even consider his résumé. He was forced to leave the real estate/construction industry altogether. Not sure of what to do or where to go, and not wanting to return to the streets, he opened the Sunday *Chicago Tribune.*

The butter company had run a full-page ad recruiting only salesmen. He sent in his résumé, which had no sales experience, but a week later, he was granted an interview. The next week, he was selling butter, a profession outside of Mr. Trent's influence.

Working for the butter company allowed him to be his own man, after being Mr. Trent's boy. The freedom of a sales position fit into his past hustler's lifestyle. Working for Mr. Trent, he had put most of his street knowledge behind him, because Mr. Trent was training him to be an assistant, and as Mr. Trent was fond of saying, "All my assistant needs to know is what I tell him. Don't think—do." The sales job, however, required him to think and stand on his own.

He had a boss, but not a boss he saw every day. He only went into the office for weekly sales meetings to get samples and make appointments. No politics, no ass kissing, no fetching coffee. He barely knew the names of the administration, the secretaries, or the other salesman, and he liked it like that. The further away people were, the less chance of them looking closely at him and discovering that he wasn't qualified for the job.

The first problem he had to deal with was learning how to dress corporate. Working for Mr. Trent, he dressed a lot like him: blazers, button-down shirts and khakis. The dress was suited more for a man in academia than business. Chance solved the problem by imitating the dress and style of television news anchors: clean shaven faces and expensive suits.

Although he had no boss physically looking over his shoulder, the pressure of making quota kept Chance working hard. After the first sales meeting where he witnessed how a salesman below quota was treated by all in attendance, Chance made up his mind right then to never be in that situation.

The salesman was a recent college graduate who had been given a territory his father retired from. This was Chance's first time observing white people treating each other harshly. The young college graduate was supposed to have made twenty sales calls that week. He'd made seven.

Chance was shocked to find out that two weeks prior, the kid's father had done the route with him and introduced him to the principals of the accounts, and he was further shocked to find out that each salesman had been introduced to the principals on their routes. Chance had not been introduced to anyone on his route. He was given a route book, a map, a video to watch on products, ten cases of samples, a pat on the back and a company gas card. He made all his sales calls the first week, however, and sold fifty-five cases over quota before he knew what quota was.

When the college kid reported that he had seen only seven accounts his first week on his own, all the tableside conversation during the meeting stopped. The room became silent. The eyes in the room went to the kid then the director.

The weekly meeting was held in the company's boardroom. Thirteen studded high-back leather chairs surrounded a long, dark granite table trimmed in leather. The company employed twelve salesmen in the region and a sales director. It became obvious to Chance that the sales director wanted no friends. All he wanted was productive salesmen.

The director always took the head of the table. The sales manager took the foot. The kid was sitting to the right of the sales manager at the far end, away from the director. The director would ask each salesman to verbally report how many sales calls were made the week prior, and of this number, which were new business. Everyone was expected to meet with established accounts. The question was asked to monitor new business calls.

So, when the college kid said, "I got around to seven of my established accounts," he said it with such enthusiasm that the director asked, "You mean seven new accounts?"

"No," the kid said. "The seven people I spent time with were old accounts. I hung out at their plants, got to know some of the production people, and I even went drinking with some of the drivers. It was cool."

"Cool? Did you get any additional business, an increase in orders?" the director queried.

"Nope, I actually found some surplus at Mr. Sullivan's plant. He's been ordering way more than he needed. He was pleased about that."

A full plastic water bottle sat to the right of the director. He slung it from a sitting position. Chance noticed the spiral on it was perfect when it blazed past him. The capped end caught the kid dead in the forehead, right above his left eye.

The director stood up out of his high-back chair with finger pointing. "Get your stupid ass out of here! This is a place for salesmen! The customer services sluts are around the corner. Get the fuck out!"

There was no hesitating. Everyone in the room except Chance broke out in laughter, and it wasn't nervous laughter. They were laughing from their guts at the college kid. The red spot the water bottle left no longer stood out on the kid's forehead. His whole head was red. He jumped up from the table and fled.

No, Chance would never be below quota. After his first six months, his sales secured him the number one position among the salesmen. He won the trips, got the bonuses and the plaques. He did notice, however, that he was not invited to the country club for a round of golf and drinks as other top producers were, and the invitation to travel to Vegas with the company owners and top producers was not extended to him, the stated reason being that he didn't play golf. He made the money, but he hadn't made the team.

Mr. Sharp's offer to head a team appeals to Chance, once the fear around the offer settles. Parked in the butter company's lot, Chance looks through the trunk of his BMW. He really has nothing to return to the company. He used all this week's samples, and he no longer uses a route book. He reaches around to his wallet and retrieves the gas card. The gas card, the letter of resignation and his last check is all the business he has with them.

Chapter Six

Sharon decided to turn a trick with the cabdriver
that wouldn't keep his eyes on the road. She didn't do it
for the money. She did it to quiet the voices inside her
head. They were arguing too much, and she knew sex
would silence two of them. The voices had been
continuous from Cherry's apartment to the cabstand.

The little burned girl wanted her to go back and see if
Cherry was okay.

The mailman wanted her to get on a Greyhound bus
to anywhere and leave the city in case Cherry was okay.

The old lady schoolteacher wanted her to go to a
hospital and get herself and the baby checked out.

The buck-eyed cabdriver didn't seem to care that her
nude body was splattered with blood. Once he realized
she was naked under the trench coat, he could barely
keep the cab on the street. His eyes kept darting up to
the rearview mirror. Despite the bickering voices in her
head, she managed to tell the cabby that looking was
free, but what he really wanted cost fifty dollars plus the
cab fare to where she was going.

He drove two blocks away from Cherry's building and
parked alongside the public park and climbed into the
back seat with her. It didn't matter to him that it was 11
a.m. on a sunny Sunday morning. All he saw was
Sharon Bate's young, tight, bare body under a trench
coat and in four-inch spike heels.

Once the cabdriver's organ was inside her, she only
heard the little burned girl whimpering. The quiet in her

55

head calmed her. The only outside sound she heard was the cabdriver's heavy panting. She took a deep breath and exhaled.

Being with Cherry was over. No more riding in the Benz and going to fancy places. No more orange scent. She wanted to think of what else she would be missing, but the cabdriver's panting distracted her. His groans and pants annoyed her, and she suddenly didn't want to hear them.

It wasn't a voice telling her to ease the butcher knife out of the trench coat pocket. She thought of it all on her own. She wanted to do it, to stick it into his back while he was humping into her, panting like a dog and stopping her from thinking about Cherry.

She wondered if he would keep humping after she stuck the butcher knife in his back. With her small, childlike hands wrapped around the thick handle of the blade, she pressed the point of the knife down hard into his back. He kept humping like he didn't feel a thing. She wrapped both hands tighter around the handle. Looking over his shoulder, she could only see the handle and a small portion of the wide blade. He humped two more times after she pushed the blade into him the first time, but he didn't hump, pant or groan after the second, third and fourth time.

She emptied his pockets of over two hundred dollars and drove the cab with him lying dead on the back seat. She drove to an alley three blocks away from Linda's apartment.

While walking the trash-littered blocks to Linda's place, six cars pulled over to her, but once she told them fifty dollars, they kept driving. She was back on Madison Street. It was lucky for them, she thought, that they didn't want to spend the fifty dollars, because she liked how it felt to put a butcher knife inside a man while he was putting something inside of her.

When she got to Linda's project apartment, she collapsed on the leather-look sofa. The voices wouldn't ease up inside her head. They were asking her questions and giving her commands. She cried to stop from responding.

She felt Linda watching her. When she looked up, she saw Linda gasp at the dried blood that was splattered across her nude body. Sharon watched her eyes go to the bloody butcher knife she held tight in her fist. She saw the uneasiness in Linda's eyes. Instead of sitting on the couch next to her, Linda sat in the easy chair, putting the glass coffee table between them.

"It was Cherry, wasn't it? What did he do to you?"

Sharon heard the question, but she didn't like the look on Linda's face. Linda never looked at her like that.

The mailman didn't like the look either. He said she was probably going to call the police. He told Sharon to go over there and stab her.

The old lady schoolteacher said she looked afraid, and justifiably so.

The little burned girl said stab her, so the apartment would be all theirs.

Sharon didn't want Linda to be afraid of her. She put the butcher knife on the coffee table and sat up.

"Cherry found out I was pregnant."

"You're pregnant?"

"And he . . . he . . . he . . . wanted to beat my baby out of me. That's what he said he was going to do."

"Did he hit you in the stomach?"

"No. He didn't hit me at all. He was beating the shit out of Janet and I snuck up on him and her. I got both of them. Ain't nobody going to hurt my baby. Me and my baby going to be together."

"Are you sure you're not hurt, Sharon? Is any of that your blood? We should go to the hospital."

"Naw, I ain't hurt. I don't need to go to the hospital, but I do need your help, though. I need to stay here. Can I live with you until my baby comes? I can work 'cause I ain't showing. The mens still want me, and I can take you to the places where Cherry took me—places where they pay fifty dollars for a date. I can make some good money before my baby gets here. I'll be making money for my baby." She rubbed the small raise in her belly. "It's going to be a boy, and he's going to be the best pimp in Chicago. We can both teach him things, Linda. You and me, we can show him how to be smooth instead of mean. We can make him a finesse pimp."

"How you know it's a boy?"

"I know because it's already in my mind to give him my money. I got a pimp growing inside of me."

No! The old lady schoolteacher protested. *This child will be more than a degenerate.*

Just another street nigga, the mailman said.

He's going to be a singer, the burned girl sang.

Sharon jumped up from the sofa, screaming, "No! All of y'all shut up. My baby is going to be a pimp, the best pimp that will walk these city streets. Now, all y'all shut up."

Linda sat stiff in the easy chair. "What's wrong with you, girl? Did Cherry have you on some stuff? I think we better go to the hospital."

Sharon dropped back down to the sofa and realized Linda had heard her talking to the voices. Only her mother and her brother and sisters knew she heard voices. It was a secret that they kept in their family, like her fourteen-year-old brother peeing in the bed.

"Cherry didn't give me no stuff. I'm okay . . . it's just sometimes . . . I hear voices." Sharon folded her feet under herself and started rocking back and forth, while sitting on the couch. "They try to tell me things to do and say. And sometimes they just talk. Right now they saying my baby ain't gon' be no pimp. They wrong. They be wrong sometimes."

"Voices?" Linda sat up on the edge of her chair with interest. "They ever give you the policy numbers? You know that's how Maggie hit and got herself on up out of here. Yeap. She said the voices gave her the numbers straight. Nasty ho won ten thousand dollars and didn't look back once. Left her furniture and everything."

Sharon watched Linda nodding her head and saw her expression change. Linda was no longer looking at her with fear.

"You know I always thought it was something extra going on with you, but hell, everybody got something. But I'm telling you this, the very next time you hear them voices, you ask them for the policy numbers. You hear me? You ask them right off." Linda raised her big frame out of the easy chair.

"Come on, girl. Let's get you in tub and cleaned up. We going to take a couple of days off then me and you are going to catch us some fifty-dollar tricks, because Lord knows I did that in my life."

"It's good money on the North Side, Linda, and them white men's gonna like you 'cause you got big titties. Womens with big titties make a lot of money. Wait and see," she said as Linda led her to the bathroom.

Chapter Seven

After sitting through all three of her competition's presentations, Patrice wonders what she had worried about. Not one used a Power Point presentation. They all read their proposals and didn't supply the audience with any written marketing material. The focus of the presentations was on what they had done in the past, not what they could do for this campaign. They had come camping but didn't prepare for bear, as her father would say.

Two of Patrice's staff members arrived dressed in business suits with four-color marketing materials in hand. Before she takes the podium, she signals them to pass out the folders. Once everyone has a glossy package in hand, the projection screen is lowered and the lights are dimmed.

Her Power Point presentation reviews what the mayor and his wife want to occur with the churches. The plan is simple: one church, one school. Each church is to adopt a public school and somehow help the students. What was lacking was the how.

Patrice proposes homework centers, monthly fieldtrips and gender-based activity clubs: girls' volleyball leagues, boys' touch football leagues and co-ed bowling. Of course, each church could tailor their own programs. All she offers is a template.

She concludes the presentation with the outreach benefits for the churches and the educational benefits for the children. She purposely makes no reference to the public relations benefits for the mayor's office. She ends the presentation with the money. The grants are already established through the city's Human Service programs and her staff has been trained on how to fill out the appropriate paperwork. All that is required of the church leaders is to fill out the interest form in the package they were given and submit them.

She didn't expect applause, but it is given when the lights are brightened. Patrice notices the big smiles from the mayor and his wife. The fat assistant gives her the thumbs up. She steps graciously down from the podium. She doesn't return to her table with the other firm owners. She takes a seat at the mayor's table. The deal is done and she knows it.

*****

Chance expects to turn in the resignation letter and leave, but he is stalled when the director's secretary informs him that an exit interview is mandatory. He's been sitting in the reception area for over forty-five minutes and is becoming a bit pissed. Just as he makes the decision to leave, the secretary comes and escorts him to the director's office.

On his large desk, made small by his huge office, the director has both a PC and a laptop. He is keying away on the laptop when Chance enters.

"Have a seat, Bates."

Chance had thought one day this office would be his when he believed all that was required to advance were good sales numbers and bringing in new accounts. He'd even mapped out the changes he would have made to the windowless office. All the seaside pictures would be replaced with portraits of his ancestors who had risen to greatness: Malcolm X, Thurgood Marshall, Harold Washington and Harriet Tubman. He had planned to bring in a couple of his African masks and his Mandigo warrior's shield. A mud cloth rug would have covered his desk, but those thoughts stopped when he wasn't invited to Vegas. He hadn't thought of quitting, and he accepted the fact that he wasn't going to rise beyond being the number one salesman. The good money he earned made it an easy fact to accept.

Last year with bonuses, Chance had earned over $110,000. He personally knew of no black man his age making that much money—illegally or legally. If he didn't rise to management, so be it, as long as his bank account kept swelling.

He sits in the office chair before the director, watching him key away on the laptop, and says nothing, but he can't help but notice the strong scent of Musk deodorant. Not since his time in lock-up has he smelled the fragrance. There, the inmates got it free, so many wore it, but more didn't. It wasn't a popular scent among the young black men behind bars. There is no accounting for taste. The director obviously likes the smell.

The director stops typing. "Had to get that done, Bates. You know how I am, once I get started on something. I have to finish it. You're leaving us, huh? I must say, I didn't see it coming." Although he is speaking to Chance, his eyes are still on the computer screen.

Chance looks into the director's narrow face. He is a thin man who, Chance found out last month, runs marathons and cycles for miles. He looks to be in his early forties. He seldom says more to Chance than, "Good morning, good numbers," and "See you next week." How could he have seen anything he had coming? The director doesn't know him.

"At first I thought you were part of that thing going on with old man Sharp. He bought out Better Butter." He looks up from the laptop to Chance with inquisitive gray eyes. He passes his fingers through his thinning blond hair and looks to the seaside picture on the wall to left of Chance.

"That was until I read your letter. But even if he did hire you as a salesman, there would be nothing I could do about it. You didn't sign an exclusivity statement with us barring you from working with a competitor in our industry. I got to be honest with you, Chance. I didn't think you were going to make it with us. That's why I didn't bother with having you sign the thing." He hunches his shoulders and smiles thinly. His eyes return to the laptop screen and then to the resignation letter to the side of the laptop.

"Going to work in the music industry, well, that makes sense for a smart guy like you. Blacks are doing great things in that industry with Puff Daddy and everyone." He hasn't looked at Chance directly for more than three seconds through the whole one-sided conversation until he asks, "If you can squeeze in the time over the next couple of weeks, do you think you could come and introduce your replacement to the principals in your territory?"

He has to be kidding, is Chance's thought. He stands and says, "I'll try my best." He extends his hand for the director to shake and leaves. He makes one stop at the customer service department and leaves a note on the college kid's desk, asking him to give him a call.

****

Eating a big breakfast is all that is on Patrice's mind while she is waiting for her Bentley to be pulled from the garage. Her assistants had gathered all the forms—a hundred percent response. She is floating on air.

The curly haired, ham-hock-colored parking attendant with the French accent walks past her. He goes across the street to the bus stop. Staring at his swagger of a walk and his muscular behind, she thinks, maybe a quickie? Maybe she should take him home and get him to hum her name in French?

No, she's still good in that department from Raymond. She's going to eat.

When she walks into the slightly crowded Pancake House, she's not surprised to see her father sitting alone at a booth. There was a time it would have been him and Chance sitting in the booth. Since he fired Chance, he seldom has breakfast with his assistants.

"Baby girl, come on in here and join your pops for breakfast. It's on me. I heard things went as expected with the mayor." He announces his greeting for all to hear, with emphasis placed on *the mayor*. "People saying you knocked their socks off!"

Patrice can't help but grin at her robust and loud father. He reminds one of a college professor, but sounds off like a ringmaster. He is never meek when he is speaking of her accomplishments. The waitress seats her at his booth and goes to get coffee.

"Hey, Daddy," she chirps before adjusting herself in the booth space. "Yes, things went well. Who told already?"

"Baby girl, I have had at least five calls telling me how professional you were. The first call was from the mayor. 'You should be extremely proud of that young lady, Trent.' Like I need a white politician telling me I should be proud of my own blood. He kept going on about how professional you were. I guess they were expecting you to get up there and speak with broken English and slang. You showed them, baby girl. Did you have any problems from the preachers?" Her father sips his coffee and looks directly into her eyes.

"A hundred percent response, Daddy. No one balked." She smiles at him. Her father is wearing one of the light blue oxford shirts she bought him last father's day. He'd asked her for white shirts, but she decided to get the light blue ones, and he wears them so often that she is certain he likes them.

"I told you. They can talk all that Jesus stuff if they want to, but they dance for dollars too."

"I'm not agreeing with that, Daddy. This is a good program."

"Sure, it's good as long as they get paid for housing the thing, and it doesn't cost them a dime."

She can tell her father is gearing up to speak on the faults of black preachers. She tells him, "Dr. Talbert sent his regards."

He puts the coffee mug on the table. "What did that red-headed fool have to say?"

"Only hello."

"Red snake. You know he tried to buy out my next lecture at the university. Since the tickets are only three dollars, he figured he would shut me down. But the school moved me from the library to the auditorium. He'll buy out a hundred seats, but he can't afford to buy out fifteen hundred. And due to the tickets selling so fast, the university sprang for some radio ads. The red snake actually helped me. And you know I'm going to speak on him during my lecture."

"Daddy, please. Leave that man alone."

Patrice's light complexion comes from both her father and mother. The three of them share the same skin color. Her thick, black hair she gets from her mother, whose mother is Cherokee. Her hardy appetite and big-boned build she gets from her father.

"Man? If I believed in demons, I would say he was one. What I do is inform our people on how to make their money work for them. What he does is try to make our people's money work for him. He's lucky there is no God."

The waitress returns with Patrice's coffee and a menu.

"What did you order, Daddy?"

"Grits, a double order of bacon and four eggs over easy with wheat toast."

"I'll have the same," Patrice says to the waitress whose skirt is so high above her knees, the apron is longer than it. "Daddy, you want to split an order of blueberry pancakes?"

"Yeah, I haven't had those since Cha—" Her father doesn't complete his sentence. He looks out the restaurant window.

"You can say his name, Daddy. Chance." She chuckles at her father's discomfort. "And I haven't had them since he ordered them for me as well."

"I don't have a problem saying the boy's name. Your mother is one that says we shouldn't talk about him. He is still living next door to you, right?"

"You know he is, Daddy. You are still receiving his rent." She adds sugar and cream to her coffee.

"He's not paying rent. He's buying the unit from me, and at a darn good price, too. I still don't understand why you didn't take that unit. You two split up, and you give him the place and then move in the unit right next door. I got a good deal on both of them, but if you had stayed in the one the two of you lived in, I could have had the second one, which was my original plan. I bought those units to sell. I tell your mother you're still seeing Chance."

"Seeing him is about it." She and Chance had ended their engagement fourteen months ago and had barely said three words to each other. She sips her coffee and decides it needs more sugar. "We pass each other in the hall sometimes. He doesn't speak and neither do I." She spoons two more teaspoons into her mug.

"Well, what do you expect from someone with his upbringing? Mother a whore and father a pimp."

"He wasn't raised by his parents, as you are well aware." She gives her father a *and you know this* look, and he looks down into his coffee mug.

"The foster care system didn't do him any better. With him, dear, it was a problem of genetics. His mother is a schizophrenic." He looks up from the coffee. "Your children could have been born with mental illness. That's not the type of thing you let into your bloodline if you can prevent it."

"What about Uncle Chester?"

"Your mother's brother suffers from depression due to his finances. Last month after he got back the dividends from the stock I had him invest in, he was as happy as a lark. That boy's mother had been in an institution. The apple doesn't fall far from the tree, Patrice. You did the right thing ending it with him."

"Perhaps."

Their conversation stops as the waitress places their plates before them. When she leaves, Patrice asks, "His past and parents aside, Daddy, what did you think of Chance?"

Her father takes off his tortoise shell glasses and rubs the corners of his eyes at the bridge of his nose.

"I would have felt comfortable leaving my business in his and your hands. Chance is a smart, ambitious young man. It's unfortunate about his past and his mother, but what is, baby girl, is."

"He worshipped you."

"Of course he did."

*****

Chance has two choices: one, go into the Lincoln Park office and get acquainted with his new surroundings or two, go to the Pancake House and pick up Nadine as he promised. This morning, she flirted with him shamelessly while serving him his blueberry pancakes and orange juice. He enjoyed her flirting greatly.

He initiated the flirtatious behavior five days ago by tipping her with Hershey Kisses. He left a couple of Kisses on top of the ten-dollar tip. The next time she served him, he left a smaller five-dollar tip, but more Hershey Kisses. Yesterday, he left a hundred-dollar tip and no Hershey Kisses.

This morning when he came in, she had a giant-sized Hershey Kiss waiting for him and said, "I figured you must have ran out and I wanted you to know that I got kisses when you need them."

Her firm, pecan-colored thighs and defined calves had held his gaze this morning, and thinking of her slim body and bright smile makes his decision easy. What gives him pause is while pulling into the Pancake House parking lot, he sees Patrice's Bentley and her father's Jaguar.

What makes him proceed . . . is Nadine standing in the doorway with a cheerful and energized greeting. She's up on her tiptoes, waving, and is very close to jumping up and down with excitement. She is dressed in her black-and-white waitress uniform. He pulls up to the entrance of the restaurant and she hops in.

When he drives past the restaurant window, both Patrice and her father look him in the face. He nods his head in their direction. He's not going to let seeing them change his plans. He has a new job where he is the man in charge, not an assistant. He turns his eyes from the Trents to his perky passenger. It's time to celebrate, he tells himself.

"Hey, now. A brother is on time and it's a beautiful day. I like getting off work when it's pretty and sunny outside." She adjusts her seatbelt and rolls the window down, paying no attention to the fact that Chance has the air on.

"Spring is my favorite time of year. It's not too hot and you don't have to be worried about bees and mosquitoes." She bends over to him and kisses him on the cheek. "I told you I have plenty of kisses for you." She lightly strokes his clean shaven chin with her fingertips. "So, how did your big meeting go?"

"Much better than I expected." Experiencing her energy is stirring around his emotions. Usually seeing Patrice and her father at the same time would get him sad then angry, but with Nadine present, he isn't sure what he's feeling.

"So, the celebration is on?" She stretches her arms wide and snaps her fingers. "You said we was going to have a real good time if things went like you wanted them to." She kisses him again on the cheek and lays an arm across the back of his neck.

"What's a real good time for you?" he asks.

"Making you happy so you'll tip me like you did yesterday," she says softly into his ear.

Chance turns his head to face her to see if her expression matches such a bold statement, and it does. Although her thick lips are smiling, her eyes are calculating.

"You like the lake?" he asks.

"Oh yeah, that's why I moved up on the North Side. The beaches are cleaner," she answers.

Nadine is close enough to him where he can smell the after-meal mints the Pancake House offers.

"I wasn't going to the beach. I know this place that has a fabulous lake view. We can stretch out, listen to a little Muddy Waters, drink a little wine and get to know each other."

"Listen to a little who?"

"Some blues. You know, Muddy Waters, BB King, KoKo Taylor, the blues."

Mr. Trent had started Chance listening to blues. The Trents didn't go to church on Sunday mornings. Sunday morning was hobby time for the Trents, and Mr. Trent, a collector of 78s and LPs, would spend the day of rest playing the blues and cataloging his vinyl collection.

Mr. Trent preached that if any man wrote words that feed the human spirit, it was Willie Dixon. And the best deliverers of his soul-feeding lyrics were Muddy Waters and Howlin' Wolf. Chance fell in love with the blues on those Sunday mornings at the Trents.

"What kind of place plays blues and serves wine this time of day? That's some nighttime stuff you talking about."

"I'm talking about my place. I live right around the corner. And who says blues and wine is strictly for the nighttime? I celebrate with Muddy Waters."

"And will taking me to your place and playing the blues make you happy enough to tip me like you did yesterday?"

"I think that's going to be up to you."

She moves away from him and adjusts herself in the bucket seat. Still facing him, she says, "Do you like me, Chance? I mean I know you like how I look. I always feel your eyes all over me, especially when I wear this short skirt, but do you like me for more than something to look at? We've known each other for what, three weeks?

"I was attracted to you from the start. It ain't like I'm going over to your place for a hundred-dollar tip. Men leave big tips all the time and think that the tips entitle them to something more than pleasant service at the Pancake House. You know what I mean? I want you to know that if I didn't like you, I mean really like you, no amount of money would get me over to your place. Understand?"

Chance wants to ask her if he didn't have a hundred dollars would she still come, but he doesn't because he really wants to get with her. Her youthful energy along with her bravado and toned body is exciting him. No sense in starting a debate.

She's alive and electric and Chance needs a shock, something to stop the re-occurring funk that has made his mind a frequent visiting place. One would think the new job would have been enough, but it wasn't. The funk is still trying to come. Nadine was successful this morning in chasing his drab mood away. Maybe more time with her will end it altogether.

As of late, if Chance isn't working, he finds himself sitting on his bed looking out at the lake. He leased a sailboat last week because he figures sailing on the lake will be better than staring at it. He is in no hurry to take sailing lessons because he notices that when people go sailing, they take others with them. Chance has no one he wants to take out on the lake with him.

His friends of the past were left behind after he was released from jail and got serious with Patrice. The thugs of his street days didn't fit into Patrice's plans for him. And what Patrice suggested gradually became what he wanted. His former thug friends don't fit into his plans for himself, so presently he has no friends. Being in Nadine's company has a familiar feeling for him. She's got an "around the way girl" style about her, and it comforts him.

"Slim, if I didn't like you, I would have never tipped you. I hope you don't think I'm the type of man that has to purchase female company."

"No, I couldn't think that. I see the women at the Pancake House checking you out, and I like how you don't let them faze you. Most brothers would get the big head behind all that attention from women. I saw them leaving you their business cards and stuff.

"At first I thought you were a stockbroker or something. They act just as big a fool over them, too, but then the cook told me that you used to work for that Mr. Trent, and made the newspaper a couple of times because of the deals you pulled off."

"Those were Mr. Trent's deals, not mine," he says quickly.

"But those women think they were yours, and most men would take advantage of that. I like how you carry yourself, Chance, and I don't want you to think cheaply of me, because I think highly of you. You know I'm not a whore . . . right?"

He feels her looking at him hard. He turns his attention away from the traffic to her.

"I hope you know that. You see, me and my baby's daddy broke up five months ago and he left me with all the bills. You don't know how much that hundred dollars you left yesterday helped me out."

This time, she kisses him quickly on the lips while he drives. "Thank you." She makes it back to her side of the car and says, "You understand that I like you a lot, but I do need the hundred dollars and that don't make me a whore. You understand?"

"Slim, I been broke before. I know what you're trying to say. Relax about it. Okay?"

"So, you like me?"

"Yeah, slim, I like you."

"Cool, 'cause I like you . . . And by the way, my man has been gone for five long months, and I haven't been with another man, and this springtime air has me wanting some male company in a serious way, so I hope you know how to throw down. You know what I'm saying, Chance?" Her bobbing leg and her white waitress shoe catches his eye.

"Yeah, slim, I know what you're saying."

Last night the model Chance took to dinner made it clear after their meal that she was available to go back to his place, but he wasn't interested. Women like her who make having a BMW and living on the lake requirements for dating, have not been able to chase his funk away.

After dating six of the rich model types, he knows where the elite dine, who does their hair, what wine is hip, which designers are in, which broker should handle his portfolio and which area of the city is best to live, but none of the model types can tell him which rib joint on the North Side had the best sauce, what band is at Buddy Guy's, the name of a good booster who got suits, a bar with a fast pool table, a produce stand that sells fresh mustard and turnip greens, or a good steppers set. And none of them knows people that play Dominoes or Spades.

Patrice, who is just as financially well off as most of the model types, knows all these things. He doesn't know if Nadine knows them, but being in her company is better than being in the company of the model types. And besides, she's chased the melancholy away once already.

Nadine makes him feel that having a BMW and living on the lake is nice, but not mandatory. The only mandatory requirement he feels with her so far is the ability to throw down, and that ability he was born with.

*****

The nerve of him, Patrice thinks, *and with that dark, bald-headed, skinny-ass heifer. He saw us sitting here and to just drive by with not even a wave.* She is fuming mad and is clanking her fork on the plate while she's in thought.

"Baby girl, I got to go. Are you leaving?" her father asks, standing away from the table. No, she isn't leaving, and once he leaves, she's going to order more eggs, more bacon, more grits and another order of pancakes.

"Not yet, Daddy. I'm going to finish my coffee and make a couple of calls."

"Okay, sweetness. Don't sit here too long pining away after that boy." He smiles, pulls a twenty and ten out of his wallet. "This is for the breakfast. Don't forget we have a 3:30 this afternoon with the printer." He bends and kisses her on the cheek.

"I'll be there, Daddy." She watches her father walk out of the front door.

The nerve of Chance, she thinks, to disrespect her like that and in front of her father. What was on his mind? Pussy. That's what is on his mind. Doing it to that illiterate, skinny, bald-headed waitress.

"He told me he didn't like thin women," she says out loud. But then, he told her a lot of things.

It was the afternoon of her sixteenth birthday party, and after her father called her his "chubby princess" in front of over 200 guests, she made the decision to run away. Yes, he had hurt her feelings, but that wasn't why she ran away. She ran because she was tired of being predictable.

She cried in front of the guests, left the party and went home to her room. Her father came home and apologized profusely. Her major birthday present was the senior trip to Spain the next year, but to show that he was genuinely sorry for what he said at the party, he bought her a new Ford Mustang in addition to the trip to Spain.

When she saw the sun gleaming off the car, she forgot that she swore to her mother she would never speak to her father, no matter how much he apologized. She screamed with gleeful excitement, hugged and kissed her father, who looked at her mother and winked.

When Patrice saw the wink, she was instantly aware that her father predicted her forgiveness as he had predicted every move she made her entire life.

She got behind the wheel of the Mustang and didn't smile. She rolled the window down and yelled to her father, "I hate you," and drove off.

She had no destination and no money. All she knew was that she had to go away to someplace where he wouldn't imagine her being and do things he wouldn't predict. She drove from their Country Club Hills home to the West Side of the city, from the west side of Chicago to Evanston, and from Evanston to the south side.

She was stopped at a light on Fifty-first and King Drive when her driver's door was snatched open, a large gun was put to her head, and she was ordered out of the car. She didn't move. She was ordered again, and that time a slap accompanied the order. The passenger door was suddenly opened and a skinny little black boy in a White Sox jersey jumped in the car and told her to hit the gas. The bigger boy holding the gun grabbed hold of her plum-colored birthday dress and tried to yank her from the car. The boy on the passenger side put his foot on the accelerator pedal and pushed down.

The Mustang sprang forward and her birthday dress gave way, leaving the top of her dress with the boy with the gun. The skinny boy drove the car from his side and yelled to her to close her door. She did, and grabbed the steering wheel. The skinny boy took his foot off the pedal because she was mashing down hard on his foot. She drove in a panic, ignoring the skinny boy's directions to slow down. It wasn't until he yelled, "Girl, stop da car. You got away. Please don't kill us," that she slowed.

She didn't stop, but she heard him. And hearing him made her notice the red light that was ahead on Fifty-first and Cottage Grove. She stopped for the light. When the light turned green, she made a right turn then another immediate right into the public park. She pulled behind a parked car and put the Mustang in park. The tears flowed, and she cried like she hadn't cried in years. Not since childhood whippings.

"Damn, you got snot and shit comin' out your nose. Whatcha crying like dat fo'? Whatcha doin' over here, anyway? Y'all Puerto Ricans live way down da other way. Whatcha get lost or somethin'?"

All she could think to say through the sobs was. "I'm not Puerto Rican. I'm black."

"You ain't black. Black girls don't have hair like that. You a Puerto Rican, Mexican or somethin'. Here, wipe ya nose with dis." He dumped a paper bag filled with small manila envelopes. "Snot hangin' all off your damn nose. You too pretty to be lookin' like dat dere."

"What?"

"Wipe ya nose."

He shoved the bag into her hand. She took it and wiped her nose and blew into it.

"If you black, what's ya name?"

"Patrice."

"See, dat ain't no black girl name. Black girls don't be named Patricia."

"What's your name?"

"Chance."

"Black boys aren't named Chance, either."

"Yeah, you right. I know another nigga named Chancellor, but I don't know another Chance. I guess a black girl can be named Patrice. But you ain't black, 'cause ya hair too long and pretty, and ya skin too light. And damn, look at dem big titties."

Patrice looked down and saw that she was sitting in half a dress and her brassiere. Instinctively, her arms covered her chest.

"It's too late to try and hide dem now. I been lookin' all dis time."

A predictable Patrice would have continued to cover herself. This Patrice relaxed her arms and said, "You're right, and besides, you only looking at my brassiere. My bikini shows more than this."

"Ya what?"

"My bikini. My swimsuit."

"Agh, what womens wear on da beach. Yeah, dey be damn near naked out dere. Especially dem white girls." The fuel gauge on the Mustang sounded and the light came on. Chance looked at the dashboard and said, "You 'bout to be out of gas."

"Out of gas! How do you know that?"

"Dat's what dat ding sound was, and see dat little light by your gas gauge? It's on. Ain't dis your car?"

"Yes, but my father just gave it to me."

"Damn! Your daddy gave you a brand new ride?"

"I can't run out of gas, because I have no money!"

"Shit, you kinda fucked up, ain't cha? Call ya daddy. I know if he rich enough to buy you a new ride, he can give you gas money."

"Yes, well . . . I'm not speaking to him anymore. I will never talk to him again."

"You mad at somebody dat bought you a new ride? Damn, dat's evil. Go on and cut da car off while I come up wid a plan. Save da little gas we got."

Patrice liked the sound of "we" coming out of his mouth because she had no plan. Her only choice if she ran out of gas would be to call one of her friends, who would eventually become a link for her father. She couldn't reach into her world at all if she was going to be new and unpredictable. She turned the key back, cutting the car off, and waited to hear Chance's plan.

"We close to da university. If we drive along da parkway, I'm bound to see one of my white boy customers. Dey usually have to come to da park to get my smoke." He held up one of the manila envelopes.

"Dey pay top price too. Yeah, let's cruise along da parkway. I'll get you some gas money."

She was about to start the car and pull off when a young white guy tapped on Chance's window. "Agh, hold up. We ain't got to move." He rolled down the window and the white boy said, "Man, C. I'm glad you're setting up closer. I really didn't feel like hiking all the way to the other side of the park. Smart move. I'll tell the guys to look for you over here."

"Cool. How many you want?"

"Five."

The white boy handed Chance five ten-dollar bills and Chance handed him five of the small manila envelopes.

"So, tell the guys to look for you here?"

"Yeah," Chance answered thoughtfully. "Yeah, dat'll work." He grinned and rolled up the window. "I never thought about movin' closer to dem. Sittin' on dis side of da park, dey will see me befo' any of da other smoke dudes. Damn, you might be good luck, Patrice." He reached over and squeezed one of her filled brassiere cups.

She drew back to slap him, but noticed he was actually looking out the window and not at her. He squeezed her breast as a simple gesture, almost like a pat on the back. Another white boy was approaching the window. He purchased three of the small manila sacks from Chance.

"Agh, shit. You is good luck." Chance reached over and squeezed her breast again. Within thirty seconds, a black and white boy were at the window. Chance had four sacks left in his lap. The two students bought all that remained.

"Whoa. I ain't thank I was gonna sell out dis quick. It's time to re-cop! Lets go put five dollars in your tank den go to da weed man."

"Are we selling drugs?"

"Nope. We sellin' weed."

"Oh, okay."

While they were at the gas station, Chance bought her a T-shirt with the Chicago skyline on it and said, "Ain't no sense in every nigga walkin' down da street gettin' to look at you. Put dis here on." He threw the T-shirt into the car and went to pump the gas.

The weed man lived in the Stateway Gardens Housing Project, and Patrice had never been in the projects a day in her life. She didn't know whether to ask to sit in the car or go with him. Chance made the decision for her. "Come on, you stay wid me and ya gonna be all right. Lock da doors."

After they walked through the metal detector, she stopped at the security desk, expecting to have to say something to the guard. Chance grabbed her hand and pulled her past the desk. On the graffiti-scarred elevator, she couldn't help but say, "Oh my God, it reeks. Don't the maintenance people use disinfectant?"

Chance didn't answer her question but asked his own. "What does *reeks* mean? I heard it before."

"It means it stinks to high heaven."

"Oh yeah. Da elevators smell like piss all da time. I just be happy dey be workin'. Eleven flights is a lot of stairs, and if you think da elevator reeks, you ain't ready fo' da stairs."

The weed man's apartment was nicer than what Patrice expected. Matter of fact, he had exactly the same furniture that her mother had chosen for their den. The black-and-gray-striped cloth furniture matched the concrete half-bricked walls of the apartment better than it did the walnut paneling in their den. Chance told her to have a seat on the couch while he and the weed man took care of a little business.

Patrice noticed that the weed man had a Sony Trinitron, a Kenwood stereo receiver and Bose speakers. She was reaching for the remote to the Sony when out from of one of the two bedrooms came a fuzzy-headed baby in a walker.

The baby had its head tilted back and was sucking hard on an empty plastic bottle, which it held with one hand. When the baby saw Patrice, it squealed with happiness and propelled across the tiled floor toward her with his mouth wide open, showing one bottom tooth. Once the baby got within Patrice's reach, she couldn't stop herself from picking up the smiling bundle of happiness.

The baby was dressed in a diaper and thick booty socks and smelled of fresh baby powder. Patrice guessed by the fuzzy head and broad shoulders that the baby was a boy. He dropped his bottle and began pulling at Patrice's T-shirt, obviously trying to get to her breast.

"Paco!" A woman stepped from the same bedroom the baby rolled out of and at first glance, one could have easily mistaken her for Patrice. The two women looked hard at each other.

"Come to me, Paco."

Patrice put the baby back in the walker and he jetted to the woman in the doorway. She picked him up from the walker and opened her robe. He greedily fed. The woman snorted in Patrice's direction and slammed her bedroom door shut.

When Chance and the weed man came from the other room, Patrice saw where the baby got his broad shoulders. The weed man was big enough to have played professional football, and next to him Chance seemed tiny.

Before they boarded the elevator, Patrice took a deep breath and tried to hold it. She was doing well for a couple of floors, but when the overhead indicator lit up with the number six, she could no longer hold her breath. She had to exhale to inhale.

Chance chuckled and said, "I would say you gonna get used to it, but you won't. Dese elevators always stink."

When the elevator opened on the ground floor, Patrice was standing right in front of the man who had snatched her car door open and put a pistol to her head. He and Chance greeted each other at the mouth of the elevator.

"What's wid you, Magnum?" Chance asked. They met palms and hugged each other chest-to-chest.

"Chillin', C. What's wid you and the square broad?" The man nodded his head in Patrice's direction.

"She wid me."

"Word?"

"Yeah."

"All right. I know my nigga, C, know what he be doin'. Is Big Time upstairs?"

"Yeap."

"Cool."

"Later."

"Later."

As Patrice and Chance exited the elevator, Magnum walked on. Patrice didn't say a word as they walked to the car. She waited until they were inside the car with the doors locked.

"That was the boy that tried to take my car!"

"Yeah, dat's Magnum . . . and Patrice, it wasn't just him gonna take ya car. Me and him was gonna jack you, all right. But uh . . . once I saw ya face . . . I knew I wasn't never gonna take nothin' from you. All I'm gonna do fo' da rest of my life is give to ya fine ass."

He reached over and kissed her thoughts away.

"Miss, here is your other order of bacon and eggs. You did say to go, didn't you?"

Patrice hadn't said to go, but after thinking about her past with Chance, she is no longer hungry. What she feels is lonely. She pays for the breakfast and walks outside to her Bentley. For some reason, the car looks shorter. She steps back and sees it is on four flats.

"Now, how the hell could that happen?"

Chapter Eight

Having a baby wasn't what Sharon thought it would be. When she was younger and cared for her little brothers and sister, her mother or another sibling was there to help. Keeping babies was fun when they were warm, soft and liked being cuddled, but not when they cried. Her mother always knew what to do to get them back to being happy.

When her baby cried, no one was there to help her. The one time Sharon asked her mother for help, she flatly refused, hurting Sharon's feelings. Pride and the voices in her mind wouldn't let her ask again.

Babies cry . . . a lot. And when her baby cried, the voices inside her head would start arguing. Each said it knew what the baby needed, and each was persistent in expressing that he or she alone had the remedy to the baby's malady, filling Sharon's mind with noise and confusion.

For the first two months, she and Chance didn't leave Linda's apartment. The old lady schoolteacher told her that outside air was bad for babies, so Sharon kept Chance covered up on the bed. Linda had put a queen-sized bed, a television and a hotplate in the back bedroom for Sharon and Chance.

Linda was hardly ever at the apartment once Sharon brought Chance home, and when she was there, she slept. The North Side of the city proved very profitable for her, so much so that she was usually up there for two or three weeks at a time. She told Sharon that the North Side, with its fifty-dollar tricks, was the best thing that ever happened to her, and that since Sharon had told her about it, she never had to feel rushed about leaving the apartment. As long as she needed a place to stay, the back bedroom was hers.

Sharon spent the first two weeks after the delivery in the queen-sized bed. Having a baby hurt . . . a lot, and she was in no hurry to move her sore body, despite what the nurse advised. The skinny, gray-haired nurse at the hospital told her to start walking around a day or so after she got home. Sharon stayed in bed. She would sit up to feed and change Chance when he cried, but that was it.

It took her two weeks to get up and turn on the television Linda gave her, and she only did it because lying in bed and looking at the people outside her window had made her sad. The illness, the poverty and the filth of the neighborhood made her cry. Then the old lady schoolteacher told her that sloth led to illness and laziness led to poverty, and if she continued to lie around, the life outside her windows would be hers.

Sharon stopped crying and began to do exercises with two of the weight reduction programs on television. After the exercise programs, the soap operas came on, and at first Sharon didn't pay much attention to them, but after a couple of days, the soap operas quickly became the highlight of her television watching.

The people she saw on the soap operas were much easier to look at than the people she saw outside her window. The people she saw out her window had stoops in their backs, scars on their faces, broken teeth, limps, crippled hands, bad skin, crossed eyes, nappy hair, scabbed sores, discolored lips, body odor, swollen stomachs, fat ankles, puffed-up hands and yellow eyes. The people on the soap operas were clean, had pretty hair, beautiful smiles, trim bodies, big houses, whole families, manicured fingernails, flawless white skin, the best clothes and busy, exciting lives. They didn't stand around for hours like the people outside her window. They went away from their homes and did things. These people she cared about. The people outside her window worried her.

Some looked so feeble and sick that she thought a strong wind would break their backs, and others looked so dangerous and mean that after they passed, she went to the front door and checked the deadbolt. She had seen the people outside her window all her life, but after spending time with Cherry on the north side of the city and after having the baby, everything and everybody in the neighborhood looked worse. The people on the soap operas looked how she thought people should look, and that's who she chose to spend her time with. Her days were spent in front of the television.

The mailman told her to watch the news programs, but she never did. She began to stop listening to him because almost everything he told her to do required her to leave the apartment. The little burned girl and the old lady schoolteacher enjoyed the soap operas with her. The only happenings she cared about in the world were on the soap operas.

From spending such a great deal of time with the good-looking, clean, happy, well dressed, rich people of the soap operas, it became obvious to Sharon that she had more in common with them than the people outside her window. She had ridden in a Mercedes, worn fur coats, drank Cognac out of a snifter, shopped at Marshall Field's, eaten lobster and steak, had facials, manicures and pedicures and had spent time in the company of rich men. She was better than the life that was outside of her window.

The young women on the soap operas lived the life she wanted. Their mothers cared about them. Their fathers bought them presents. Their boyfriends went to college and became doctors, lawyers and mayors. And the soap opera girls only had to have sex with their boyfriends; their boyfriends who became their rich husbands.

Having sex with only one man seemed a lot easier than what she had experienced. She could no longer remember how many men she'd slept with. Before she turned to the stroll it was four, and after being on the stroll, how many no longer seemed important. Only how much mattered, so she stopped counting how many.

The closer she got to being healed, the healthier she felt, the more the mailman told her it was time to go back to work. The doctor had done some minor surgery on her privates because Chance had ripped her a bit. He called it a "husband's knot." He told her that no one would be able to detect that she had a child, at least not through intercourse. It took her a minute to understand that intercourse meant having sex. He told her that her first experience after the surgery might be as painful as the first time she had sex. She doubted that.

The mailman told her she was a virgin again and she could make a lot of money with her doctor-tightened coochie. Sharon liked the idea of being a virgin again, but no longer liked the idea of going back to working the streets. The streets damaged people, and the evidence was outside her window. If she got back her virginity, which the mailman took when she was eleven years old, why give it back to the streets for money?

The young women on the soap operas got rich husbands with their virginity. Why should she settle for fifty dollars? Cherry taught her that youth was valuable. The young women on the soap operas showed her how valuable.

When Sharon wasn't in front of the television, she was in front of a mirror. The most apparent difference between her and the young women on the soap operas was skin color. Other than that, she felt their equal.

TONY LINDSAY

Having a baby cleared the few pimples she had, and her
skin, although dark, was blemish-free, and her teeth
were white as sugar. If not for the dark skin, she felt she
was just as pretty as the white girls.

Her face was just as slender as theirs. Her lips were
as thin and her nose was as narrow and pointed as any
of the young, rich-husband-getting women. Her hair,
which she had not had done since she had Chance, was
worn in five long braids that hung past her shoulders.
Her hair had never grown so long before. Having the
baby grew her hair.

The little bit of a stomach she had after having
Chance was gone, because like the young women on
television, she became a vegetarian and exercised daily.
A constant worry was her breasts possibly sagging after
the milk was gone. They'd become so big with milk that
she was certain they would drop some. To combat the
problem, she kept a supportive bra on 24 hours a day,
except when feeding Chance. The young women on the
soap operas had bouncy, firm breasts. She couldn't let
hers sag if she was to get a rich husband. She had to
look like those women and sound like them.

She began practicing their tone of speech and
substituting the words she would normally use with the
words and phrases they used; "ain't" became "aren't," "a
good day" became "a pleasant day," "yeah" became
"certainly," "feelin' good" became "feeling well."

The mailman told her she was thinking foolish, and
all that a rich man wanted from her was sex. She was
being stupid not to go out on the streets and get some
money with her doctor-tightened coochie, because the
money she had wasn't going to last much longer and she
knew Linda wasn't going to take care of her. The least
she could do, he told her, was to go out and get on
public aid to have something to help her when her
money ran out.

87

Sharon ignored him because she didn't want to leave the television. In front of the television, her plan to marry a rich husband was valid, but if she went into the next room away from the television, the mailman began to make sense. However, as long as she was watching the soap operas, her plan was sound and promising, until Chance cried.

The young, rich-husband-getting women didn't have babies. They had bouncy, perky breasts, long windblown hair and no children. She could get her hair done and keep the bra on, but what was she to do with Chance?

That's why she had to stay in front of the television and couldn't leave. Her plan wasn't whole. If she waited and watched the soap operas closely, she would figure it out. She was pretty enough. She was thin enough. Her hair was long enough. Her speech was clear enough and her coochie was tight enough. She qualified for a rich husband—except for Chance.

She was lying in her bed at the county hospital when the nurse came into her room to get Chance. The gray-haired nurse held Chance in her arms and whispered, "I hope God gives you a chance, my beautiful black child." Sharon had no name for her son until then. The only name she could think of was Thomas, the name of her father who she had never seen. Chance was a much better name.

She no longer wanted him to be a pimp because there were no pimps on the soap operas. She didn't think about what he would become. All she wanted from him was not to cry during the soap operas, but he always did. She tried to pump milk from her breast into a bottle and give it to him, but he wouldn't drink it. He would only feed from her breast, which meant she had to hold him during the soap operas.

The little burned girl liked it when she held Chance in her arms. She would hum and sing lullabies. She continued to tell Sharon that Chance was going to be singer. Sharon only hummed the lullabies to Chance hoping he would fall asleep.

It was important for the room to be quiet while she watched the soap operas, because she had to pay close attention to learn how to live like the young women, and she had to listen closely to the new ideas that came into her mind, like living in Boston or Hollywood. In those places, there where a lot of rich, prospective husbands for her to choose from, and there, no one knew that she was once a prostitute and not a virgin.

For traveling money, she had what was left of the money she'd earned on the North Side with Linda, before Chance was born, the money she took from Cherry's hoes and the cabdriver, and the money Linda had in the freezer, wrapped in butcher paper.

The old lady schoolteacher told her to look inside the package one day when she was getting ice for lemonade. There was over $2000 inside the bundle. Linda had more money in the bank. Sharon was sure she wouldn't mind loaning her the money until she found her rich husband. Besides, she would pay her back with interest.

Her plan became whole in the middle of Chance's fourth month of life.

The little burned girl protested it the most, calling her a selfish bitch that would burn in hell.

The old lady schoolteacher said perhaps it was for the best.

The mailman was happy she made a decision to leave the apartment, and didn't care about what or who she left behind.

Linda had come home for a couple of days and was intent on Sharon going out and enjoying herself. She even bought her a new sailor-styled blue dress, some nylons from Marshall Field's, a black wool coat, a cream scarf, a pair of black flats and a cream cashmere glove and hat set.

Sharon couldn't have asked for better travel wear. The only thing she wished was different was the hat. She wanted a pillbox hat. Having that would have made her ensemble perfect. The plan was coming together. All she had to do was follow the path.

Linda came home fussing over Chance like he was the Crown Prince of London. She bought him over twenty new outfits and insisted that he sleep with her, allowing Sharon to have a night out. She even got Chance to feed out of the bottle.

Chance and Linda would be fine together, Sharon thought. Once she found her rich husband and he fell madly in love with her, she would send for them both, but Linda would have to tell him that Chance was her son and Sharon was the aunt. It would work out that way. She'd seen it on a soap opera.

Standing at the door dressed, she adjusted the borrowed package of cold cash under her left arm. She'd sewn it inside the coat's lining. Inside the right pocket of the nice wool coat was the butcher knife. She didn't have a purse. Her money was stuffed beneath her left breast. She'd put toilet tissue and Band-Aids over her nipples to absorb some of the leaking, so as not to stain her new blue sailor-styled dress.

The little burned girl was screaming for her to go back and get Chance.

She ignored her, walked out the door into the cold winter night without a goodbye to Chance or Linda.

At the entrance of the stairwell, she saw the little burned girl standing there. She hadn't seen her since she found her smoldering on the steps over seven years ago. She heard her daily, but never saw her. But there she was, standing in her path.

It's wrong. Leaving Chance is wrong. He's your son, not Linda's.

"You don't know anything. I will get him later. Move out my way!" She tried to push past the little burned girl, but jumped back when she felt her warm fingers wrap around her arm.

You're going back to get your son now. The little burned girl pushed her back toward Linda's apartment. *Go get your baby!*

"No!" Sharon yelled, running hard past the little burned girl into the stairwell. "I'm going to Hollywood."

The little burned girl had followed her all the way to the el station, saying nothing, just dogging her steps. On the el ride, she sat next to Sharon on the train, shaking her head from side to side, repeating, *He's your baby. He's your baby.*

Sharon looked around to see if any of the other passengers could see or hear the little burned girl, but no one appeared to be bothered by her. Sharon didn't understand why a girl whose skin was blistered and melted and whose clothes were burnt to a crisp wouldn't get people's attention. Her presence made Sharon change el cars three times before she got downtown to Clark and Lake.

The bus station annoyed her, not only because the little burned girl continued to dog her steps, but because of the people waiting for buses. They looked no better than the people she saw outside her window, even though most of them were white. They too had swollen ankles, scars, and bad teeth.

The one-way ticket to California cost less than the wool coat Linda bought her. Sitting on the bench in the waiting area, she pulled the tag from the coat. Most of the benches were filled. She shared hers with a young mother and her three sons. The little burned girl sat on the floor at her feet. Sharon pretended not to see her.

There was enough space between Sharon and the small family that she didn't have to interact with them. She'd purchased a *Life* magazine and was totally captivated with the pictures in the story about Hollywood wives.

A man sat in the space between her and the family, and placed his hand on her thigh. "Hey there, baby. Damn, imagine seeing you here. It must be my lucky day."

Sharon didn't recognize the man.

"We met at a bar on Rush Street. Cherry hooked us up, remember?" He was a skinny white man with an afro, and his trench coat was dirty with numerous coffee stains.

"Yeah, we had a good time that night. My district manager was being transferred to Jersey. I was with you, and he was with the blond. Oh baby, that was a good night." He tightened the grip on her thigh.

His filthy hand was on her new nylons from Marshall Field's. She let the magazine fall to the ground. Her right hand went into the coat pocket and her fingers wrapped around the handle of the butcher knife.

"Where are you going, darling? I'm heading out to California. Lost my job about two weeks ago. I decided to start over out west. Are you headed west?"

The little burned girl snickered. *You are leaving your son to go to Hollywood to be with dirty white men like this?*

Sharon didn't answer the white man or the little burned girl. With her left hand, she brushed his hand from her thigh and stood. She bent down and retrieved her fallen magazine.

"Now, I know you are not trying to highbrow me. Not after the good time we had." He stood with her. "I asked you where you are traveling to. Where are you going?"

When she turned to leave, he grabbed her shoulder. All she meant to do was stick his hand with the butcher knife to get him to let her go, but the knife went through his hand into her shoulder. She yelled in pain and pulled the knife free. She would have run away, but he slapped her.

She attacked him with the knife, and when the police came, he couldn't be identified as black or white. All they saw was red.

In Sharon's mind, she boarded the bus to Hollywood, got there and met the mayor's son. It took four days of dating for him to profess his never-ending love. She didn't get the opportunity to send for Chance, because she'd gotten pregnant during the honeymoon and decided it would be best to leave her past behind.

In reality, she was charged with the murder of the man in the bus station and sentenced to a state institution for the criminally insane. She spent the next twenty months of her life living inside her own mind.

Chapter Nine

Chance hadn't showered with a woman since Patrice, but Nadine insists he join her and he's glad she does. Nadine has no hair to worry about getting wet. Hers is cut shorter than Chance's. It reminds him of when he lived in the center and all the boys got their hair cut with number one guides on the hair clippers. Someone has taken a number one to Nadine's hair.

When she tells him to soap her body, she means her entire body, and the soaping gives way to caressing. He is soaping the top of her head, the back of her neck, her shoulders, her back, her firm butt, between her butt cheeks, the bottom of her butt and her thighs. He lowers himself to get the back of her knees, her calves, and her ankles.

"Now the front, Chance. You have to do my front."

He raises and starts with her neck and the top of her shoulders. He slides the bar across her breasts, flicking each nipple. He soaps under her breasts and between them. Chance drops the soap bar and caresses her breasts with the remaining lather. He allows the water to rinse the lather away. He doesn't want to move from her breasts. Her nipples are extended. He takes one into his mouth.

"If you keep sucking on them, you are going to get more that you expect," Nadine whispers.

Chance has never seen nipples as thick as hers. They are as wide as nickels. He sucks harder and a warm, bland liquid fills his mouth. He's tasted mother's milk before, so he swallows and the water continues to cascade over them, rinsing the soapy lather and milk away. He puts her breasts together and tries to suck them both at once. She giggles.

"You have more of me to wash."

He retrieves the bar from the floor of the shower and glides it across the little pug of a stomach she has. He lowers himself to her thighs. She leans against the shower wall and opens her legs. Chance parts her lips with the bar, thumbs the hood of her clit back, and with the corner of the bar, he flicks gently. Nadine pushes forward and he drops the bar again. His tongue is where the bar was. He keeps the hood back with his thumb and holds her clit with his lips while his tongue twirls it.

"Ooh, baby," she says.

With his other thumb, he opens her, and inserts his index finger. He spins his finger while pulling harder on her clit. Her knees buckle and she slides to the floor. He stands.

She starts at his feet with the bar, soaping his toes then his ankles. When she gets to his knees, he feels his meat touching the top of her head. She looks up and takes him in her mouth. She knows how to twirl her tongue too. He bends down and scoops her up.

They tumble into his bed, wet kissing—kisses, kisses and more kisses; long tongue kisses, short pecks and long, loud smacks. They hug tight and kiss hard, neither wanting to stop. Chance feels her hand on his meat. "You are a big boy, Mr. Chance. From the back first. I want it doggy style." Her request is not made quietly.

She gets on her knees in the middle of the bed and lowers her head to one of his pillows. Chance gets behind her. For a second, his mind goes to the rubbers he has in his nightstand, but the fat, wet coochie in front of him is calling him louder than the rubbers. He wants to feel it skin-to-skin.

There is no resistance. He slides straight into her wetness. When he tries to enter fully, she says, "Not all of it yet. I don't like pain. Ease it into me, big daddy".

He backs out a little, leaving in the head and a little meat. He works her walls. "More, Chance." He goes in halfway and works where he is. "More." He goes in fully. He lifts up one of his thighs, letting him get in deeper. The deeper, the tighter. She tries to ease away, but where he is feels too good. He grabs her waist and holds her in place.

"Stroke me, Chance. Stroke me like I'm yours."

Chance isn't stroking, he's humping. He is in too deep to stroke, and doesn't want to back out. He lies across her back and wraps his arms beneath her and humps. When he humps in, she pushes back. They have a lasting groove going. Now it's more sweat than water making them wet. He feels it coming, so he humps faster. She must feel it coming too, because she's matching his speed.

Chance feels a gush of wetness and Nadine collapses. He didn't nut. The gush is from Nadine. On his knees, he sees liquid spraying out from between her thighs. He touches the liquid. It's not pee, it's slippery. For some reason, this excites him more. She's lying face down in his bed. He opens her thighs and goes into the gush.

"Ooh . . . don't you make me love you."

Chance is stroking now. He's pulling back, almost out, and going back in fully. He starts counting his strokes to divert his mind from his approaching orgasm. He is trying not to cum because he wants her to gush again, but at stroke fifty-three, he goes too deep and gets into her tightness and explodes.

"Ooh, you shouldn't have done that like that."

Chance doesn't pull out. He stays inside her. Lying on her back, he feels her walls tighten and loosen around his meat. He's not soft, but he's not all the way hard. He rubs around inside her. His mind goes to her milk-filled breasts and he thinks about her being fertile. The thought excites him. He can afford a child if he wants one.

She pushes her butt up into him and rolls. He rolls with her. He doesn't want to come out of her. He starts a slow hump until he feels himself thicken. He's making small circles with his hips. He needs a son; every man needs a son. He feels his meat expanding. He's hard again and she knows it.

She rises up on her knees and Chance is back to humping. He wants to kiss her.

"Lie down and roll over, baby."

She lies on her back and opens her thighs wide. Chance lies on her. He slides his tongue into her mouth and his meat into her wetness. Their embrace is tight. He feels her thighs wrap around his waist. He buries himself inside her, planting his seed—deep. They stay connected at the hips and attached at the lips.

Two hours later, Chance wakes up alone. "Nadine," he calls. No answer. He gets up and walks through the condo. He's alone. He goes to his dresser drawer. All his jewelry is there. He goes to the closet and pulls his wallet from his suit coat. All the cash is there. Not even the hundred dollars is missing. He looks around for a note and finds none.

"Damn."

He goes to the bathroom, washes his meat and gets back in the bed. The scent of Nadine is dominant, and he likes it.

When Chance wakes up, he thinks he's dreaming. Next to him on the bed is a blue plastic baby carrier with a baby in it, and he thinks he smells chicken frying. He goes back to sleep. When he wakes again, the baby carrier and baby are still on his bed, except the baby isn't in the carrier. The baby is asleep, next to him, on a little baby-sized pillow.

The series *Soul Food* is playing on his plasma screen and Nadine, who is wearing a pair of cut-off blue jeans shorts and nothing else, is lying on the other side of the baby. Her head is opposite his and the baby's, and before her is a huge platter of fried chicken wings. In front of his closet he counts four large green trash bags, which are filled with something. Chance decides not to comment on the bags or the baby. He's learned that when dealing with women, it's better to wait for an explanation than to jump to conclusions.

He turns to the end of the bed where Nadine is and takes a chicken wing from the platter. On the floor in front of the bed, Nadine has a paper bag that she's using to toss the chicken bones in. There are no bones on the platter.

"So, you finally woke up, huh?"

"Mm-hmm. Somebody knocked me out pretty good."

She smiles a blushing type smile and darts her eyes away from him to the television. She can't be much older than twenty, Chance thinks. He is going to wait for her to bring up the bags and the baby. He devours the chicken wing, tosses the bones in the paper bag, and picks another wing from the platter.

He hasn't stretched out in his bed and watched television in over three months. It feels good. His eyes move from the television to her bare upper torso. She has small breasts that hang, but they are very solid and milk-filled at the bottom. He rolls closer to her, lays his head next to her right breast and starts licking. She pulls away.

"Why you gonna start up again?" she asks, smiling.

She doesn't wait for his answer. She takes two of the four pillows off the bed and makes a pallet for the baby on the carpet. She places the platter of chicken wings on the dresser and puts the baby carrier on top of one of the plastic bags. She slides out of her shorts and climbs into the bed.

A sixty-nine isn't what Chance has on his mind, but it's obviously what Nadine has on hers. She's rolled him over on his back and is lying on top of him in reverse. Her mouth has surrounded his meat and her thighs are on the side of his head. Chance puts a pillow under the back of his head for support, and pulls her to his thick, flicking tongue.

*****

Patrice stands in the Pancake House parking lot watching the tow truck driver load her Bentley on the flatbed, after waiting an hour and fifteen minutes for him to arrive. She can't decide between calling a cab and going to the office or walking home and taking a nap.

She is too pissed off to work after seeing Chance with the waitress, and the wait for the tow truck didn't improve her disposition a bit. She doesn't even want to think about how much four new tires will cost her, nor does she want to think about who might have slashed them. She is comfortable with thinking of it as a random act of envy. Composing a list of suspects would take her too long. Many people think of her as an adversary.

Her two-way pager is humming in her purse. She digs to the bottom of the bag and pulls it free, expecting a message from her office. The text message she sees causes her to gasp: BITCH, NEXT TIME I'M GOING TO CUT UP YOUR FAT, LYING ASS.

"Who would . . .?" she asks the air. She looks around to see if anyone is staring at her.

NO, YOU DON'T SEE ME NOW, BITCH, BUT YOU WILL, another message reads.

Whoever it is can see her, and she doesn't want them to see her panic. She checks for a signature on the messages. None.

She responds back: WHO IS THIS?

DEATH, it reads.

She cuts the two-way off and flips it closed. Again, she scans the sunny lot and street. No one is looking in her direction.

The tow truck driver walks to her and says, "This is going to Exotic Motors, right?"

"Yes, on Clark Street."

"Do you need a lift over?"

"No, I have a way, but thank you."

"Somebody is upset with you, lady, to cut your tires like that. They sliced the tire wall, making sure you can't repair them."

"Yes, well, that's not your concern." She turns abruptly from the driver and walks back into the restaurant.

What nut's cage has she rattled? She has no idea. She walks back into the restaurant. She decides to walk to ladies' room when her cell phone rings. The small screen displays: PRIVATE CALL.

She pushes the answer button.

"It's going to take more than cutting off your two-way, fatso. I'm in your life deep."

It sounds like a black man.

"Who is this?"

"Let's not be redundant. I already told you who I was."

"Why did you cut my tires?"

"'Cause your fat ass wasn't available."

"Why would you want to hurt me?"

"'Cause you need to die. Black bitches that don't respect black men should die."

"What have I done to you?"

"You know!"

The glass door behind her shatters. She hunches down. The cash register becomes speckled with bullet holes. The cigarette packages and potato chips are shot up. She drops to the floor. The man standing behind the counter is hit twice in the chest. He falls back against the cigarette rack and slides down. She can see his face in the space between the bottom of the counter and the floor. He is praying.

Through the speaker of her cell phone she hears, "I ain't playing with you, bitch!"

She hears no more bullets hitting, no more glass shattering, but she doesn't stand. She crawls out of the waiting area toward the booths and tables, dragging her attaché case and purse. She leaves the phone. The people in the eating area are not totally aware of what happened. They are still sitting in booths and at tables. It isn't until a waitress screams out after seeing the man behind the counter shot that they become riled.

The moment Patrice stands from the floor, the large side windows of the restaurant are shot out. She dives to the floor again, accompanied by the other patrons and staff. This time, the shots are heard. Loud explosions bang through the restaurant as if the shooter is standing in the eating area.

Patrice feels it, but there is nothing she can do to stop it. Urine releases from her bladder. From outside the window, she hears, "Come on out, Patrice. Don't get innocent people killed. Come on out here and die like the proud black woman you are. Show the world you got balls, bitch." The voice is familiar to her.

Everybody on the floor hears approaching police sirens.

"Before nightfall, you will be dead. That I promise you, you fat-ass, ho."

A car door is slammed and spinning tires are heard. Patrice rolls off her stomach and looks down at her skirt. Thank goodness it's dark blue; the wet spot isn't showing. Gradually, people are rising from the floor, cautious and apprehensive about standing. Patrice rises, not in view of a window. There is a wall between her and outside.

The police are entering the restaurant. People are being ordered to sit and stay, but many are leaving out the side door. Patrice sees her cell phone getting kicked across the floor by a couple of different feet. She goes and scoops it up from in front of the register. The man behind the counter looks dead to her. His open eyes are not moving.

The people leaving out the side door seem to have the right idea. To her, there is nothing she can tell the police, and she doesn't want to be involved in a murder investigation. She looks around the restaurant to see if anyone knows who she is, and more importantly, is if anyone knows she is the Patrice the shooter was calling for. She sees no one. With phone, attaché case and purse in tow, she makes it out the side door.

She walks diagonally across the parking lot to Belmont Street. She hurriedly walks east down Belmont. She sees a black BMW like Chance's approaching, but it isn't Chance behind the wheel. It's the skinny, bald-headed waitress. For an instant, she thinks of jumping in front of the car, forcing her to stop, but the smell of her accident creeps up to her nose. The foul scent quickens her steps towards home and her shower.

*****

When the phone rings, Chance is startled from his sleep. It's not the ring of his house phone. His first thought is that it must be Nadine's phone, but the ringing is coming from his bedroom closet. He stands from the bed and stumbles to the closet, stepping over the baby's car seat and plastic bags.

The ringing is coming from his suit jacket. It's the phone Mr. Sharp's secretary gave him.

He flips it open and answers, "Hello."

"Good morning, Mr. Bates. I expect to see you at the North Side office within the hour."

Click.

It was Mr. Sharp. Chance looks over at the alarm clock on the bedside table. It reads: 4:30 a.m. He flips the phone closed.

"Damn, it's early."

He looks down at the empty car seat then he looks over at the bed for Nadine and the baby. Neither is in the room. He stretches, yawns, and walks naked through the condo. He hears bare feet on the kitchen floor. He finds Nadine standing over the sink, rinsing out bottles. She and the baby are dressed, except for shoes.

"Hey," he says.

"Hey to you too. We didn't wake you up, did we?"

"No, my new job called and woke me up."

Nadine is holding the smiling baby in her arms. The baby doesn't look like her to Chance. It looks Asian.

"Oh, so they gonna have you coming in on Saturdays?"

"I couldn't tell you, slim. Why are you up so early?" He walks over to her and kisses her on the forehead. He even gives the milky-mouth baby a peck on the cheek.

"This is the time a Pancake House waitress starts her day, and I got to get Andrew to his sitter." She adjusts the baby on her shoulder. "Are you leaving soon? Maybe you could give us a lift." Her free hand drops down to Chance's meat. "You shouldn't walk around slinging all this beef. You put thoughts in a girl's mind."

He kisses her again on the forehead and steps to the side of her caressing fingers. He decides it's time to bring up the plastic bags she has in the bedroom.

Standing behind one of the two kitchen chairs, he asks, "Nadine, what's with all the bags?"

"Oh, that's my stuff. I used your car while you were 'sleep yesterday and went and got Andrew."

"You did what?" Chance doesn't even let a valet park his car. He grips the top rail of the chair tightly, but keeps a calm expression on his face.

"I hope you don't mind. It's just that you were sleeping so good that I didn't want to wake you up, and the keys were right there, so I grabbed them and left."

He sees her looking to see if he minds. He's trying to look like he doesn't, but the BMW is his pride and joy. He has over $15,000 worth of extras on the vehicle: the more powerful sports engine, the ground effects package and bulletproof windows. The bulletproof windows were something he and Magnum agreed to get on their cars when they were kids. He has no need for them, but he ordered them anyway. No one has ever driven the car but him.

"No big deal," he says, avoiding her gaze. He relaxes his grip on the chair.

"I had some stuff stored over the babysitter's and she asked me to take it with me. Well, really she told me to take it with me since I was driving. She acted kind of strange when she saw me get out of your car. I was going to tell her it wasn't mine, but she turned so green with envy that I left it alone.

"I lived with her when I first moved to the North Side. My place is too small for all my stuff. That's why I kept some things with her. When she saw me in the BMW, I guess she figured I could afford to haul my belongings off of her porch. I didn't argue with her, but all those clothes won't fit into my studio . . ." She looks up at Chance with requesting eyes.

Chance releases the chair altogether. Storing clothes is better than moving in. "Yeah, all right. You can put them in the empty bedroom."

"Thank you. That's sweet of you. And what about a ride to the sitter and work?"

"Let me shower and dress and we're gone."

"I would join you in the shower, but the early morning is me and Andrew's time. This is our cuddle time. Ain't that right, boo?" she says to Andrew, who responds with cheerful gurgles. "You know I hate having to leave you, but mama got to do what mama got to do. Ain't that right, boo?" More gurgles and happy waving of arms from Andrew.

"Well, I don't want to be the one to break that up. I'll be ready in a minute."

In the shower, Chance realizes that this is the first morning in weeks that he woke happy. No funk is in his mind. He actually feels cheerful and relieved. He thought for sure Nadine bringing in bags was a move-in play, and he isn't sure how he would have reacted to that.

True, he enjoys being with her enough to maybe let it happen and he has more than enough space in his condo, but he is tired of following when it comes to women. He promised himself after Patrice that he would allow no other woman to lead him.

The few girls he had before Patrice, he told what to do. He gave the orders to women as he saw other men in his world do. The life Patrice exposed him to was different and unknown to him, and he had no choice but to follow her and her father's lead. He followed more than he cared to.

Nadine, however, is from his world. With her, he can lead. This thought causes him to smile. He really isn't cool with her driving his BMW, but she did it to go get her son. He is cool with that. Andrew sure is a happy baby, he thinks, but that's because he's got a good mother. Good mothers make happy babies.

A good mother.

Chance turns the shower to full force, stopping the thought of his absent mother from creeping into his mind. He is feeling good, and he wants to keep feeling good.

Chapter Ten

When Sharon Bates returned to reality, the psychotropic medication she was given over past the twenty months received the formal credit. However, in her mind, it was the scent of barbecued ribs that pulled her from her life in Hollywood.

At times in her psychosis-created life, she would smell barbecued ribs when there were no ribs present. She would be dining at an exclusive restaurant with her trim, proper and rich husband, eating baked eggplant, smelling barbecued ribs. On another occasion, her rich husband had bought her a beautiful crystal bottle of cologne from France, but when she sniffed it, the smoky aroma of barbecue permeated.

She loved barbecued ribs, but in her psychosis-created life, she didn't eat meat, and she certainly didn't eat barbecue. However, the aide who was assigned to watch Sharon on the midnight shift at the institution did eat ribs, and brought a half-slab order with her every Friday night.

Sharon Bates was on one-on-one observation 24 hours a day. She was always to be in view of an aide, largely due to Sharon's semi-conscious state. Physically, she was in the institution. She walked through the ward and sat in the dayroom. She was assisted in her bathing and took her medication and ate meals, but she did not hold a conversation with those outside the life her psychosis had created.

She sat for hours in the dayroom in front of the television, but none of the programming registered in her mind. She was in Hollywood living "the good life" with the mayor's son.

On the Friday night that Sharon returned to reality, the aide had pulled her order of ribs from the greasy brown paper bag, peeled the wax paper back, and set the steaming barbecue ribs atop the bedside tray. She'd placed the small paper cup of coleslaw to the side of the ribs.

The meal was sitting on Sharon's bed tray, but the aide had positioned the tray so the she could eat from it while she sat at Sharon's side. What made her rise from the meal was some grime on the top of her Pepsi can. She'd gone to the sink to rinse the top of the can.

When she turned from the sink, Sharon Bates, her patient whose eyes hadn't shown any response to conversations in twenty months, was bent over the tray, wide-eyed and focused. She had a rib bone in her mouth, and she was stripping it clean of meat. Barbecue sauce was covering both of her dark, smiling cheeks.

The aide's first impulse was to scream for the nurse, but Sharon was enjoying the ribs so much that she allowed her to finish the entire meal, including the coleslaw, fries and Pepsi, before she notified the nurse.

During the next six months, Sharon became the poster-child for the wonders of psychotropic medication. Her debilitating illness had been stayed by the advancement of psychiatry. She was proof that the medication worked.

When questioned by doctors if she still heard voices, the old schoolteacher told her to say no. When asked if she still had visual hallucinations, she answered no on her own, because she no longer saw the little burned girl, but she did hear her and the mailman.

The Hollywood life was completely gone, and she accepted what the doctors told her about how it was created in her mind. The trauma of being attacked in the bus station along with the postpartum depression of childbirth was too stressful for her mind to handle, so she went inward, the doctors told her, and created a better life.

As the days passed, she could remember less and less of her Hollywood life, and the reality of life in the institution set in her mind. She was on a ward with ten other patients—all were convicted of homicide—nine men and one other woman besides her.

She and the other woman, Elaine, shared the same doctor. Elaine, an inch shorter than Sharon's five-two frame and five pounds lighter than her 115 pounds, told her that she and Sharon were guinea pigs for the new medicine, and since it worked, they both would be getting out soon. Elaine also told Sharon that she knew she still heard voices just like she did, because "the shitty-ass medicine doesn't really work."

They were sitting alone in the ward's dayroom when Elaine told her, "Don't bother to deny it. I see you trying not to respond. If the aides were doing their jobs, they would see you too. See, you give it away when you look around as if you've heard something. See, how I do it is, I ignore all sounds from people that are not right in front of me. If I don't see their lips moving, I'm not acknowledging them. I don't look around to see if people are talking to me. See, that's what you do, and that's how you are going to get caught. Do you understand?" Sharon had returned to reality three weeks ago, and these were the first words Elaine had said to her.

Her first thought was that Elaine, dressed in the same green hospital gown and beige slippers she had on, was working for the doctor, and her giving her advice was a trick of some kind.

"I don't hear voices anymore. You are making a mistake. The medicine worked for me," Sharon declared.

"See, that's why I don't like helping you nappy-headed black girls. You are all ungrateful liars," she said, pointing her finger at Sharon's forehead.

They were sitting on the couch closest to the television. Sharon had been alone in the dayroom most of the morning. The men didn't move around much until after the p.m. medication. If she wanted to, Sharon could have grabbed Elaine's finger and bent it back until it snapped. She didn't because she was certain Elaine worked for the doctor.

"I'm not lying," Sharon answered, ignoring the finger in her face and putting her hand on her braids. The midnight aide had braided her hair that morning. It wasn't nappy. She had five long ponytails, four of which hung past her shoulders. Elaine's hair was what needed grooming. It was wild and all over her head; stringy brown strands cut short.

"You don't have to lie to me," Elaine whispered, leaning closer to Sharon. "I didn't ask you if you heard voices. See, all I did was tell you how to avoid looking as if you do. Because if they find out the medicine didn't work for you, they will start looking closer at me. See, and I am not about to be stuck in here because your slow black ass couldn't pull it off. Do you understand me, Sharon Bates?" Her breath smelled like stale coffee.

Sharon nodded her head and scooted to the end of the couch, putting two cushions between them. That morning, and her overall time on the ward, had been calm. She hadn't felt like fighting, fussing or stabbing since she came back to reality. And she wasn't about to let this pale little woman upset her.

"Good. See, now if you do as I say, we will both be out of here before the year is out. You would like that, wouldn't you?"

Again Sharon nodded to the affirmative. It was the intensity with which Elaine spoke of being released that caused Sharon to listen to her. Maybe she did know something.

"See, we are going to be friends, Sharon Bates. You and I are going to be closer than two peas in a pod."

Sharon didn't want to be Elaine's friend. She'd heard the nurses and aides talking about her. She'd killed her mother-in-law at Thanksgiving dinner and told the police the turkey told her to do it. Sharon heard voices, but she didn't have talking turkeys telling her what to do. She turned her attention to the television news and tried to ignore Elaine.

"So, you stabbed a person, too, didn't you? I don't remember doing it . . . do you?"

Sharon nodded her head and turned from the television to Elaine. She did want to talk about that. She wanted to talk about the memories that began flooding her thoughts about a week prior, but she didn't want to talk about them with the doctor or a nurse.

She remembered Cherry, Janet, the cabdriver and the white man with the afro. She remembered every stab, every slice. She remembered how the blood squirted, spilled and splattered. And it all made her laugh.

She knew that laughing wasn't the proper response, but she couldn't help it. She remembered the events in a humorous light. She saw Janet's huge breasts flying all over the bedroom with the large leopard bed. She saw Cherry trying to dodge the butcher knife and cover his privates, but the cabdriver, the one she stabbed leaving Cherry's apartment, made her laugh the hardest, largely due to what the mailman said: "He came and went at the same time." She thought that was clever.

The mailman was becoming the voice she heard the clearest. He was the only one who wanted her out of the hospital and back to work on the streets.

The old lady schoolteacher talked about her leaving the city and starting a new life, but had no plan as to how.

The little burned girl only talked about her getting out and finding Chance.

What she thought about when the voices were absent and she wasn't being tickled by stabbing memories, was getting out of the institution and getting some money. And the fastest way she knew to make money was prostituting on the North Side.

She was afraid to think about finding a rich husband in Hollywood or Boston because she didn't want to fall back into a fantasy world. In the real world, she knew how to work the North Side. After she got some money, she would decide whether she would stay in the city.

"I don't know how I would react if I remembered doing it. She was my husband's mother, for God's sake, and I killed her. See, he will never forgive me." Elaine's head hung.

"You really don't remember it . . . any of it?" Sharon asked.

"No," Elaine answered.

"But you remember the turkey telling you to do it?"

Elaine lifted her head and faced Sharon. "You have been listening to the nurses. It wasn't the turkey. The voices I hear can come out of anything. That day, they came out of the turkey and told me to slice my mother-in-law's throat. I can recall hearing the voices, but not doing the deed.

"I don't hear one or two voices independently. I hear a choir of voices singing, and they sing their commands loud. Since I've been on the ward, I've heard them singing out of a cockroach, out of doctors and out of the priest that comes on Sundays. The choir is losing power, though. It isn't as loud and can't make me do things anymore. Yes, I still hear it, but I can ignore the commands." Elaine began rocking on the couch.

"See, it's like this. The choir was singing out of the television when I first walked in here, telling me to kill you because you were going to mess up and keep me in here. I didn't kill you, did I? See, the choir doesn't tell me what to do anymore."

"I'm glad," Sharon said, looking back to the television. Elaine wasn't a person she could share her thoughts with, because Elaine was crazy for real.

"Did you know the man you killed?" The speed of her rocking increased.

Sharon had to remind herself that Elaine, the police, and the hospital staff were only aware of one of the people she stabbed: the white man with the afro. No one had asked her about Cherry, Janet, or the cabdriver.

"No, I didn't know him, not really. He said I turned a date with him, but I didn't remember it."

"Turned a date?"

Sharon didn't turn from the television to answer Elaine. "Yes, I do escort work."

"Oh really. Do you think I could make a go of it?"

"I thought you were married."

"Would you stay married to someone who killed your mother because a turkey told her to do it? The doctor thinks I don't know about the divorce, but I know my husband. The divorce is done. And as far as the escorting goes, I'm just asking do you think I could do it."

"With the right direction and management, a thin, young white girl like you could make quite a bit."

"Do you have a manager?"

Sharon turned from the television because the mailman suddenly became loud in her head. He told her to say, "No. I run the agency, and matter of fact, we are looking for new talent."

"And how does one apply?"

"Have you ever turned a trick?"

"Only with the patients in here."

"The patients?" she questioned, slightly shocked and a little disgusted.

"Yes, the patients. These men have things of value: cigarettes, desserts, and one can get weed. But honestly, I don't do it for the things as much as I do it to stop from being bored. See, I like the sneaking and pulling it off without the staff knowing. And the skinny one, Nathan, has a huge pecker. I have never seen one as long as his."

"But the men here walk around like zombies."

"Oh please. We are not the only ones acting like the medicine works. See, most of them don't even take the medicine. They puke it back up or never swallow it. See, being here is better than being in prison. A couple of them like each other, but most of them will pay to play."

"Desserts and cigarettes? You're selling your stuff kind of cheap. A professional doesn't do it to stop from being bored. It's always about the money. No money, no honey. If you hold out for cash, I promise they will deliver."

"But I like doing it with Nate," she said, grinning.

"Then let Nate be your manager. If you want me to manage you, you have to hold out for cash. And that includes Nate. The patients aren't the only men in here."

"The staff? You been tricking with the staff?"

"I didn't say that. I said that you are selling your goods too cheap, and the patients ain't the only tricks available. Let's say staff was interested and they found out the patients were getting you for a pack of cigarettes. Believe me, all they will offer will be a pack of cigarettes."

"Will you show me how?"

"Maybe. But you got to understand I handle all the money. You'll get a share, but it comes to my hands first."

"When do we start?"

"First you got to show me that you can hold out for cash. Start charging the patients twenty dollars a date and bring me the cash, then we will talk about you working like I know how to work."

"A test, huh? I like tests."

Even though Sharon thought Elaine was crazy for real, she followed her advice. She was trying her best not to respond to the voices she heard in her head. If and when she did slip, Elaine was there to make her conscious of it. Soon, not responding to them on the ward and being in the privacy of her room became easier. She could hear them without having to talk back to them.

It became the two of them together, watching each other for telltale signs of responding to hallucinations. Sharon became just as adept at detecting when Elaine was trying to ignore her choir as she was at spotting Sharon's responses. Elaine would sit prone and stiff and not respond to anything. If she was looking at television relaxing and the choir sang, she would sit straight up and try to act as if she was looking at the television and not listening to anyone. Sharon would make her way across the room and tell her, "Your stuff is showing," which was the code phrase they used.

The phrase developed because at times, sitting around in the hospital gowns, one's "stuff" did show. And Sharon didn't want Elaine's or her own stuff to show without getting paid. The male patients were having a hard time coming up with the twenty-dollar price tag Sharon insisted on for Elaine, so she began charging them five dollars for peeps in the dayroom. The men would pay five dollars, and either she or Elaine would sit wide-legged across from them, giving the payer a full view while he masturbated under his hospital gown.

This arrangement worked until Elaine saw Nate's club. She couldn't look at it without having it. When she sat wide-legged in front of him, he would flip up his gown, showing her his erection. After she saw that, there was nothing Sharon could say that would stop her from leaving the dayroom with him.

It wasn't within the year as Elaine said, but they were released within two. It wasn't a trial with a jury like Sharon expected. It was a competency hearing. Her doctor and five other doctors asked her the same questions they'd been asking her for three years. She gave them the same answers: No, she didn't hear voices. No, she didn't see things that weren't there. No, she had never been to Hollywood and no, she didn't want to hurt herself or anyone else. Yes, she was very grateful for the medicine and would continue to take it once she was released. What she didn't expect was to be questioned about her son, Chance.

No, she hadn't forgotten him. No, she didn't think she was able to take care of him. Yes, her doctor and the social worker told her that he was in foster care. No, she didn't want to hurt him.

She wasn't lying. She didn't desire to hurt him. She couldn't plan her actions on the outside with him in her thoughts. Her plans had no room for a child. What she was preparing to do was make as much money as she could, as quickly as possible. From Elaine's continuing interest in working for her escort service, along with the mailman's coaching, the idea of having other girls working with her began to form.

The idea became concrete after Elaine was released and moved into a two-bedroom condominium provided by her husband's divorce settlement. She got a condo on the plush Oak Street, a Volvo and a monthly allowance. The allowance was enough to maintain the lifestyle he had provided for her before she was institutionalized. Elaine didn't join Sharon's escort team out of financial need. She had other needs that she hoped the service would fulfill.

If it had been a male and a female patient who wanted to live together, the doctor would have not have approved it because of the relationship implications. But since both patients were females who had shown phenomenal improvement while on the new medication, and both were scheduled three times weekly for intensive outpatient treatment, their housing request to live together was considered therapeutic and thereby approved.

When Sharon Bates walked through the tall doors of the institution and down the stairs to the sidewalk, she had the wool coat Linda had bought her across her arm, and a plastic bag from the institution with her personal belongings and identification in it. The summer sun was blazing bright through the ozone, and the humid air was heavy on her shoulders. She would have thought of the day as stuffy, if not for the fact that the breath she took was her first free breath in over five years.

She almost didn't recognize a polished Elaine, who was sitting on the hood of the baby blue Volvo, smoking a cigarette. Elaine was released two months prior, and the months of freedom showed. Her hair was feathered and dyed blond. The pale skin was replaced with a golden tan, and a pair of Ray-Ban aviator sunglasses covered her light brown eyes.

"See, I told you to sell that coat or just leave it. Why on earth would you walk out into the July sun with a wool coat over your arm? It's bad enough you're wearing an outdated, although cute, little sailor suit. Come, come, it's time for us to do a little shopping. You are ready to leave, aren't you?" she asked from the hood of the car.

URBAN AFFAIR

"What do you think?"
"I think you're ready."

Chapter Eleven

Trying to sleep is useless. Patrice is unable to nap in the afternoon or sleep through the night. But she has lived to see daybreak, despite her attacker's threat. Her father demanded that she go to the police, but she didn't. She dated the public liaison officer for the police department and is certain he wouldn't miss an opportunity to leak her name to the media, embarrassing her as she did him.

It was his fault. She met him when he was at the Piano Bar, bragging about the size of his manhood. Once she got him back to her place, even fully erect, he didn't have half of the ten inches he claimed to have. When he went to bragging again at the bar, she called him a damn liar, loud enough for all to hear. He called her fat, tipped over her drink and left. Some people just can't handle the truth.

The truth was, he was good with the five or so inches he did have, and if she weren't expecting ten, the five would have sufficed. Men . . . why do so many lie about their size? Could the liaison officer be the one that shot at her? No, he isn't crazy.

Patrice rises from sitting on the corner of her king-sized bed and walks into her living room. She grabs the sound system remote from the arm of her yellow leather sofa, selects disc three, which is Anthony Hamilton's "Comin' From Where I'm From." The smooth R&B tenor whispers from her eight speakers. The volume is set on one. She keeps it there and sits on the tan carpet in front of her sofa. She and Amy went and had pedicures two days ago, and the polish on her right baby toenail is already chipped.

"Damn."

She doesn't want to admit it to her father, but the shots have her afraid. Good and scared. Whoever it is really wants to do her harm. The most a man has ever done to her is threaten to smack the shit out of her. No one has ever put his hands on her except for Chance's friend, Magnum, but she was a kid then. Yesterday, this fool shot at her and slashed her tires and said she knew what she did. She can think of nothing she's done to a man that would justify getting shot.

The carpet feels soft on her thighs. She's glad she went with thick nap as opposed to the long shag. She's gotten busy a couple of times on the carpet and never got a carpet burn. The naps are cushy.

Yes, she has bruised some male egos, but only of those who tried to hurt her or lie to her. The only man she can think that would have a reason to hurt her is Chance. She broke his heart and she knows it, but Chance still loves her. Of that she is certain. The evidence is the fact that he remains in close proximity. She knows he has received several profitable offers on the condo, but he hasn't sold it. Like her, he doesn't have a clue as to how to get past their differences.

These are differences that others claimed would tear them apart and stop a marriage from working. The others are, specifically, her father and mother. She can clearly hear what her mother had to say when she told her she was marrying Chance. "You can't fit a square peg into a round hole. There is a reason for the class system, dear. Helping the less fortunate is a good thing, but doing it through marriage is a bit extreme. You did wonders helping him with his speech and dialect. We allowed you to date him. A little slumming around builds one's character, but you don't bring the cute mongrel puppy to the show, dear, because his bloodline is tainted."

At this moment she needs Chance—tainted blood and all. She needs his protection. He will be able to deal with this nut shooting at her. He probably would have ended the situation right there in the Pancake House parking lot.

The way this nut spoke, he is obviously from the streets. And street people respect Chance, even if her parents don't. Her father's way of dealing with such a threat is to call the police, but as she learned from her time with Chance, the police don't help everyone.

She didn't understand that in the beginning. She was brought up believing that the job of the police is to serve and protect. And they do serve and protect people of her parent's stature. When her mother was pulled over for driving under the influence, she wasn't taken to jail. One officer drove her home in the squad car while the other drove her car home.

When she and Chance were pulled over and the police found her open beer in the car, they poured the beer out and slapped Chance around and took him to lockup for eight hours. It took a year and over a $1000 to clear his driver's license.

Chance's acceptance of the unfair treatment shocked her more than experiencing it. He told her, "Da police protect citizens from criminals. I'm not a citizen in dey eyes. I'm a criminal. And since I really am a criminal, it's my job to be on da lookout for dem. I am da bad guy, and if you wid me, you da bad guy too. And smart bad guys don't drive around wid open beer in da car.

"I try to make myself invisible to da police because when dey pull me over, dey lookin' for my weed, my pistol and anything else dey can find to get me off da streets. Now, if you gonna be wid me, girl, you got to get smarter."

On the streets, Chance was known to be smart and he was respected. They called him C. They were developing into quite a team on the streets, once she realized she didn't know a thing about his world and started listening to him. They probably would have still been out there had she not got them in the mess that sent Chance to county jail.

During her short time as a runaway, Chance had gotten her two new outfits, complete with underwear. He had to buy the outfits because she refused to wear clothes that weren't clean, and since they slept in her car, they had nowhere to wash clothes.

She wasn't expecting to have to sleep in the car, and didn't quite understand why Chance didn't have a place to stay. He made money. Why didn't he have a place? The first morning she woke up after a fitful night of sleeping in the bucket seat, she asked him, "So, tell me again why you don't have an apartment or someplace to stay."

Yawning and stretching his arms over the seats and almost reaching to the car's back windows, he answered, "'Cause we didn't make dat much yesterday. Not enough to spend fifteen dollars to sleep overnight. Winter will be here in a minute, and I want to have a real place befo' it hits. If I keep spendin' fifteen dollars a night, I won't be able to save up da security and first month's rent. I don't have a place because I'm livin' real low-budget right now."

"So, where do you normally sleep?" She looked out the driver's window to the morning sky; no clouds, but the sun wasn't bright yet.

"Here and dere with friends. At da park, you know, wherever."

"That doesn't seem very safe." She rolled her window down in case her breath was smelly. She didn't want him to be surrounded by her morning mouth odor.

"Safe? I ain't never thought about it being safe or not. It just is what it is. I sleep where I can."

"Where do you keep your stuff?"

"What stuff?" Chance sat prone in the car and raised the seat.

"Your clothes and belongings."

"Here and dere. I got my good pieces in da cleaners. I got a little bit of stuff over Big Time's place: a couple of jeans and a leather jacket. Everything else is wid me."

Chance reached inside his White Sox jersey and pulled into view his three thick gold chains and extended his hand, displaying his diamond pinky ring and gold watch. Then from the small of his back, he retrieved his .9mm pistol.

"Dis here is da important stuff and it stays wid me." He put the pistol and chains back where they were. "I live out here on dese streets, baby. I ain't got no address. Not yet anyway, but I will have one befo' winter sets in."

"Where does your family live?"

"Everybody ain't got a family, shorty."

No family. That stopped her questions for a minute. She couldn't imagine not having a family. Chance was such a small kid. How could he have survived the streets with no family, no one to look out for him? One of her thighs made two of his, and his arms, although very muscular, were as thin as corncobs. There must be someone, she thought. He just didn't want to talk about them. Everybody has a mother.

"Where is your mother?"

Chance, who was counting the marijuana-filled manila envelopes, said, "I heard she went crazy after havin' me, and the state locked her up. I ain't never seen her, and ain't never missed her. All I got is me, okay?" He didn't look up from his counting.

"Cousins, aunts, uncles?"

"If dey out dere, dey ain't never reached for me. All da family I got is Magnum, Big Time and a couple of otha niggers on dis here end." He rolled down the window and spat. "We got eight bags left, and I already got re-cop money plus thirty dollars. Dat means I can add a hundred dollars to my movin' money. Shorty . . . if bizness stays dis good, I'll have a place befo' da leaves fall.

"Whatcha gonna do today, shorty? You goin' home to Daddy or you gonna stay another day wid me? If you stayin' out here wid me, we got to go get cleaned up and get some breakfast, den go over to da park. Today is da Bud Billiken parade. People gonna be out dere early lookin' for da good weed. So, what's wid you, kid?"

Patrice wanted to go home to sleep in her bed, bathe and put on one of her new birthday dresses. She wanted to see her mother and tell her that she was okay. She was certain that her mother had worried herself sick.

"If you want to go home, dat's cool. You don't owe me nothin'. I know your daddy got to be lookin' fo you and da car. You betta go on home. Come back to da parade today and we can hook up later. Go let ya peoples know you aw'ight." He was putting the manila bags into another brown paper bag and again not looking at her while he spoke.

"Do you want me to leave?" she asked.

"Naw, shorty. I likes ya company."

She was expecting him to try something the previous night, and if he had, she was certain she could have stopped him. That was before she knew he had a gun, but he didn't try anything. All he did was rub her thighs, kiss her a couple of times and tell her how pretty she was with such light skin. After the kissing and caressing, she wanted to do something more with him, but they both went to sleep.

They spent the night parked on 53rd Street in front of one of the university's buildings. Chance said they would be fine there as long as the car seats were let all the way back. That way, no one could tell that they were in the car.

"Where are we going to freshen up?" she asked, letting him know that she was going to stay with him.

The smile that crossed his skinny, dark face went from ear to ear. Patrice noticed that his thin eyes smiled too, and even his narrow, pointed nose wrinkled a bit with the big smile.

"Da same place we eat at—Micky D's."

"How are we going to wash our clothes if these are the only clothes we have?"

"Your clothes ain't dirty."

"They may not look dirty, but believe me, they are not fresh."

She noticed the day before how soiled his Calvin Klein jeans were and wondered if he had gotten them dirty that day or if the grime was from several days of wear. After spending hours in close quarters with him, she knew it was the latter. Chance had an odor about him.

"Fresh and dirty is da same. Your clothes is fine."

"My clothes are not fine," she said with attitude and rolling eyes. "I know when my clothes aren't clean. And if you were a woman, you wouldn't think fresh and dirty were the same thing. I need clean, fresh clothes and underwear. Do you understand?" She'd unintentionally raised her voice, and in the car, the volume boomed.

"Yeah, yeah, aw'ight. Damn. Hold your horses. You ain't got to get all huffy and loud. We can go get you some new stuff before we go to wash up. I didn't smell you, so I didn't know you was all funky and stuff down dere. But I can get you some clean drawers."

He grinned.

"What? I am not funky down there." Her head started bobbing. "And if I were . . . you would never know, and don't be talking underneath my clothes. Down there is none of your damn business. How dare you!" She grabbed the door handle of the car to leave, but remembered where she was. Her back was to him.

"Damn, shorty." He reached for her shoulder and laid his hand on it easily. "I was only jokin'. Calm down, my bad. I didn't mean to be talkin' under your clothes. I was just jokin'. We gonna go see Juanita, aw'ight? She sells ladies clothes."

"Juanita?"

"Yeah, Big Time's woman. She's a booster."

"A what?"

"She steals clothes and sells 'em for half da ticket price. But first let's cruise by da park and see if we can get rid of a couple of dese bags befo' we go up to Big Time's. Is dat okay wid you?"

Patrice turned to face him. "That's fine." She sat upright, adjusted her seat and the rearview mirror. Before she started the car, she asked, "Do you really like my company?" No one had ever told her that.

"Yeah, we cool, shorty. You just a little spoiled, but we gonna work on dat."

"Spoiled! What do you mean spoiled?"

"Just start da car, shorty, befo' we miss da people-goin'-to-work money."

"The people-going-to-work money?"

"Yeah, da early people dat buy a bag to take da work with dem. I got about fo' customers like dat. If I get out there about seven I can catch 'em, and like I said, today is Bud Billiken, so we might get rid of all eight bags dis morning. Let's roll, shorty."

"The Bud Billiken parade. That's the parade with all black people, right?"

"Yeah."

"I've never been to it. I heard about it, but my parents don't attend. We go to the Christmas parade."

"No stuff? I thought all black people went to da Bud Billiken parade."

"Not all black people."

She started the car and drove to the park, and as Chance said, people were out and about, setting up for the parade and their own smaller cookouts. Grills, folding chairs and tables were being put in place. Families appeared to be vying for positions between trees and near waterspouts.

She heard the PA system being checked, radios being played, and mothers calling after small children that were running through the park as if it were the afternoon. Volleyball nets were going up and softballs, Frisbees and footballs were being tossed through the early morning air. She sat in the car and took it all in. Never in her life had she seen so many black people up and about, and so festive so early.

Ice cream trucks were out and doing business, and a couple of mounted police rode through. She counted over seven different family reunion T-shirts, which were all yellow or red. One family, however, the Hurstuns from Alabama, wore sky blue.

Chance hadn't been gone twenty minutes before he returned, excited. "Sold out and didn't walk a block. We got to get over to Big Time's and right back out here. Today gonna be a hellava day." He joyfully kissed her. "We gonna make some money," he sang.

The scene in Big Time's building parking lot was pretty much the same. People were hauling grills, blankets and chairs to their cars. Everyone in the community was getting ready for the parade. Upstairs in

Big Time's apartment, the mood was just as busy. Five other women were there getting new outfits to wear to the parade, and three other smoke dudes were waiting to get served by Big Time.

Juanita's clothes were of good quality. She sold Guess jeans, DKNY tops, Pelle Pelle shorts and tops, Fila tennis skirts and the cutest Nike jersey dresses. And best of all, she had plus sizes. The sundress Patrice chose with the underwear came to fifty dollars.

Chance was gearing up to complain until Juanita told Patrice that if she babysat Paco that night, the clothes were free. Chance agreed for her, and he also asked Juanita if they could freshen and change clothes in her bathroom, because he wanted to get back out to the park.

The other shoppers and smoke dudes were gone. It was only Juanita, Patrice, Big Time and Paco in the apartment, and Big Time was in one of the bedrooms getting Paco ready for the parade. Juanita was sitting on one end of the couch, folding white clothes out of a laundry basket. Patrice was sitting at the other end with her new dress in her lap.

Juanita said she didn't have a problem with Patrice using her shower and bathroom, but she refused the courtesy to Chance because "Boy, you don't know to flush a toilet. Three times your nasty, foul ass messed up my bathroom. I told you last time never again, and I meant it. Go on down the hall to the abandoned apartment. The water is on down there. You can go down there and wash your ass." She tossed him a face cloth from the basket of white clothes. "And you can grab that bar of soap off the kitchen sink. You ain't gonna do nothing but wash your face and under your arms, anyway."

Chance caught the face cloth and went into the kitchen and got the bar of soap. Then he sulked out of the apartment.

Patrice was embarrassed for him.

"Girl, I'm glad he got a girlfriend. Maybe he'll take better care of himself. A helluva hustler he is, but that boy hate to stop and wash his ass. He'll run for two or three days straight then want to come in here and sit his smelly ass on my sofa. No, no, no, not here.

"Big Time has to make him wash up just like you do a little ol' boy. And girl, when he takes a dump, he lights up the whole apartment. Don't get me wrong, young lady, I like C. Big Time treat him like a little brother, but the boy just ain't got no home training. He eats without washing his hands, farts in mixed company, and he will dig a booger out of his brains and wipe it on his pants. He needs a nice young lady like you to house-train him.

"Shoot, Big Time wasn't much better when we moved in together. He didn't even own a toothbrush. All these niggas from this neighborhood know how to do is make money. Don't none of them know a thing about living in a nice place. They will sleep outside in the park or anywhere. Will have a pocket full of money and won't rent a room.

"I got tired of Magnum and C sleeping here. I told Big Time his homeboys had to sleep someplace other than my sofa. Both of them follow behind Big Time like he's they daddy, and I guess for the most part, he is. But I ain't they mama, so I ain't got to be bothered with they asses.

"I told Big Time that whenever they spend the night over here, he had to sleep out here on the sofa with them. And I tell you this, young mama, they ain't slept here since I said that. Them two smelly boys can kiss my half Puerto Rican ass. I wasn't having them stinking up my nice place. I wasn't raised like that."

Patrice knew no Puerto Ricans personally, and the ones she knew from school sounded Mexican. Juanita sounded black; blacker than her.

"You go in the bathroom and get yourself together. After you come out, we can talk some more. I'ma tell you all about that little nasty-ass C."

Once Patrice was in Juanita's bathroom, she understood the woman protecting it. It was a small female retreat that was painted a soft pink. The shower curtains were white, and the shower rod had a pink cover over it. The white tub had pink and white flower decals on the side, and the shower mat was made of pink rubber flowers. Her porcelain white sink had a pink flower painted in the bowl. The sink held dainty, little white shell hand soaps in a dish. She had a white-and-pink striped towel set with matching face cloths. The tile floor was covered with a shaggy pink bathroom rug. The medicine cabinet mirror was surrounded by pink and beige quarter-sized seashells. The white toilet had a cushy pink seat and lid, and the potpourri-filled glass dish Juanita had placed on top of the medicine cabinet gave the small area a wonderful floral scent.

Patrice removed her heeled sandals, stepped into the tub, and opened the window. She didn't want the bodily functions she had release fouling the ambiance of the room. Nor did she want to get on Juanita's "no home training" list.

She showered using the towels Juanita gave her and she made sure the bathroom was left like she found it, wiping excess water from the face bowl and using the pink toilet brush to remove the tracks her bowels left in the toilet bowl. Juanita would never call her nasty.

When she came from the bathroom to the living area, she saw Chance sitting on the couch, and he looked much better. He had on clean jeans and a clean black Nike jersey with all-white gym shoes that looked new.

She sat next to him on the couch and noticed he smelled better too.

Dressed in her new sundress, which matched her old sandals perfectly, she wrapped her torn birthday dress, the Chicago skyline T-shirt Chance bought for her, and her old underwear into a tight bundle. She sat next to Chance, waiting for him to comment on how good she looked in her new off-white linen sundress. Juanita didn't sell bras, so she wore the same brassiere from the day before.

"You look good in dat outfit," Chance said, smiling when she sat next to him.

"You look nice too."

They were alone in the living area.

"Where is Juanita and Big Time?"

Chance grinned. Patrice was beginning to recognize the tight lip, top-row-of-teeth-showing grin as his devilish grin. He nodded his head toward the bedroom door. "Listen close and you can hear what dey doin'."

She didn't have to listen close. The moans came through the door loud and clear.

"Ooh, they're doing it!"

"Yeap, dat's why I'm glad Big Time gave me my work already. Dey will be at it fo' hours. He said dey was going to meet us at da park in a little while. Dat ain't gonna happen. Dey will be fuckin' da whole mornin'. Naw, we ain't gonna see dem at da park dis mornin'. We probably won't see dem 'til time fo' you to baby sit." He stood to leave. "Let's roll, shorty."

"Don't call me shorty. I'm taller than you."

She was a good four inches taller than him, she noticed while following him to the door.

"Yeah, but you younger dan me, so you still a shorty to me. Shorty."

The park was crowded at ten in the morning, and people continued to come. Chance had gotten a colorful Flintstone blanket from Juanita. He spread the cartoon blanket on the grass under a huge maple tree, carving out space between two picnicking families.

Patrice sat on the blanket while Chance went through the park, getting rid of his work. The family that was setting up on her left, the Bostons who lived in Chicago, wouldn't let her sit alone. They sent children over with pops and chips, and before long, she was helping the ladies clear off tables and uncover food.

They sent her down to the spout for water, and once they found out she had a car, she was sent to the store for ice, seasoning salt, lighter fluid, plastic forks and paper plates, because Selma, their sister who drank, forgot every damn thing.

Patrice got new recipes for potato salad and fried corn casserole, and she learned how to cube a watermelon, along with the right way to cut a chicken for the grill and how to season spare ribs. They tried to teach her how to play Bid Whist, but she couldn't understand why low cards could beat face cards. By two that afternoon, the Bostons had officially adopted her and Chance, and they were both expected at the Sixty-third Street Tabernacle for Sunday morning service.

Patrice rises up from her Berber carpet and her memories of Chance. She decides to go over to his place and tell him what happened to her yesterday; about the nut shooting at her. Perhaps he can offer some advice, and maybe even help her figure out who it is. There really is no one else who can help her in this type of situation.

She goes into her bedroom and slides into a robe. She checks her reflection in the vanity mirror. She gathers her hair and pulls it together, so it will hang over her right shoulder, and she decides to open the robe a little more. Chance responds better when cleavage is present.

She's standing in the hall about to knock on Chance's door when it opens. Standing before her is the bald-headed waitress with a baby in her arms, and Chance is behind her, carrying a baby's car seat. He's dressed for work.

If she weren't standing directly in front of them, she would leave without saying a thing. The sight of the skinny table server gets her angry. And she's wondering whose fucking baby it is. No way it's Chance's. It's not dark enough, of that she's certain.

She utters her first words to Chance in over a year. "Hello, Chance. Something happened yesterday and I need your . . . your input on how I should handle it."

She gathers her robe, covering her cleavage, because the bald headed waitress is staring at her exposed skin with daggers in her eyes.

Chance doesn't seem shocked to see her at his door. He answers as if they spoke yesterday. "No problem, Patrice."

Nadine walks past them, slightly bumping her.

She and Chance are left facing each other. Neither looks away. He looks good in that tan suit. Damn good. When they were together, getting him to wear a suit was like pulling teeth.

"But I see you're leaving," Patrice says. "Would you mind if we met later?" She lowers her hand, allowing her robe to open again. She sees his eyes gravitate. She can still control some parts of him.

"No, not at all. Would this evening be fine after work?"

"Yes. I won't be going out, so when you return, please, stop by."

"I will. I will most certainly do that."

*****

Chance can think of no other word to describe the vast, half-a-football-field office space designated for him and his staff, except "fly." The East Lake Bakeries North Side office is all loft space with brick walls, exposed beams and a twenty-five-foot high ceiling. Chrome spotlights hang from the high ceiling by thick black electrical cords. Chance always thought that lofts were dark and dusty, but this place has little, if any, noticeable dust, and the hanging spotlights have the place lit up like a dentist's office.

"Do you like it?" Amy asks. She is Mr. Sharp's daughter and is showing him the space.

"Yes. I will be very comfortable here."

"Good." Amy obviously wasn't planning on working today. She was sitting on one of the two steps that led into the East Lake offices, when Chance walked up.

She is dressed in gray sweat pants and an over-sized white T-shirt. Her straight, black hair is pulled back in a long ponytail. She is wearing running shoes with no socks and is walking on the back of them, and she also smells of gin.

"The office supplies and furniture catalog is on the small table in the corner." She gives a faltering point to a table across the room. "A phone should be over there somewhere. Order what you want to fill the space. I wrote the company's account number on the cover. Daddy said to get everything you need, and he wants you to review and be familiar with the files that are also on the table."

Chance can see the files and the phone, but he doesn't see a chair.

"Is your father here? I was expecting to meet with him."

"No, Mr. Bates, my father is a very ill man. My mother won't let him work on the weekends. He has had three heart attacks and two cancer surgeries. His doctor forbids him to work more than three hours a day through the week. We have all been trying to get him to retire, but he won't.

"My mother probably heard him on the phone with you and canceled his plans. That's why he called me and told me to let you in. I live three blocks west of here. These are your keys, and the alarm code is 1123." She drops a ring with four keys in his hand. "I'll show you later all that they open, and please, if you have any questions, save them for Monday. I need to leave.

"I don't do A.M.'s, and I certainly don't do 6 a.m., and I try my best not to work on the weekends. So this is a double no-no for me. The catalog company takes orders on Saturday. They will have what you order here by Monday morning. See you in the P.M. on Monday, Mr. Bates."

Chance notices that she doesn't extend the tour to her work area. He wants to see how she filled her space. That would give him some direction with his.

"He said order what I need. Does that include computers and such?"

"Of course, Mr. Bates. Order whatever you think you and your staff needs: desk, phones, computers, printers, chairs. Go office shopping." She turns and leaves, not looking back.

Chance is standing with the keys in his hand, looking at her back walking out of the loft.

"Oh." She turns around. "Father is going in the hospital for a week. His secretary will be working with you during that time . . . Yes, I believe that is all he wanted me to relay. Bye-bye." Again, she turns and heads for the door, this time not stopping.

No boss for a week. Mr. Sharp didn't look sick to Chance. He was robust and challenging. His demeanor did not match that of an ill man.

Office shopping. This is not something Chance is skilled at or cares to do, but he knows someone who would enjoy it. Chance walks across the hardwood floor, liking the slapping sound that his leather soles make on the floor. He picks up the phone and dials Patrice's number. Since she has broken the yearlong silence between them, the call is an easy one to make. Her phone is picked up on the second ring.

"Patrice?"

"Yes?"

"It's Chance."

"Okay."

"I got a situation where I need your . . . your business expertise. Can I pick you up in about fifteen minutes?"

"Sure. I'll meet you downstairs."

When Chance hangs up the phone, his attention goes to the files on the table. He recognizes the majority of the company names on the labels of the files. Looking through them, he notices contact information and past buying history from his old employer. The files even contain his old company's order sheets. At least sixty percent of the files are customers from his route. A smile opens his face. These people he could sell easily.

Chance stops at the florist and buys a single white rose, has the thorns removed and a thin, white satin ribbon tied around its stem. He's never picked Patrice up for a date without a flower or flowers. He hadn't bought Nadine a flower. For some reason, he didn't think of it. Why hadn't he extended that same courtesy to Nadine? This isn't even a date, and he is stopping to get Patrice a flower.

Nadine didn't ask one question about Patrice when he dropped her off this morning, and Chance appreciates that. So far, Nadine is drama-free. And the smile she gave him when he handed her a check for $300 to help her catch up on her bills makes him feel good. No, not good; manly is a better word.

He feels like a provider because she really needs the help, and he is able to help her. Giving her more than what she was expecting shocked her to joyful tears. The only time Patrice ever needed his help was when he first met her, and even then, she only needed him for a short time. Her intelligence showed on the streets too.

The way Chance remembers it, the trouble really started after the Bud Billiken parade, when Patrice went to babysit Juanita's and Big Time's son. They had a bunch of fun that day at the parade. Plenty of money was made, and they became a couple.

It was the best time Chance had ever had at a Bud Billiken parade. Thinking back, he contributes his good time to being with Patrice. He'd never taken a date to the parade before. People treated him differently while he was in Patrice's company. Being with her, families invited him to join them in their picnicking. He played cards, softball and ate like he was part of a family.

He taught a couple of little boys how to throw a Frisbee and swing a bat. He even changed a toddler's diaper. It was a good time, and he was sorry to see it end. Big Time and Juanita never made it out to the parade. When evening came, Chance rolled the blanket up, and he and Patrice headed over to their place to baby sit.

Big Time, who in Chance's seventeen-year-old eyes had it made, was not a happy man. He often told Chance he hated living in the projects and he hated hustling instead of working. He wanted to be like his father, a bus driver for the Chicago Transit Authority who owned three apartment buildings. But Big Time started "the game" young and was the first to admit he didn't have the patience needed for a regular a nine-to-five.

"I been making fast money since I was eight years old. Shit, I was making my own scratch before I even knew who my daddy was. A store buggy full of pop bottles and a hot car radio fed me before him. I don't hold anything against him, though, and like you, I think squares live a better life, but I always thought it just wasn't for me."

He passed the joint to Chance. They were sitting on the couch in the living room while Patrice, Juanita and his son were in one of the back bedrooms. Chance admired how Big Time dressed. He was wearing a pair of black tailored pants, and the matching short-sleeve jacket was across the arm of the couch next to him. He had on a red silk T-shirt and a forty-inch gold chain with a gold-and-jade marijuana medallion hung around his neck.

Chance had brought up the subject of living a square's life as opposed to a thug's. He was telling Big Time about all the fun he had with the squares at the Bud Billiken parade and picnic.

"Now, my daddy, he used to hustle, but once he got that good job with CTA, he squared up quick. My uncles couldn't even get him to go to the racetrack. He cut all his outside women loose, including my mama, and settled down with his wife.

"He only has daughters with his wife. If I had been a girl, I probably wouldn't have known who he was, but being his only son, he kept me in his life. My mama says he couldn't deny me if he wanted to, because me and him is the only two tar-black niggas with acorn heads in Chicago.

"It's not a problem for some people to square up, to go legit. If I wasn't so good at what I do, and Juanita wasn't such a damn good booster, we would have squared up when Paco was born. That's what we said we were going to do, but I'm telling you the honest to God truth; when that alarm clock went off at 5:30 the Monday morning when we was both supposed to get up and go look for jobs, shit, she beat me to cutting that loud sucker off.

"We riding good. We eating good. We go on two vacations a year and our crib is laid. Yeah, it's in the jets, but we got everything we need and want in it. Shit, we do our business in the jets. She's from the jets and I am from the jets. Her mama live upstairs, my mama live downstairs. What the fuck. This funky motherfucker was home."

Chance heard him say "was" and listened closer. Big Time was telling him something. He hit the joint twice and passed it back.

"The thing that I hate the most is that the police can take everything I got in a second. If I get busted, everything I got in here, my truck and my Caddy, is theirs. And the lawyers are going to take all the cash the police don't take. The system is raw on a thug hustler like me." He inhaled deeply from the joint, smacked his full lips and exhaled.

"Everything I got can be gone in the blink of an eye. It's not like that for my old man. His shit is legit. He's got property, bank accounts, a good job and a lawyer on retainer that calls him Mr. Olden. I'm not Mr. anybody, and that's the shit I hate." He passed the joint back to Chance and opened a book of Tops rolling papers. "You finish that one." He reached under the couch and grabbed a Ziploc bag stuffed full of green weed. He stuck two Tops papers together and rolled another joint.

"What we do ain't easy. It ain't easy to make something out of nothing every day of the week, but, C, no respect comes with living this type of life. At least not from the squares. Yeah, we build a rep, but that don't mean shit outside of the hood. Downtown, you and I ain't shit but two other street niggas for them squares to laugh at. And they laugh at us just like we laugh at them goofy-walking motherfuckers. And white squares walk the worst, holding their asses all tight and shit.

"And, you know, it wasn't until I spent time with my old man as a man, did I know that squares didn't like us. They're jealous. They jealous of our lifestyle and mad 'cause we don't have to get up all early every day. Mad because they think we don't have to answer to a boss. They think our life is all fun and games and that we're lazy.

"But you let one of them have to stay up two or three days selling weed to pay the rent, and see how easy they think this hustling lifestyle is then. You let one of them have to worry about the stick man or crooked-ass cops taking their goods and see how simple this lifestyle looks to them then." He pulled a small box of wooden matches from his pants pocket, struck a stick match and put it to the joint. "A square wouldn't last a day doing what we do. Their life is way easier.

"Juanita doesn't know this, C, but yesterday I gave my daddy thirty-two grand to get me a building. Shit, I'm twenty-seven years old, man, and I can't get a phone or a light bill cut on in my name. Yeah, I'm hood rich, but that don't mean shit in the real world. My daddy's lawyer's going to hook it up so it looks like he bought me the building. It's going to be mine. I'm about to be a property owner."

Chance put out what was left of the joint in a gray clay ashtray with BAHAMAS etched in the side. He was trying to listen to Big Time, but the green weed had him wanting to chill.

"He told me a couple of months ago that if I showed him I was serious about going legit, he would help me. After I gave him the thirty-two grand yesterday, the old nigga got tears in his eyes and started talking about getting me on with him at CTA. He said if I get my system clean, he would get me a shot. Smoking this one here with you is my last one." He passed Chance the other joint.

"What I'm trying to tell you, C, is that I'm about to retire, my brother. I spent all afternoon on the phone with travel agents. Juanita thinks we're going to Puerto Rico on a simple vacation, but, C, they got a doctor down there who can get your system clean in three weeks: fat cells, hair cells, everything. When I come back, I'm moving into my building and going to work with my old man."

Chance held the joint without hitting it. Big Time was retiring?

"I'm going tell Juanita tonight over dinner she can get on with me or move on. I love her, man, but this is for me and Paco. I don't want him to have to make something out of nothing every day of his life. I want him to start his days with something. That's how people get ahead, C, when they got something to start with.

"He's going to be able to afford to go to college. He's not going to have to worry about the police and lawyers taking his shit. He's a greedy little dude, C. I can tell if he starts in the game, he'll never leave it. I'm going to start him out legit, and pray he stays that way. Give him what I didn't have: a chance."

"But who am I supposed to get my weed from?" Chance passed the joint back without taking a pull.

"I was trying to figure that out. I was going to put either you or Magnum on to the weed connect. I can't put both of y'all on. And I was thinking more toward you, because you think and you're not as hot-headed as Magnum. But I was worried that Magnum would get jealous and fuck with you about it after I was gone."

"I can handle my own."

"I know, C, but I didn't want to start no bad blood between y'all." Big Time heavily inhaled the joint, causing the red glow to move up half of it.

"It won't be no bad blood. I'll give him the same deals you gave him."

"Yeah." He exhaled. "But he will look at it like you profiting off of him, when y'all was once equals. Just like you would if he got the weed connect. It's a move up." He tossed the joint in the clay ashtray without putting it out. "You know what I'm saying?"

Big Time had a point. He would be pissed if he had to cop from Magnum.

"What about you hook me up with the weed connect, but me and Magnum split the profits? We both run what you built."

"Yeah." A big smile crossed his face. "I like that. That's thinking. Page that dude and get him up here. We'll get this all straight right now."

"No! That's not fair." It was Patrice. She and Juanita entered the living room.

Juanita, who was dressed in a blue duster and had Paco in her arms said, "Man, who is talking about 'will have to get on or move on'? I gave you a son! I ain't no damn hoochie mama who you make decisions without. I'm part of this. You ain't been telling me what I will do and what I won't do."

"Hold up, it's men talking up here. Y'all better get on in the back." Big Time tried to stand, but Juanita put Paco in his lap.

"Men my fat ass. You sitting up here, *Edward Olden, Jr.,* trying to plan my future. You ain't that big-time.

Nigga, when you was selling joints in high school, I was there. When your ass was so hungry you was cross-eyed, it was me that snuck my mama's tamales out to you. When your ass didn't have no boots for the winter, I went up in the store and stole you some.

"Nigga, we been a team since catch-a-girl-freak-a-girl, and I let your slow ass catch me. Ain't no 'get on or move on' between us. I gave you the son you trying to provide for. How dare you plan a damn thing for him or you without me?" Juanita stood above Big Time with her finger in his face and her other hand on her hip.

"Us two against the world. Ain't that what you was saying this afternoon when your ass was knee deep in my pussy? Us two. Us two. Nigga, please. And for your information, your daddy called this morning and was telling me shit about the building on 86th and Jeffrey, and how much better it's going to be for us to raise Paco away from the projects. He respects me as your woman, as the mother of your son, like I thought you did." She huffed and sat on the couch between Chance and Big Time.

She looked over at Patrice, who was still standing, and said, "Don't believe shit that come out they mouth when they be fucking. It's all lies." Then she started crying.

It was Big Time's turn to huff. He reached into his tailor-made pants pocket and pulled out a small black velvet box. He placed it on the coffee table. "Did my daddy tell you about that too?"

Even though she was crying, Chance noticed her eyes had focused on the box, and so did Patrice's, as she sat in the armchair.

"Daddy was supposed to be calling to find out the date we going to arrive in Puerto Rico. He wants to be there for the wedding."

"What?" Juanita's black eyes didn't leave the box.

"Yeah. That's why your mama is going. She's arranging the church and getting all your family together."

"What?"

"Yeah, I figured I might as well be legit all around. That is . . ." He got off the couch and put Paco in Chance's lap and got on his knees. "If you want to marry a square dude like me." He picked up the box from the table and opened the lid.

It was the biggest diamond Chance had ever seen. Patrice gasped.

"Oh, Edward!"

Big Time picked Juanita up from the couch and gave Chance a wink. He left Paco with Chance and Patrice in the living room.

"We ain't gonna see dem until tomorrow," Chance said to Patrice while he laid a sleepy Paco out on the couch.

"That was so sweet. He loves her." Patrice was crying. "And she loves him, and they got a wonderful little boy, and they're going to get married and move into a new house."

"Yeah, all dat is cool, but we had business to discuss. He coulda called Magnum first and we coulda got it all straightened out. They leavin' tomorrow. It might not get right 'til he gets back. And three weeks is a long time to go with no weed to sell."

"Well, if you tell him in the morning that you want to meet the connect and run things yourself, you won't have to wait and talk to Magnum."

"What?"

"Do it without Magnum. Big Time must think you can, or else he would not have offered it to you."

"You don't know what you talkin' about. Me and Magnum is boys."

"Someone has to be the boss. If you two are really friends, you being the boss shouldn't matter. And I bet if Magnum was given the opportunity you have been given, he would take it."

Thoughtfully, he answered, "Yeah, he would."

"So, why don't you? You're in the right place at the right time." Patrice moved from the armchair to the sofa and sat next to Chance. "Don't turn your back on opportunity. My father says it doesn't knock often."

"Opportunity, huh?" he whispered in her ear, almost kissing her.

"Yes, Chance. An opportunity."

"It's kinda like right now, me and you got an opportunity to get together." He put his arm across her shoulder.

"What?"

"You heard me. Me and you got our opportunity to get together. Paco is 'sleep. They ain't coming out until the morning, so me and you can move this table out the way and stretch out on this rug and take advantage of our opportunity."

"Juanita would object."

"Shorty, Juanita in there takin' care of her business with her man, like you should be doin'."

"You're my man?" she asked with mock attitude.

"Yeap. That be me."

Chapter Twelve

It was a two-bedroom condominium with living room, dining room, kitchen, sitting room and two baths. The walls were sandy beige throughout, with high stucco ceilings. The dark brown carpet ran through the connecting hallway to all the rooms except the kitchen and bathrooms. Those floors were covered in a beige-and-forest-green star-patterned marble tile. The tile had been recently waxed, so the heavy smell of floor wax was throughout the condo.

The only windows in the condominium were in the kitchen and the bathrooms. The layout of the place reminded Sharon a lot of Cherry's apartment. One entered in the living room, the dining room was beyond that and the two bedrooms were to the left down the hall. The kitchen sat to the left of the dining room.

All the furniture was dark. A green velvet sofa and loveseat along with a black velvet armchair occupied the living room. The walls were bare and there were no coffee or end tables. There was one tall Tiffany-shaded brass lamp in the far corner of the room.

The dining room was completely empty of furniture. The kitchen held a white stove, a white refrigerator, a white microwave and a chrome sink. There was space for kitchen cabinets, but none had been installed. No kitchen table or chairs. Newspaper was taped over the curtain-less window glass.

Sharon was following behind Elaine, who was showing her the place. She had her arms full of shopping bags from Marshall Field's and Lord and Taylor. She stopped in the kitchen and asked, "Where is your kitchen?"

"You're standing in it."

"Tables, chairs, curtains, dishes, you know, your stuff?"

"See, I decided that I will no longer cook. There is to be no cooking done in here. Nothing will be cooked at any time. No microwaving, no boiling, no baking and for God's sake, no frying. The refrigerator is used to store wine and spring water only. Eating is to be done outside of our home. There are several very good restaurants and diners within walking distance."

"You don't eat or cook in here?" Sharon asked.

"No," Elaine replied.

"Why?"

"It's just safer that way."

"The choir?" Sharon questioned.

"The choir," Elaine repeated.

"Well, maybe you won't hear them as much with me here."

"Maybe. Come, let me show you your room," she said dryly.

The little burned girl told Sharon to take her new stuff and leave.

The old lady schoolteacher told her to call the doctor and see if he could find her a safer place.

The mailman told her to stay put.

Both bedrooms were identical and just as bare as the rest of the condo. Each had a walk-in closet, attached bath and a queen-sized bed in the middle of the room with no headboard. A plain white fitted sheet and cover sheet were all that draped the beds. Elaine's walk-in closet, however, was full of clothes and shoes, but none of the items were scattered about in the bedroom. Her bedroom, like Sharon's, held only a bare bed without a pillow.

"I didn't know how to furnish them since we are going to be conducting business in them. I didn't know if I should decorate them feminine fancy, sultry sexy or bondage freaky. See, my thinking was we could decide together. What do you think?"

The mailman screamed, *Bondage freaky!*

The little burned girl whined to leave.

The schoolteacher said, *If she going to stay, go with feminine fancy.*

Sharon didn't care. She hadn't thought about décor. Her mind was on where to go and how to recruit more girls. Her plan didn't include her doing much "dating." She was going to leave that to Elaine's hot little self and whatever new girls she found, but sultry sex did sound better.

Because the voices were so loud in her head, particularly the mailman, she was thinking it was time to take her medicine and lay down for a nap.

"Elaine, you wore me out at the stores, and thank you so much for buying the nice outfits, but I need to take my medicine, take a nap and plan our evening. Tonight is a working night, girl."

"Already? I thought you would want to wait a couple of days."

"Money doesn't wait. The sooner we get started, the quicker you learn."

"I hope you're thinking about places where there are some black men. I haven't been with nothing but white men since I been out, and I got sorta into black guys on the ward. Don't get me wrong. I had fun with the white guys, but I'm missing that deep penetration that Nate gave me."

Through her sly smile, Sharon noticed Elaine's teeth had been whitened since her release.

"Did you charge them?"

"Who?"

"The white guys you been with since you been out. Did you charge them?"

"Of course."

"Then where is my money?" Sharon squared off in front of Elaine.

"I spent it on your clothes," she said smartly.

Sharon didn't think twice about her action. She slapped Elaine so hard she fell to the chocolate-brown carpet. She then kicked her twice in the stomach.

Sharon squatted down to the floor to Elaine, grabbed a handful of her blond feathered hair and yanked her head up to her mouth. She spoke harshly and quietly. "You don't spend a damn dime before it touches my hand. You understand me, bitch?"

"What?" A confused, frighten and dazed Elaine asked.

Sharon bounced Elaine's head off the carpeted floor twice. "Every damn dime you get, bitch, comes to my hand first." She dragged her by her thin hair to the bed and slung her on top of it. She straddled her and slapped her repeatedly, saying over and over, "Every damn dime you get, every damn dime you get . . . comes to my hand first."

Sharon rose from the bed and riffled through the shopping bags, pulling a Louis Vuitton belt from the one of the bags. She ripped a docile Elaine's skirt and blouse off and beat her all over her body with the belt.

Standing over Elaine on the side of the bare bed, Sharon ordered her to take her panties off and open her thighs. When she was slow about complying, Sharon ripped off her panties and forced a whimpering Elaine's thighs open.

With her forearm under Elaine's neck, Shawn pinned her to the bed. Sharon forced one finger into Elaine and worked it around until she felt moistness, then she inserted three. After repeated insertions of the three, Elaine's whimpers turned to gasps. When the area was slippery wet, Sharon balled her small hand into a fist and went into Elaine.

"This here is the only big black dick you're going to take free, bitch."

Elaine slung her thighs wide open and took Sharon's arm almost to her elbow. After ten full thrusts, her orgasms came steady and hard. Sharon removed her fist and Elaine coiled up in a ball and shuddered, again and again.

Sharon didn't want her to rest.

"Bitch, get your ass out of the bed and go stand in that closet, and I betta not hear a damn sound until I tell you to come out. Move, ho!"

Elaine tried to jump out of the bed, but she collapsed.

"To the closet, bitch," Sharon snarled.

On her knees, Elaine crawled into the walk-in closet, pulling the door closed behind her.

Sharon went into the attached bathroom and washed Elaine's wetness from her hand and slender arm. She couldn't stand the smell of another woman on her. Satisfied the scent was gone, she went to Elaine's room and retrieved her purse, which she carried back to her room. Sitting on the bare bed, she went through the purse, taking credit cards, car keys and $600 in cash. She opened her checkbook and was shocked to see that Elaine had over $14,000 in the account. She called her out of the closet.

"Ho, come here!"

The door cracked open, but Elaine didn't appear.

"Bitch, don't make me come and get you."

Elaine walked out of the closet, eyes wide open. Sharon looked through the purse and found a pen. She tossed her the checkbook and the pen, which fell to the floor at Elaine's feet.

"Ho, pick up the damn pen and checkbook and write me a check for thirteen thousand."

"But this money is from my ex-husband. I didn't get any of this from turning tricks," Elaine offered in slight protest.

Sharon snatched the belt from the bed and quickly stood. "Ho, I didn't ask where the fuck the money came from."

Elaine snatched up the pen and checkbook up, and began writing while she kept an eye on the belt in Sharon's hand.

"And when you finish, you're going out to buy some food and shit for around here. I want bacon, eggs, hamburger meat and steaks in that refrigerator, and a gallon of motherfucking milk and box of Captain Crunch. Hurry up with the damn check."

Elaine tore the check from the book and handed it to her.

"Bitch, give me the checkbook too." She snatched it from Elaine's hands. "You have no damn money unless I give it to you." She threw Elaine's ripped clothes from the bed to the floor. "Now get dressed and get your ass to the store."

Sharon sat on the bed. She handed Elaine eighty of the $600 she took from her purse.

"And don't take all day. When I wake up, that damn icebox better be full."

Elaine put her clothes on and back together as best she could. She held the eighty dollars tight in her hand and fled for the door. The door to the condo hadn't closed before Sharon was up and ripping out the lining of her own winter coat, trying to get to the two thousand plus dollars she'd taken from Linda five years ago.

It was still there. She put that money with the cash from Elaine's purse. She grabbed the plastic bag she was issued from the state and checked for her own identification. It was there. She dumped all of Elaine's contents from the purse and filled it with her own belongings and identification. She took Elaine's credit cards and her identification.

With one swing of the arm, she grabbed all the bags of new clothes off the floor. She decided to leave the Louis Vuitton belt. She was out the door and in a cab in less than three minutes.

Her first stop was First Standard Bank, where she cashed the check without a hitch. She was expecting to hear the voices offering directions and opinions, but her head was filled with only her own thoughts. The cabdriver who had waited for her protested when she gave him the address of the projects on Western Avenue as her destination. She offered him a twenty-five dollar tip plus fare, and his protest stopped.

She didn't know if Linda still lived there or not, but she walked up the stairs hoping she did. She turned more than one head in the stairwell with the Marshal Field's and Lord and Taylor bags. When she got to the second floor landing, she thought she caught a glimpse of the little burned girl, but it wasn't her. It was a cute little girl with multicolored barrettes in her hair, playing with her toddler brother.

Linda's door was open, but the screen door was locked and a big steel blade floor fan was on full blast, blowing air out from the kitchen. Sharon smelled ham hocks simmering. She knocked hard on the screen door.

A man's head instantly popped up from the leather look sofa. The high arm of the sofa had his and Linda's upper torsos hidden. Sharon spotted their nude legs hanging to the side of the sofa.

"Come back later," an unseen Linda yelled.

"No, bitch, I got to come in now!"

"I know it ain't." Linda jumped up from the sofa, naked. "I'll be damned. Look at your thieving, crazy ass. And in the same damn sailor outfit I bought you. And look like you been shoppin'. Bitch, you better have my money."

Sharon watched Linda walk her hefty frame to the screen door, grinning. She hadn't lost a pound. She unlatched the screen door. The embrace was warm and their tears genuine.

"It's good to see you, girl."

"You too, Linda. It's so good to see you."

The man, who had put his pants and tee shirt on, walked past, saying, "Linda, I'll get with you later to finish."

"What?" Linda snapped. "Nigga, you nutted. Don't be tryin' no slick shit with me. You came befo' she knocked on the damn do'. Get on out of here." She held the door open for him. "Don't piss me off today, Tommy." She latched the screen door behind him. She turned and looked back at Sharon. "Is something for me in those bags?"

"Not unless you can get into a size three."

"Not in this life. Come on in here, Ms. Ann, and catch me up on you."

Linda pulled the sheet off the sofa that she and Tommy had lain on. The smell of sex was dominated by the simmering ham hocks.

"Sit on down. Let me put this sheet in the laundry. Hold on a minute." She ran in and out of the bathroom and returned dressed in a white terrycloth robe. She joined Sharon on the sofa.

"Baby, you know the police and the social workers came up in here and took Chance two days after you cut up that white man in the bus station. And it wasn't anything I could do to stop those people from taking him. I told them you had family in the building, but they wasn't trying to hear it. And I don't think your mama ever went down to check on him. So . . . Chance is in the system, baby." Linda hadn't met eyes with Sharon the entire time she spoke of Chance. "You know I couldn't keep him, and I hope you ain't mad at me about it."

"I know he's in the system." Sharon had her eyes on the far wall. She hadn't come looking for Chance. "The doctors told me. And how could I be mad at you? I'm the one that left him on you. It should be me asking you if you're mad at me."

The friends' eyes met. They were best friends before they knew what the term meant.

"Well, since you're asking, what possessed your frail ass to steal from me?" Linda said with challenge in her voice.

Sharon quickly opened Elaine's purse and brought out Linda's cash, plus what was left from the $600.

"It's just like I took it, same bills and everything." She laid the bills out on the table.

Linda's mouth opened in a huge smile. Sharon saw every tooth and the one empty space in her head.

"Damn if it ain't the same bills. You know I mark my bills right here in the corner. You see my little loop circle on each one. Now, these other bills here, they ain't mine."

"Oh those . . . that's the interest on the loan," Sharon explained with a smile.

"Loan? Bitch, you stole that money. But I'ma take the interest all the same." Linda scooped up the bills and hugged Sharon tight. "Girl, you always been good with me. My money plus some. Now, that's how a real bitch gets the books straight.

"Did you know you made the papers? Girl, every nigga around here and on the strip was talking about you like they knew you personally. Yeah, you was a celebrity for a little while.

"It's good to see you, girl. So, did you escape or get released?"

"I got released, but I just blew it." Sharon relaxed and sat back on the leather-look sofa. There was a time she envied every piece of furniture in the apartment. It was better than any she'd seen in her life. Her mother's furniture was from the Goodwill and pieces they had found in empty project apartments.

"What do you mean?"

"I ripped off this white chick who I was supposed to live with. She wanted me to hook her up with hoeing, and I was going to do it until I saw the chick had $14,000. Then plans changed.

"I was laying the law down to her wannabe ass, and I went through her purse and saw all that money in her account. I figured, why be bothered with working her when I could take what I wanted right then. She was too hard-headed anyway, and she was black dick crazy. Ho wanted a big black dick worse than she wanted money."

Linda sat prone with interest. "You took the whole fourteen grand?"

"Damn near."

Linda made clucking sounds with her cheeks. "You think she's going to the police?"

Sighing, Sharon answered, "I don't know. But I think I need to put some space between me and her, but I don't want to go too far because I need to stay in touch with my doctor."

"A shrink or a regular doctor?"

"A shrink. The medicine he gave me worked some. It's new, and I think he's the only one who got it."

"Damn . . . okay, so tell me exactly what you did to the white chick. Did you use a weapon to take the money?"

"No . . . I was laying down the law with a belt, and I did fist fuck her."

"Shit. What was you gonna do, pimp the ho yourself?"

"Yeah."

"Damn. Did anybody else see what happened?"

"No."

"Is she bruised or marked at all?"

"Maybe some whip marks from the belt."

"That's nothing. Then it's basically her word against yours . . . and she was in the crazy house like you, right?"

"Yeah, but like I said, she's white and her husband got money."

"Oh . . . yeah. You might be kinda fucked then. But you know what? She might not report anything. Shit, girl, truth be told, she might be waiting for you to come back and fist fuck her again. With them little baby hands you got, she probably liked it."

Linda reached over and held up one of Sharon's dainty hands and snickered.

Sharon snatched her hand away and laughed. "She did like it. Look like she nutted to me."

Sharon began going through the shopping bags.

"What made you think about pimpin' her, anyway? Are you sure all you got in there is size three stuff?"

"Yes, three's and two's. What made me think of pimping her? She asked me to. I told her I did escort work and she said she wanted to get into it."

"Helping her get into escort work is not beating her with a belt, fist-fucking her and taking fourteen thousand dollars from her. That's pimpin' her. What made you think to pimp her?"

"When she asked me to set her up with escort work, I told her I had to manage all the money and she agreed. I guess it started then. I kept all the money from the tricks she turned in the mental hospital." Sharon stopped pulling the new clothes from the bags.

"And when she told me she'd been turning tricks on the outside, I was expecting the money. Then she said she spent it on buying me clothes. Linda, I snapped. I did to her what Cherry would do to me if I spent his money before he got it. I whipped her ass and fucked her hard.

"When she said she didn't have my money, I wanted to beat her ass. It was like she hadn't listened to anything I told her on the ward. She knew the money was supposed to come to my hand first. I figured if I didn't beat her, then she would keep fucking up.

"The law had to be laid, and it had to be laid hard. I wanted her to know that we weren't playing a damn game. Just like I got the money on the ward first, the same rules applied on the street. I couldn't beat her on the ward for fucking that skinny-ass Nate for free, but I wanted to." She pulled a white silk blouse from the bags and fingered the material while it was in her lap.

"So, what you're saying is that you was pimpin' her on the ward, and she's used to you gettin' her money. Sharon, think. That dumb ho ain't gonna report you to the police or doctors. She waitin' for you to come back and tell her what to do next."

Sharon turned her attention from the blouse and asked, "How do you figure that?"

"Just think about it, girl. After Cherry whipped your ass and fucked you hard, what did you do? You sat your ass still and waited for him to tell you what to do next, because you loved him and you wanted to make him happy and do whatever he told you to do.

"And . . . you didn't want him to beat your ass again. That white ho is just like you was when you first met Cherry. She lookin' for direction. Shit, she might even be in love with you, but one thing you know for sure, she's

URBAN AFFAIR

afraid of you. You done broke the ho in. You can work her or walk away without fear."

Suddenly Sharon heard the mailman telling her to go back and work her.

The old lady schoolteacher told her to leave Elaine and Linda alone, and go see her doctor.

The little burned girl told her to go see her mother, and find out if she could help her find Chance.

She ignored all the voices.

"Linda, I need a safe place to stay just for a couple of days." Sharon began to fold all the clothes she took from the bag, and placed them next to her.

"You know, girl, you must have got God on your side, because I'm getting ready to drive out to Gary, Indiana to live. You can stay here. I don't care.

"My grandfather died a month ago and left me his house. I drew my money out of the bank this morning, bought me some white gym shoes, a pair of blue jeans, that plain, white cotton shirt on the chair and a used Chevy. I am going away from this place dressed different and with a new attitude. I'm leaving as soon as my ham hock splits open in them black-eyed peas.

"That's gonna be my last meal here. And I ain't coming back and I ain't taking shit with me that ain't on me. I'm going to secretary school out there. Been accepted and everything. And, girl, I'm going to find me my own husband." Linda stretched her legs out and crossed them at the ankle.

"I'm tired of other women's husbands. I'm twenty-three years old, a young tender to those that don't know me, and I know my coochie is just as good as any of them square broads. And if those stiff-ass bitches can find a husband, I know my slick, Chicago ass can find me one of them hard-workin', big-check-makin' steel mill men. Girl, I hear it's still a few niggas out there workin' at the mill and driving Cadillacs.

158

"And you want to hear somethin' stupid? In the back of my mind, I always thought I was gonna meet me somebody that would take me away from this type of life. I know it sounds crazy, but I thought I could find me a good man hoein'.

"The only good men I met were always other women's husbands. The rest was selfish bastards that would stick their dicks in a rotten tomato just as soon as a woman. And that includes them fifty-dollar North Side tricks you put me up on.

"Girl, the money was good up there, but them North Side men too freaky for me. Want to eat your coochie while you on your menstrual, want to piss on you or have you booboo on them, and damn near every one of them wanted me to stick my finger in their butt holes while I gave them head—just plain nasty. Ain't no good men out there trickin' off; only freaks and husbands.

"This is one big girl who has had enough. And I'm leaving all this shit here too; sofa, TV, rugs, everythin'. I don't want nothin' that's gonna remind me of what I been going through. I'm tired of this damn city and how it has made me live.

"My granddaddy left me his house. I got a house, girl. It's got four bedrooms and it's on the corner. He left it to me because he was still mad with my father for kicking me out. At least that's what one of the lawyers told me. It's my house, though. The lawyers came up here last week and told me.

"Girl, with a house and a education, I'ma get me a good man."

"You will, Linda. I know you will." Sharon thought of the plan she had formed in her mind when she lived in Linda's apartment with Chance and the television, and understood Linda's wanting.

"Yeap, that's fo' show. So, yeah, girl, you can stay here no problem."

"Damn, Linda, I don't want to stay in the city either. If you leaving, I want to leave with you." Sharon wasn't thinking about leaving the city just then, but if Linda was leaving, why not leave with her? Gary, Indiana wasn't Hollywood or Boston, but it was away, and she wanted away.

"Oh no, girl, ain't nothin' personal, but I'm startin' over and I'm startin' over alone. What I am sayin' is that you can have this place, furniture and all, and the rent's good for the next six months."

"You're giving me this place?" Sharon said, looking around.

The little burned girl said, *Take it.*

The mailman said, *Take it and use this and Elaine's place for the escort service.*

The old lady schoolteacher said, *Take it and then call the doctor and tell him you decided to live on your own.*

"Yeah, if you want it."

When she was seventeen, she thought Linda's apartment was the epitome of living well. At twenty-two, all she saw was a project apartment with a phony leather couch.

"But I want to go to Gary with you. I want to start over too. I want to go to school and find me a husband too."

If Linda thought she could find a man with her stuff, Sharon felt certain her "husband knot"-tightened, virgin-like vagina could get her a man as well. She hadn't put as much as a tampon inside her in five years.

"Girl . . . you ain't ready for all that. You was just whipping some ho's ass this mornin'."

"You were just turning a trick, and you say you're ready. Besides, I got my own money. I won't be a burden, I promise. I just want to start over too. I want to leave this city too. I want to go where people don't know me.

Take me with you, please." Sharon didn't see Linda's eyes giving an inch, so she added. "We can buy new clothes with the credit cards."

Sharon saw Linda looking at her folded pile of silk blouses.

"Damn, girl, I wasn't plannin' on nobody goin' with me. If you go, you gonna have to take GED classes to get into the school."

"I don't care. I'll do whatever has to be done to get a fresh start."

"What about your doctor? The one that has the medicine that stops you from being crazy."

"If I need it, I'll figure out a way to get it."

"You don't even know how much money is on those credit cards."

"Girl, I told you her husband has money. We can buy whatever we want with these cards."

"Damn . . . you my girl from way back. All right then, but we ain't hoein' out there. We gonna be two college girls livin' square. You hear me?"

"You're saying I can go with you?" Sharon was perched on the edge of the couch anxiously.

"Yeah, shit . . . you talkin' about buyin' a bitch a new wardrobe. Hell yeah, you can go. I knew I was cookin' for two when I put them good luck peas in the pot, but we ain't buying no damn butcher knives! You hear me? Not nay butcher knife!"

Chapter Thirteen

Patrice is standing outside the entranceway of her condominium, dressed for business. Chance told her he needed her business expertise, so she dressed appropriately in a brown pinstriped skirt suit with a yellow, high-collar blouse.

She discarded the blue suit she'd had the accident in the previous day. She wrapped it, the panties, the bra and the slip in three green plastic garbage bags, and shoved them down the disposal chute. She only wishes she could get rid of her fear as easily. Patrice is afraid while standing in front of her building.

Yesterday's attack stayed in her mind. Still unable to identify the person who shot at her, she is unable to focus on work or anything else, except the threat. Chance's request is a much needed distraction.

The morning dew is starting to dry up and there is no traffic on Marine Drive. Gray clouds mask the sky; however, the air is fresh and she hears sea gulls, sparrows and robins. A bluebird is timidly perched on the mailbox on the curb. A small boxer puppy with a leash but no owner has come up to her and is sniffing at her open-toe slide-in shoes. He must like what he smells because he begins licking her toes.

The puppy is too cute not to pet. She bends down and rubs his little golden head. She looks up and down the block and sees no one. Just as she makes the decision to pick up the puppy, Chance pulls up. The BMW is the perfect car for a man as upwardly mobile as she feels he is. She scoops up the puppy and gets into Chance's car.

She doesn't wait for him to come around and open the door as is his custom. She wants to hurry and get into the car, because a black sedan with tinted windows and large silver rims has slowed to a stop across the street.

It reminds her of Raymond's car, the man she'd given the Viagra, which caused him to have a heart attack. It isn't until now that she gives Raymond a second thought. Damn. He has a reason to want to hurt her. Why hadn't she thought of him? She slams the passenger door and tells Chance, "Lock your doors and pull off!"

Chance puts his car in drive, but not soon enough. Shots are fired from the black sedan's half-rolled-down driver's window. The driver gets out of the Chevy and fires directly on Chance's car. Chance pulls ahead three car lengths and makes a U-turn on Marine Drive, facing the sedan.

He quickly goes into his glove compartment and retrieves his .9mm. He exits, firing his own weapon. He hits the attacker in the shoulder and thigh. Chance continues walking toward the fallen attacker, shooting. The attacker, Raymond, discards his weapon and holds his hands up.

"Don't kill me, please. Please, man! I love her so much. We're in love, man. She's my woman."

That doesn't stop Chance's approach.

Chance runs to him and kicks him in the head then begins to pistol whip him in the middle of Marine Drive. Patrice jumps from the car and runs toward the two men. She wraps her arms around Chance, pulling him away from a down and badly beaten Raymond.

"We have to leave, Chance!"

"No, Patrice . . ." Raymond babbles. "Don't leave me here like this. You don't love him. We belong together. It's about me and you."

"We have to leave now, Chance!" she screams.

Instantly, Chance looks around for witnesses. The only moving thing he sees on the block is Raymond and a scurrying boxer puppy. He allows Patrice to drag him to the car. She gets behind the wheel and Chance slides into the passenger seat. She mashes the gas and the BMW responds with a cat-like leap.

"Take the drive to North Avenue. I got to get rid of the pistol," he orders.

Not another word is spoken until they get to the North Avenue beach.

"Wait here."

Chance exits the car and runs across the sand to the water. He slings the .9mm as far into Lake Michigan as he can. He turns, and Patrice is standing beside him with a box of shells and the other clip. He takes them and slings them into the lake as well.

"I'll get you another pistol, Chance," she whispers.

"Oh yeah, you will."

She hugs him tightly and says, "Thank you."

She feels his arm wrap around her just as tightly. His hands drop down to her butt and his grip is serious. He's pulling her into his erection.

"Morning joggers," she informs him.

"Not at the Drake."

If someone offered her $10,000, she couldn't tell them if there are people in the lobby of the Drake or not, if the desk clerk is male or female, or if they take the elevator or the stairs to the suite. What she can tell them is that once the suite door is closed, Chance rips her Jones of New York suit coat open, tears her high-collar blouse to shreds, and pops the hooks from her pushup bra. He scratches her thighs and her butt, yanking her pantyhose off.

He is no gentler with his own clothes. Material is ripping and tearing until they both are nude. He doesn't try to pick her up. He shoves her down in the bed and pounces on top of her. He slips into the grooves of her body that they'd made years ago.

She doesn't stretch her thighs wide. She opens them to where she is comfortable and his waist fits perfectly. She doesn't have to wonder what to do with her hands. They hook precisely on his shoulders. She doesn't have to turn her head to the left or the right, searching for his lips. They are where they are supposed to be. When he exhales, she inhales. When she groans, he moans. When he quivers, she shivers.

*****

Thoughts of a homecoming for some would include the smell of baking bread, or seeing a loved one's face, or even the annoying reminder of stepping on a squeaky porch step. Chance has no such memories of a homecoming. When he thinks about home, he thinks about the youth center. When he thinks about family, he thinks about Magnum and Big Time.

While laid atop Patrice, the softness of the encompassing mass of her subdues his mind. Wherever his hands wander, her subtle skin tells him this is where he should be. Her pleasurable gasp drives him to stay deep inside her. There is very little movement in the bed, just her holding him close to her, and him giving all he has in return.

If he were not so lost in his homecoming, he would hear the door chimes of the suite, but he doesn't. He doesn't even hear the hard, rapid knocks. What he does hear is the door being kicked in and the suite's bedroom window shattering. Eight police officers are barging into the bedroom of the suite, and two through the window with weapons drawn.

Reacting more than thinking, he rolls from the bed to floor and begins his attack from there, sweeping three officers from their feet. When he stands, he has a policeman's service revolver and a baton. He strikes one standing officer across the forehead with the baton, and he puts the revolver to another one's head.

"Y'all better back da fuck up out here befo' I blow this pig's brains against dat wall." It isn't Chance talking. C is back.

Weapons drawn, none of the standing officers move.

"It doesn't have to go this way, Mr. Bates." The officer speaking is the one Chance has the revolver on.

"Y'all already makin' it go dis way, comin' up in here like Nazis."

"We thought it was a hostage situation."

"What!"

"You shot a man on Marine Drive, Mr. Bates. We thought this woman was your hostage."

Chance notices the officer is trembling as he speaks, and looking around, he counts six guns on him. Patrice has wrapped herself in a sheet and is mouthing for him to calm down.

"How do you know my name?"

"The doorman at your building reported the shooting. He was coming on duty and saw you force this woman into your car."

"What?" Patrice says, shocked.

"Yes. And his story was corroborated by your boyfriend, who Mr. Bates allegedly shot and beat."

"My boyfriend. That man was stalking me!" Patrice yells, standing from the bed. "He shot at me yesterday at the Pancake House. This is a horrible mistake. You've been listening to the wrong people."

"Wait a minute," Chance says with a grin on his face. "You're telling me that you think I beat a man in the middle of Marine Drive, then kidnapped his girlfriend and checked into the Drake Hotel with her as a hostage?" Chance lowers the weapon. "Take me to jail so I can call my lawyers and sue the hell out of you dumb-ass cops."

The last time Chance was in the county jail, he and Magnum went together. They had tried to kill each other over Patrice. The last person he expected to see in the dark, dank bullpen of the county jail was Magnum.

"I know damn well that ain't my pussy-whipped-ass nigga, C. Hell naw!"

The man speaking has a full, ragged beard and a bald head, and when he stands from the bench, he is wider and taller than the teenage Magnum Chance remembers.

"Get da fuck outta here, Magnum. I know that ain't you!"

It's only them and one other man in the bullpen. The other man is asleep on the bench across the cell. He is exhaling pure alcohol fumes. Despite the fact the last time Chance and Magnum saw each other, each swore death to the other, they hug like brothers.

"My nigga," they both say in a tight embrace and release each other.

"Man, last time I saw you it was pistol play. You drew down on your boy."

"Shit. How I remember it, Magnum. Your pistol was out, too, my brother."

"Yeah. We was both gun slingers back then. You still with that babe?"

"Just got back with her this morning and had a pistol play that got me up in here."

"You got to be lyin'!"

They sit on the empty bench across from the passed out man.

"No. I wish I was. Some dumb-ass nigga that's been stalking her tried to unload a clip on her."

"You ain't got to say what you did. I bet you still got that .9mm. Is the stalker alive?"

"Alive and lying his ass off. Said I attacked him and kidnapped Patrice."

"Damn. Well, I know your rich, square broad got her lawyers on the way."

"Brother, I got my own lawyers these days."

"No shit. You livin' like that?"

"I'm living very well, my brother."

"What, you got into the cocaine rock game like everybody else?"

"No, no, my brother, I been squared up since I got out after our little altercation."

"Little altercation? Nigga, we shot up the mothafuckin' projects. Went down ten flights of stairs shooting at each other. I know I went through two clips."

"Yeah, me too. And ain't it funny how they managed to pull both our slugs outta that cop's ass? I swear I didn't shoot at him."

"Me neither. I don't think me or you shot him. We made the mothafucker a hero, though. I think he's a captain or some shit now."

"They only held you in here a couple of hours, right? Didn't you get shipped to juvenile?"

"Yeah, and Big Time's mama came and agreed to be my guardian. I only did fifteen months. I heard they had you in here for two years."

"No, it was two and a half, and it was the worst time of my life. And that was with Big Time reaching in and keeping the booty busters from going up in me, but his lawyers couldn't get me out because I was seventeen. It was Patrice's pops that pulled the freedom strings."

"Yeah . . . it was like you just disappeared after you got out."

"Man, when I got out of here, I didn't want to hear nothin' about game, hustling, street life, none of that. All I wanted was for me and Patrice to make babies. She and her pops had other plans, though, and all in all, they were good plans. They kept me out of jail and a brother got a college degree."

"You bullshittin', nigga. You got a degree?"

"Yeap."

"What, you got a company and shit too?"

"Nope, not yet, but I am a manager."

"Nigga, can you get me hired?"

It is a sincere question, and Chance sees the need in Magnum's eyes. Chance looks hard at his one-time friend's rough exterior, and remembers there was a time he looked just as thuggish.

With a shave, a good suit, a little language coaching and his own personal sales coaching, Magnum can transform. Chance decides to say, "I can bring you on as a sales trainee, but the hours is like seven a.m. to six p.m. while you training. And I'm the trainer, so you will have to accept me as the boss."

"Shit, them ain't no hours. You know how we used to crank it twenty-four/seven. And this ain't back in the day, C. I ain't got no problem working fo' you, man. But do you really think you can get me on fo' real, C, with my record and everything?"

"Brother, yes. And if you work half as hard at learning how do the job as you did for Big Time, you will easily make fifty or sixty thousand your first year."

"How much do I get paid to be trained?"

"Entry level is thirty thousand."

"What! Nigga is you tellin' me you can get me a legit job payin' me thirty thousand dollars a year?"

"Yes, my brother, that's what I'm telling you."

169

"When do I start?"

"When do you get out of here?"

"They just waitin' for my fingerprints to come back clear. I got picked up on a warrant from St. Louis that was cleared two months ago. Chicago Police still had it in their system."

"If you get out today, come by my place. Thirty-four sixteen North Marine Drive, number 2311."

"Damn, C, you ballin' ain't cha? Ain't nothin' but rich folks livin' up there."

An officer is at the bullpen's dark green gated door. "Chance Bates, your bail has been posted. You're out." He slings the gate open.

"Come see me, Magnum. For real, brother."

*****

Patrice didn't contact the lawyers Chance told to her call. Instead, she called her father who got his lawyers on the case. She and her father are at the police station's front desk waiting for Chance to be brought out.

"Does he know I'm out here?" her father asks.

"No, Daddy, I haven't spoken to him since he was arrested."

"This is the second time I have gotten this young man out of jail at your request. There won't be a third. Why you kept in touch with him after he went to jail the first time, I never understood."

"He went to jail, Daddy, when he was seventeen years old, because he was defending me. I kept in touch with him because I felt it was my fault."

The station is close to empty: two officers behind the desk and Patrice and her father in the waiting area. Patrice wishes there was a crowd. In a crowd, her father wouldn't ask questions, and she doesn't want him to ask her what she and Chance were doing at the Drake Hotel. She has no answer for that question, for him or herself.

"And the man he shot, did he know him?" Mr. Trent removes his tortoise shell glasses, pulls a handkerchief from the inside pocket of his tweed jacket and wipes clean the lenses. He puts the glasses back on and looks at Patrice for an answer. Her father assumes Chance knows every black criminal in Chicago.

"No." She hopes short answers will stop more questions.

"That fool confessed to shooting at you yesterday, and I don't think he knew he killed the man at the register. It looks like he's going to be charged with murder."

"I don't care what they charge him with, Daddy, as long as they keep him away from me." Raymond turned out to be a good screw turned nut, and she truly could care less about what happens to him.

"So, you and Chance are seeing each other again?"

There it was. It isn't as personal as "What were you doing at the hotel with him?" but it is just as prying. He hasn't asked one question about her relationship with Raymond. His concern is her and Chance.

"He saved my life, Daddy."

She is determined not to discuss the relationship because she has no idea where it is going. All she knows is it feels right and she wants more of it.

Her father steps closer to her, so only she can hear his words. "He shot a man in the middle of the street and pistol whipped him."

"Would you rather have had that nut shoot me?"

"No, that is not the point I'm making. The point is, Chance is a violent and dangerous man."

She knows the point. She's heard them for years. Chance is a square peg, Chance has tainted blood, Chance is from the ghetto, Chance's mother was a schizophrenic murderer, and Chance's father was a pimp. Chance is not good enough for her.

171

"He saved my life, Daddy."

*****

When Chance is escorted from the bullpen through the lockup doors, he pauses when he sees Patrice and her father. He was expecting his lawyer. He nods in their direction while being handed his belongings. He becomes conscious of his shirt that he ripped the buttons off of in the hotel suite. He adjusts his suit coat to cover his untidiness.

Patrice comes to his side. "Are you all right?"

"Yes," he answers with a smile, noticing she is holding her suit jacket together as well. He turns to her father and says, "Mr. Trent, it's good to see you, sir."

"Yes, well, Patrice called me and informed of the situation. You have my gratitude for helping her. The lawyers seem positive that they can handle the whole situation as self-defense, with possibly only one court appearance from yourself and Patrice."

"Thank you." Chance extends his hand.

Mr. Trent shakes it and looks him in the eye. "No. Thank you. Your car is outside. I had it towed from the Drake here." He releases Chance's hand and to Patrice he says, "Shall we leave?"

Both men look and wait for her answer. Chance is waiting to hear her say she is going to ride with him. What he hears is, "Chance, I'll call you later this evening. Perhaps we will meet tomorrow for dinner?" Her words are to him, but her eyes are on the police station's floor.

Her father puts his arm around her shoulder and walks her out of the station. Chance stands at the desk, watching them descend the stairs. He wants to call after her, but what he says is, "Fuck that shit. I ain't going there again."

What he does is flip open his cell phone and dial Patrice's cell number.

*****

"Hello"

She wasn't expecting to hear Chance's voice.

"So what . . . what happened at the Drake was just some shit we did?"

She looks to the police station while climbing into her father's Jaguar. She sees Chance pacing back and forth through the door. This is the wrong time to talk. She can't say what she feels with her father's ear on her, so what she says is, "Chance, we have different lives . . . it was a moment and we shared it. What . . . did you think it was more than that?"

If he says it was more, she will jump out of the car and run to him. That she knows. She sees that he stops pacing.

"No, you're right, shorty. It was nothing more than a moment." He flips the phone closed and moves away from the door.

With Chance, it's "all or none," and it has been that way with him since the beginning. What did he expect; her not to consider her father's feelings? Just ignore her father's stare and leave the police station with Chance because of the time they spent at the hotel? Chance wants too much. He always has.

Hadn't she ostracized herself from her parents and friends when they were teenagers, demanded that her father get him out of jail and give him a job? Those things obviously weren't enough. Wasn't it she who insisted he get his GED while he was in jail, she who remained loyal to him while he was in jail, she who coached him in his speech, she who put the idea of going to college in his mind, and she who helped fill out his college applications? Hadn't she given him her all? But that wasn't enough, was it?

He had to have all of her—now. Well, now things are different. She has a business to run and she has responsibilities to her parents. Chance can't have all of her. She won't choose between having a full life and having him. If they are to get back together, Chance will have to accept the fact that she has a life that is bigger than him, and it includes respecting her parents. Chance blew his relationship with her father on his own.

It was Chance whose work performance dropped after their engagement ended. Her father told her he was reporting to work late, smelling of liquor, and he had no choice but to fire him. Chance bounced back, though, found another job, and bought a BMW. And she noticed he was dating two months after they broke up. He wasn't disturbed enough to curb his sexual activities. She'd heard the sex sounds coming from his place.

True, she was dating others before she broke up with him, but that wasn't her fault. Her parents kept having dinner parties that Chance wasn't invited to, and at these parties, they would entertain suitable bachelors. Most were attractive.

It was her mother who convinced her to date the bachelors, saying that if she truly loved Chance, dating the men wouldn't affect her feelings. "Keep your options open, dear. That's all I want you to do," she'd say.

Chance believed that she ended the engagement because of the information her father discovered about his parents. She didn't tell him any different. However, the engagement ended because she enjoyed exploring her options with the bachelors. She moved out of their condo to have more freedom to date, and after dating, she was no longer certain Chance was the man she wanted to marry. Her mother was right. Exploring her options was a good thing.

Patrice hadn't planned on ending her engagement to Chance. She merely wanted to extend it, giving them both time to make sure that they were making the right decision. But with Chance, it was all or nothing, so when she moved out, their engagement was over and they stopped talking.

She didn't think that would happen. She didn't think Chance would pass her in the halls and ignore her. She didn't think he would not return her calls, and she certainly didn't think he would refuse to go to the Bud Billiken parade with her, which was something they'd done every year since he got out of jail. His refusal to go to the parade with her hurt, and it was then that she realized that Chance was out of her life. Suddenly, the bachelors lost some of their appeal.

As long as she had Chance in her mind as a backup, she felt secure and dating was only a game. But once he was gone and she was left with only the dating game option, it became serious because she had to replace Chance. She soon found out that a serious game was no fun. What had appeared to be a plentiful bounty of bachelors withered when she started talking with them about future plans and marriage.

When she began to play the game seriously, she also became aware of the competition. There were only so many arranged dinner parties her parents could host where she was the center of attention. If she wanted to keep dating, she had to go out to the clubs and meet men on her own. There, she met the competition: thin women who were veterans at the dating game. Women who knew how to cross their legs at a bar. Women who knew how to get men to buy them drinks. Women who cabdrivers would pass her by to pick up. Not since high school had she felt so unattractive. She quickly canceled the club scene, at least the black clubs. She still went to the white clubs with Amy. At the white clubs, the competition was a little less steep. There, she had the black girl novelty thing working for her.

She began meeting men through work, at the grocery store, at the park, and she even met a couple of good-looking ones through an on-line dating service. Although she was dating two or three nights a week, she was lonely, and she couldn't understand why until father told her, "Baby girl, dating is not having a relationship. You have to get acquainted with these young men."

Getting acquainted required her to give the men she met some real time, and her real time went to building her business. Few of the men she met understood that, and if they did, it was because they too were driven and had tighter schedules than hers. After almost a year, the game had become taxing and she stopped looking for a serious person to be with and settled for good-looking dates. The game became fun again. She was serious about work. Men were for play.

In her quiet moments when she allowed herself to think seriously about a man, she thought about Chance and what they had and how right it was until she decided to try her options. Options. Raymond was an option, and look how that turned out. If it wasn't for Chance, he would have killed her.

"To hell with options."

Chapter Fourteen

It was a 1983 Chevy Caprice and it smelled like it was new, and the odometer read only 596 miles.

"Girl, it was the owner's wife's car. He said he didn't have a better kept used car on the lot."

Linda opened the back door of the sedan, allowing Sharon to toss her bags in the back. "At first I didn't want a burgundy car because I had never seen one this color, but once I got inside and saw how clean and like new it was, I had to have it! And, girl, you know I thought I was going to have to do a little somethin'-somethin' fo' him to drop the sticker price, but when I told him I was movin' out to Gary to start school, he was so proud of me, he shook my hand and said, 'It's good to see our young black women moving ahead. I only wish more of our men were seeking an education.' Then he dropped the price eight thousand dollars. That's been only one of the signs tellin' me what I'm doing is right.

"Passing the GED test after only two weeks of classes was another. I been scared to take that class since I was eighteen years old, always thinking I was too stupid to get a high school diploma. Sharon, it was easy. All I had to do was sit still, listen and really want it.

"And befo' I even knew about my grandfather's house, I figured my life wasn't gonna get no better without an education. And it was like once I made one decision to change, girl, shit just started happenin'.

"I was to the point that every mornin' I got up and looked out my window, I got sick. I knew I could do better. If them North Side men wasn't so damn freaky, I wouldn't have ever came back to this neighborhood. Just look around you, Sharon. This is no kind of life."

Until Linda told her to look around, all Sharon saw was a beautiful sunny day and the burgundy Chevy with a white top that was gleaming in the sun. All that was on her mind was riding in the pretty car, out of the city. She hadn't noticed the trash or the slight breeze that was blowing. Nor had she noticed the ten to twelve boys standing in the entrance way of the building, the abandoned cars next to the Chevy, the poor black dog that someone had scolded, the small group of older men and the one woman passing a bottle between them, the broken wine and whiskey bottles in the parking lot and in the trounced dirt. She hadn't even noticed the three young women in short shorts and halter tops standing across the street on the same corner where she and Linda had stood. Once she did notice, she was more than ready to leave.

"You're right, so let's leave it."

The drive to Gary couldn't have been filled with more merriment. The friends didn't rehash the time they spent on the streets. They talked about a prior time when they were girls and played hopscotch and caught lightning bugs, ate Now and Laters, sunflower seeds, sour pickles with peppermint sticks in the middle, blew Bug's Daddy bubbles and raced home from school to watch *Dark Shadows.*

They recalled the adventures of going from floor to floor in the projects; seeing Mr. Nash's fat belly in boxer shorts; laughing at the funny way the Jamaicans talked; finding kittens in the stairwell that were too young and too small to be able to climb up a step; hearing Mrs. Dottly praying to Saint Jude for the numbers. And the best part of their floor to floor adventures was finding new girls to play with.

They found Daphne, who knew how to play jacks, Thelma, who had an Easy-Bake Oven and Kimberly, who had a kickball. There was Mildred, whose mother worked at the five and dime and gave them colorful ribbons and rubber bands for their hair, and Michelle, who had a brother who died, so they got to ride his bike, which had training wheels on it.

Most of the other girls' mothers wouldn't let them go from floor to floor in the building, so the exploring of floors and eventually the other buildings was left to Sharon and Linda alone. It was only the two them that found the smoldering little girl in the hallway.

When the conversation got to that point, they had pulled up to 2301 Chase Street in Gary, Indiana, and both women where happy to end the reminiscing.

The house was a ranch styled, red brick house which was being well kept. It, and every other house on the block, had trimmed lawns. Some had sculptured hedges and lawn ornaments. The three steps that led up to the house's mahogany front door were carpeted. Neither woman moved from her car seat.

"Are you sure this is the house?"

"Yeah, that's it. The address is the same as on the papers the lawyers gave me. It just looks so much better than I remember. I was only here once when I was a kid, and it was in the winter. All I remember is snow, slippery steps, and water leaking in the kitchen."

"That's a nice house."

"Yeah . . . and it's mine," she claimed with a happy yell.

They hurried from the car to the front porch. Linda stopped before the door with keys in hand.

"Last month, I had one key on a smiley keychain. Girl, now look at all these keys. And they all go to stuff."

Sharon was expecting the house to be dusty, stuffy and have the scent of older men she had dated. The

179

sharp scent of green alcohol, Ben Gay, Vick's or some other scent of elderly ailments, is what she expected. The scent that greeted them was that of fresh cut flowers. There was a full, white porcelain vase in the foyer of the home. The tall vase was full of red roses.

There was no dust. The orange French provincial sofa and high-back chairs in the living room were covered in a thick, clear plastic, which was customized to cover each piece of furniture perfectly. The plastic covers had their own seams.

The dark cherry wood trim of the baseboards also outlined the top of the walls. The lighting of the living room was actually installed in the walls. Each corner had an electric light that resembled an oil lamp near the ceiling. A small crystal chandelier hung from the ceiling by a wire that was encased in a crystal wrap. There was a huge fireplace surrounded with the same red brick as the outside of the house, and dark cherry wood made up the mantle.

The dining room's ceiling was domed, and the crystal chandelier that hung from it was double the size of the one in the living room. A complete mahogany dining room set, including a table with eight chairs, and a buffet and china cabinet filled with china was beneath the huge chandelier. A Persian rug sewn with gold and emerald thread covered the wall next to the china cabinet. Sharon wondered why it was on the wall instead of the floor, although she thought it looked beautiful on the wall.

"Hello. You must be Linda People, Aston's granddaughter."

Both women jumped slightly, startled by the thin, tall woman dressed in a blue jean dress who stood in the kitchen doorway.

"Yes, I am."

"I'm Nora. I was Mr. People's housekeeper." She walked up to them and extended her long hand for them to shake. Each did.

"It's nice to finally meet you. You were heavy on your grandfather's mind his last days. I would come in three days a week and tidy up the place for him, not that he needed any help. The man was as neat as a pin. His conversations during the last days were about getting things in order for you."

Sharon watched Nora looking Linda over, as if she were calculating whether she was worth her grandfather's efforts.

"The directives he left in the will were for me to clean the home until the day you moved in, and he paid me well to follow his wishes. It was also his request that everything of his—clothing, medicine and such—be removed from the home before you moved in. He didn't want you to have to deal with anything. Your father came and got his clothes and jewelry. What he left was a few pair of shoes and winter coats. I donated those things to a local church."

She paused for a response. None came from Linda.

"The home services he had, I haven't canceled. I left that to your discretion. There is a lawn service. The florist brings fresh flowers to the house every two days, and there is a home security system. Milk and eggs delivered weekly, and he has cable."

"Cable?" Linda questioned.

"Cable is television programming that comes through a wire; movies and programs that aren't on regular television, but you get all the regular stations too. It's kind of nice."

"That does sound cool," Sharon agreed.

"The phone, lights and water have all been switched to your name. The property taxes are paid for the year. Oh, and he told me to give this to you personally. I asked did he have a letter to go with it, he said no, but to tell you he was sorry for not being part of your life. He was quite clear in stating that your father was not to get this."

Linda unfolded the document. It was the life insurance policy, with her as the beneficiary of $15,000.

"Damn! What he didn't do while he was alive . . . he sho' is doing now." Linda folded the paper and put it into her purse.

"Yes, that's how he wanted you to feel," Nora said, smiling warmly. "He did ask, however, that you put his wife's portrait up. Where you put it is up to you."

The tall Nora walked to the corner and uncovered a huge portrait against the wall on the floor.

"For years, it was on the wall where the Persian rug is. Then a month before he died, he took it down and put the rug up."

Sharon and Linda walked over to the portrait.

"She looks just like you, Linda." Sharon's eyes went from portrait to Linda.

"That's kinda freaky," was all Linda said.

The portrait could have been a photograph taken of Linda that morning. She and her grandmother shared the same thick, black wavy hair and each had it styled going to the back. They had identical thick eyebrows, matching slanted eyes and wide, flat noses all held in the same round pork-and-bean-colored face. The portrait, like Linda's face, showed the weight the woman carried.

"It's like lookin' into a still mirror."

"Yes, the resemblance is uncanny. Did you know her?"

"No, I barely remember him."

"Well, let me be the first to tell you this, although I'm sure others, particularly your neighbors, will tell you as well. It's said that her spirit is still in the house," Nora offered.

"Come again?" Linda challenged.

Sharon immediately pulled her purse to her chest and looked around. She took a step closer to Linda. She heard of old people's spirits remaining in places. She didn't know if she believed it or not, but hearing about it always frightened her.

"People that knew your grandfather better than me, tell me that your grandmother haunted him his last days. I personally think it was all the medication the different doctors had him on, but people say that he said his Linda had come back to make sure he got all his affairs regarding you in order."

"Her was name Linda too?" Sharon asked.

"Yeah, I was named after her. Hold up, Nora. You sayin' she came back to haunt him because of me?"

"That's what he told people. Let's sit, and I'll tell you what I've heard and what he said. How much credence you give to it is completely up to you."

The three sat at the dining room table in chairs next to each other. They were sitting on the window side of the room. Hearing the word "haunt" got Sharon even more on edge. She figured she had enough problems. She didn't need to be haunted. She continued to look around for any signs of Linda's grandmother.

"Let me start with what common folks call 'the dirt.' He kept him a young woman living with him until two months ago, a different one every so often. He didn't get serious with any of them until this last one. In my opinion, she came through the door thinking about her future, and his short time left on this earth.

"She was after him to marry her, so she would have a legal claim to something for herself after he was gone, and I heard her say it to him several times as plain as that. I don't believe any of the others were as educated as the last one. He could talk to her about things: world events, literature, and she played chess.

"I'm telling you this so you will understand that she did more than soothe an older man's desire for a younger woman. In the short time she was here, she had become his companion.

"Mr. People, being the fair man that he was, told her that he would make sure that upon his demise, she would be taken care of. But that wasn't good enough. She wanted marriage. And the day after he broke down to her request and agreed to marry her, people who believe in such things say that's when your grandmother came back. The young woman swears it was your grandmother that ran her out of here."

"How?" both of the friends asked.

"She said the spirit of your grandmother would do things like turn her hot bath water cold while she was in it, pull the covers off her at night and chill the bedroom until the windows frosted. And she claimed that every time she came into or left the house, she was tripped at the door. No matter which door she came in through, back or front, she would be tripped.

"Now, all of that, the young woman said she sort of overlooked, contributed it all to strange occurrences. What ran her up out of here was what happened the day the justice of the peace, a lawyer and a witness came to the house to marry them.

"Was my grandfather crippled or somethin'?"

"No, he got around good to be as sick as he was. He could and did walk. The young woman had them come here for her convenience, or so she thought.

"She claims that it all started when the justice of the peace was unable to open his attaché case. It was a simple clasp, no key or combination, but no one, including her, was able to unclasp it. Frustrated, she cut the man's leather case with a pair of sewing scissors and pulled the marriage papers from the case.

"When she handed the papers to the justice of the peace, they ignited into flames and burnt to ashes in a matter of seconds. Then a high-pitched giggling was supposedly heard through the whole house. Those that knew your grandmother say she loved a good giggle. Some say she would laugh until her eyes watered.

"At this point, your grandfather suggested calling the whole thing off. He told me he knew that giggle could have only come from one person. You see, his hot bath water had been chilled to almost ice a couple of times while he was in it as well, so he said.

"But the young woman wasn't about to give up that easy. She asked the lawyer could he draw up the appropriate substitute papers. He said he could if all that were present witnessed them. Now, this next bit I can partially confirm, because I did part of the cleanup the next day.

"The lawyer's case was already open. He removes a couple sheets of paper and a pen from his suit coat. When he goes to write, a thick liquid resembling mucus comes from the pen. He tries to write, but no ink comes from the pen, only this thick substance is on the paper.

"Suddenly, the pen erupts, not merely on the paper he's writing on, but over everyone present. The pin shoots off like a fire hose, covering everyone in the thick substance. The lawyer claimed he couldn't aim it or stop it.

"I assure you, the living room carpet was covered in the substance. At one time, the carpet throughout the home was a bright orange. Mr. People had to have the living room dyed rust after that. No service could completely clean all that . . . snot from it."

Sharon tightly grabbed Linda's arm. Linda whispered, "Easy, girl, it's okay."

"The erupting fountain pen was enough to motivate the witness' departure. She was followed by the justice of the peace, the lawyer sat shocked next to the young woman. What happened next reminded Mr. People that he was once a married man with a jealous wife.

"At that time, your grandmother's portrait hung from that wall." Nora pointed to the wall holding the Persian rug. "They were all sitting in the living room in full view of the portrait. Your grandfather says your grandmother's face in the portrait turned to him, and the smile that is painted on her face in the portrait was not on her face when she looked at him. And then again, according to him, he was not the only one who saw her turn to look at him.

"After your grandmother turned and faced them from the portrait with a furious scowl on her face, the lawyer quickly stands up from the couch and says to your grandfather, 'Mr. People, perhaps this is not the best afternoon to conduct this business.'

"He attempts to take a step to leave, but the young woman grabs a hold of his arm. She's not trying to pull herself up or anything, she just grabs him. He doesn't even try to jerk her loose. He just stands there, in your grandfather's words, 'watching the impossible.' Your grandmother's face supposedly came out of the portrait and floated from the dining room to them."

Linda and Sharon gasped.

"The lawyer was out of here so quick your grandfather didn't see him leave. He left his suit coat in the young woman's gripping hands. To the young woman, your grandmother's face says, 'Chil', it's time for you to go.'

"Your grandfather said the young woman was then slung from the sofa, through the plate-glass picture window, with the lawyer's jacket over her head. We haven't heard a thing from her since, though I hear she's been repeating the story all over town. The next day, your grandfather took the picture down and covered it up.

"Why he wanted you to uncover it and hang it up is between family, I suppose."

Linda pushed her chair back from the table. "Between family, my fat ass! You better put that damn cover back over that picture. We ain't hangin' up a damn thang," she exclaimed.

Sharon released Linda's arm and looked down at the portrait. The woman was smiling. She looked like a friendly aunt. Sharon could see no evil or ill intent in her image. If she was in the house, Sharon decided right then, that she wouldn't be afraid of her.

"According to your grandfather, covering the portrait didn't stop her from—again, these are his words, 'nagging him.' She would come to him in his dreams nightly and tell him what to do the next day. And if he was slow about rising the next morning, her loud giggle along with the frosting of the bedroom would get him up and about. He said she made sure he got things right for you.

"Now, this is something I witnessed his last days that I thought peculiar. Mr. People loved pork: pork sausages, pork roast, pork steaks and pork chops, and I did do the shopping for him. The fresh pork I bought him, I would find in the refrigerator two days later, rotten with maggots. Mrs. People hated pork, he told me. I stopped buying it for him.

"Oh goodness, will you look at the time?" Nora's eyes were on her wristwatch. "I have to get over to the school and get my own grandbabies." She stood up. "I left my phone number and my keys to the house on the counter in the kitchen. If you need anything or have any questions, give me a call. And don't think about all that spirit business. If she is in here, she has your best interest at heart," Nora said with a wink. "It was nice meeting you both." She left without covering the portrait.

Alone in the house, both Linda and Sharon's eyes were on the painting.

"Are you going to hang it up?"

"What would you do?"

"I would hang it up and see what happens. Like that tall lady said, she was doing it all for you."

"I don't believe in ghosts."

"Me neither, but like you said, a lot of good stuff has been happening to you lately. Why rock the boat by not doing what your grandfather asked? It's just a picture."

Sharon got up and walked over to the portrait. She picked it up and stood it on the dining room table for Linda to look at.

"Everybody is going to think it's a picture of you, anyway."

Linda walked over to the Persian rug on the wall and unscrewed the six hooks that held it up. It slid to the floor. There were two small holes in the center of the wall. She screwed two of the rug's hooks into the holes.

"Bring it over here."

The outline of the portrait's frame was still on the wall. They hung it where it had hung for years. The two friends stood in front of the portrait.

"If she comes outta there, I'm leaving—grandmother or not."

They stood, waiting for several slow seconds. "Okay, let's get out of here for now and go shoppin' with those hot credit cards of yours. And I need to get to a bank and open up a checking account. We got a house to take care of."

*****

Sharon was tired and her feet were hurting. The two friends had shopped from one end of the South Lake

Mall to the other. They'd made five trips out to the car to drop off bags. The backseat and the trunk of the Chevy were full. Anything they thought they wanted, they purchased. They bought clothes and shoes for business, for school, for church and for the occasional nights out on the town that Linda said they *might* have.

They decided to end the shopping spree with a trip to a beauty salon. Sharon, who hadn't gotten her hair done professionally in over five years, caught a second wind with the idea. Her head was in the shampoo bowl when she realized she hadn't heard a voice in her head since she left Chicago. Not a murmur from any of them.

Her mind was occupied with thoughts of taking the GED class and going to secretarial school. She'd gotten good grades in school and was positive she could pass the GED test. Under the hairdryer, she imagined herself walking across a stage and getting her secretarial certificate. Being a secretary was an important job. A good, honest job.

When her hair was dried and combed out, it hung past her shoulders. She decided against the straight and shiny style Cherry insisted she wore. She went with the poodle style she saw in one of the hair magazines in the salon: big curls on the top, and the sides and back hung straight down. The beautician told her that style would allow her to roll her hair up and wear it all curled if she wanted to. She liked the option.

Linda got her hair dyed light brown and cut into a mushroom style, which was curled under at the tips. Sharon thought the style made her look younger and smart. She looked like a secretary. The two friends left the salon smiling and satisfied with their new looks.

They stayed at the mall past banking hours, so Linda was unable to open a checking account. Not sure if there was food at the house to cook, they stopped and picked up a bucket of fried chicken. It took seven trips back and forth from car to house to get all the bags inside. Once in, the two collapsed on the couch in the living room.

"Girl, those cards wouldn't stop. I didn't think we was gonna get the jewelry on them." They went to a jewelry store after the salon, and each bought a pair of diamond stud earrings, thick gold bracelets and a string of pearls.

"Neither did I. But I think your idea to break them up and throw them away was best. There was no sense in pushing it. We did well enough."

"We did damn good, Sharon. I'm happy you came out here with me. All of this is better with you here. You know what I mean?" Linda stood from the couch and yawned, not waiting for Sharon's response. She walked into the dining room and flipped the light switch.

"Yes, I know what you mean, and I'm happy you let me tag along." Sharon grabbed the bucket of chicken and stood.

After the dining room light came on, Linda said, "Oh, hell naw. You see this shit?"

"This shit" was the portrait, and Sharon saw it.

Linda's grandmother's hair had changed. It was no longer black and styled to the back. It was light brown in color and in the same mushroom style as Linda's. The face in the portrait even had on the half-carat diamond stud earrings they'd just bought.

Sharon dropped the bucket of chicken. She was no longer certain that she wouldn't be afraid of the smiling face in the portrait.

"Do you see it?"

Sharon didn't answer.

"Damn it. Do you see it?"

"Yes. Yes . . . I see it."

"What do you see?"

"I see her hair is like yours, and she's wearing our earrings."

"Damn. She do got on the earrings!"

Linda backed up a step. "What we gonna do about this?"

Sharon wanted to say, "What do you mean *we?* It's your dead grandmother." What she said was, "I don't know, but we are not leaving this house. Being out here in Gary is our chance to start over. We are not leaving."

"But, Sharon, the damn picture changed!"

"So? It didn't hurt us."

Sharon picked up the bucket of chicken and walked through the dining room, past the portrait, into the kitchen. Over her shoulder, she yelled, "I'm hungry. You better come in here and get some of this chicken while it's hot."

She hadn't turned around to see if Linda was following her because she didn't want to turn around and see the face from the portrait following her as she feared it would. She felt certain that it was right behind her, and if it was, it was going to have to sling her out the window, too, because she wasn't leaving, and she wasn't planning on Linda leaving either.

Still not looking behind her, she yelled, "I know you're not going to let a picture stop you from a new life."

No response came from Linda.

"Do you hear me, Linda?"

Maybe the face got her. Maybe she was covered in snot. "Linda?"

"What? Damn, I hear you. The picture got me trippin'."

"Well, think about this: Is walking past a haunted picture as bad as standing your fat ass out on Madison Street in subzero weather waiting for a trick? Is walking past a haunted picture as bad as having a trick screw you in your booty hole for twenty dollars? Is walking past a haunted picture as bad as having to go to the clinic because your pee is burning like acid?

"Walking past a haunted picture is nothing compared to what we've been through, so get your scary fat ass in here and get some chicken before I grab one of these butcher knives your granddaddy left in here."

She heard Linda running through the dining room. When she looked up, Linda was standing beside her, and the face from the portrait hadn't followed her. She sighed heavily in relief.

"Ain't you scared a little?"

"I'm scared a lot, but I know what we left behind, and that scares me more. This is our chance, and your grandmother changing her hairstyle in a picture is not going to stop us."

"But what if she do some mo' stuff?"

"I think we can be certain that she will. But whatever she does, I think it will be for our benefit. We're in Gary because of her."

Chapter Fifteen

When Chance exits the police station, his mind is on going home to change clothes, and getting back to the Lincoln Park office. He still has to order computers, furniture and office supplies, and he has to do it alone, is what he is thinking.

As he exits the police station, he's looking up and down the block for his car. He doesn't see it. There is a dark blue BMW across the street from the station, but his car is nowhere to be seen. He flips open his phone and dials Patrice's cell to find the whereabouts of his car.

Before he can say a word, he hears, "Chance, I'm glad you called me back. I was lying. . . . It was more than a moment—way more—and we both know it. What I felt this morning in your arms was real, and I want it back in my life."

Chance wasn't expecting to hear such words from her. He has no response. The loud objections he hears from her father in the background are expected. He flips the phone closed. "I'll take fuckin' a cab," he says to no one, and walks to the corner.

*****

"Daddy, please! I'm on the phone. Chance? Chance? Chance? He hung up. He must have heard you. Drive me back to the police station, please."

Patrice closes her phone and counts to fifty in her head. She takes several deep, calming breaths and blows them out. Yelling at her father is something she hasn't done since her teenage years, and then it was done when she wanted to do or get something he wouldn't allow. Her romantic involvement shouldn't be a situation that depends on what her father will and won't allow.

"Daddy, I apologize for yelling, but you have to understand that I am a grown woman, and I'm fully capable of making decisions in my own life."

Her father doesn't respond for several seconds. She watches his jaws tighten, his temples throb, and his fingers clench the steering wheel.

"Patrice, I'm going to drive you back to the police station because you are right. You're grown. But hear this: You wear self-removing blinders when it comes to that young man. You refuse to see how he can damage your life, and how you damage his."

"Daddy, I am a twenty-five-year-old single black woman, and I want that status to change. I want a family. I want a man that loves me. I want a man to love. I allowed you and mother's judgment of Chance to end our engagement."

"That wasn't totally our doing, young lady. We presented you with choices. You made the decision to date. You became dissatisfied with Chance's social status, as you will again. There is nothing wrong with wanting love or a family, but with Chance, you're settling for less and you know this.

"After the emotions from this morning settle, you will be left with the same man you left before. It's not your heart or your head you are thinking with now, Patrice."

"Daddy!"

"It's the simple truth. You don't love Chance. You never did. If you had, you would have never attended the first dinner party your mother arranged where Chance was not present. You would have insisted she invited him, but you didn't. You went and got new dresses and attended the parties.

"As a teenager, Chance was a pastime for you. As an adult, he is your 'boy toy,' nothing more. Don't lie to yourself, and spare Chance of your whims. He deserves better, and you want more than he can ever be. You and he will never marry."

"You are wrong, Daddy, so very wrong. I haven't been happy with a man since I left Chance. I know what I'm feeling, Daddy. I am not a little girl anymore. I run my own company. I pay my own mortgage. I am successful in every area of my life except in matters of the heart, and I was happy in that area before all the others. I met the right man for me when I was sixteen years old.

"You're right. I was too young to know what I had then, but I'm not that spoiled little girl any longer. Chance moves me in ways no other man can. He saved my life, Daddy. The signs are obvious to me. He's the man I should be with. I'm getting back together with him."

"You can do want you want. You are grown."

"There he is, Daddy, going around the corner."

"I see the poor guy."

*****

Chance has gone back inside the station to question the desk officer about his car. He is told that it was towed to the front of station and they haven't touched it. He comes to the irritating conclusion that his BMW has been stolen.

Outside, Chance sees Mr. Trent's Jaguar pulling up, two car lengths from him. He notices that Patrice barely has time to close her father's car door before he rapidly pulls off. Chance stands still on the corner as she approaches.

"I'm willing to give us a try if you are."

"Patrice . . . loving you hurts. You flip-flop, and I don't know if my heart can take it."

She quickly kisses him and smiles. What he sees in her eyes makes him smile, despite his missing car. He pulls her to him and kisses her. A police officer walking past says, "Get a room."

Chance doesn't stop the kiss because he feels a release. He's been waiting too long to let go of emotions and desires he doesn't understand. If someone had asked him yesterday if he wanted Patrice back in his life, his answer would have been no. He told himself he was over her, but at least three times a week, he times his morning departure to match hers. He doesn't understand why some mornings he has to see her.

He doesn't understand why every woman he dates he compares to her: their hair isn't as black, their thighs aren't as thick, their lips aren't as soft, their speech isn't as clear, their greens aren't cooked as tender, their minds aren't as quick, their scent isn't as sweet. No, he can't replace her. But why try to replace someone he told himself he hated?

He hated how she took herself out his life, how one day, she was just gone. She no longer wanted to be his fiancée, his bride-to-be, his life partner, his best buddy. She wanted to be his "friend." He doesn't want her as a friend. He needs her as his woman, as his thinking partner. She has become part of his mind, his sounding board, and he thought he was the same for her. But he couldn't have been, because she left him and didn't ask him if she should, and he wanted to hate her for it.

She was his family, his woman, his best friend, and he found it hard to hate someone who had become all he had. But if he couldn't hate her, he would be damned if he was going to miss her. He told himself he didn't miss her. He told himself that he could hate her. He told himself that there were other women in the world that could fill his needs.

His needs, for a while, he thought were all physical, so he found women to take care of his physical needs, but he was still wanting. He couldn't label what he wanted, so he started shopping: plasma television, Rolex watches, Gucci sunglasses, the BMW. And these things would satisfy him for a short while.

After he got the BMW, he started taking road trips on the weekends: Detroit, St. Louis, Cincinnati, and Atlanta. He met women in all the cities, but none he wanted to make part of his life. He told himself he needed to take a longer vacation. Going abroad appealed to him. However, he had never been as lonely as he was in London. When he came back from London, he brought a funk back with him that he was unable to shake.

He would wake mornings so heavy in sadness that he was barely able to get out of the bed. It was during these still mornings when he would hear Patrice moving about in her condo. If he listened closely, he could figure out where she was in her preparation, and if he timed it right, he could pass her in the hall on his way to work.

He thought himself pathetic for going through such extremes for glances of her, but the planning got him out of the bed and out the door. He didn't speak to her during these calculated departures, and would ignore her slight greetings because he told himself he hated her. His eyes, on the other hand, would send a message to his heart that it was time to be happy. He would suppress the happy feeling and try to change it into anger.

Every so often, the happy feelings would be too strong to suppress. These days, he would call the florist and order her dozens of roses, only to cancel the order moments later, when he got a hold of himself and remembered it was she who left him.

Working was his saving grace. He was good at his job, and that kept his self-worth up. He was worth something in the world, despite the fact that he was worthless to Patrice. The large paychecks and bonuses confirmed his worth. He may not have been the man she wanted, but he was "the man" on his job.

The man she wanted, he suspected, was the type her parents wanted her to marry. She'd confided in him about her parents' objections prior to their engagement. They laughed together at the objections because they were in love, and they knew they could make a marriage work. Her parents' objections strengthened their commitment to one another. Then her father found the identity of his biological parents, and proved him unworthy through genetics. He felt certain Patrice would laugh at the discovery. She didn't.

She never told him that the information was her reason for calling off their life together, but it was days after her father found the information that she wanted to change her status from his life partner to a friend. She no longer desired to be his fiancée. She no longer desired him. So he told himself he didn't desire her, and tried to bury the emotions he had for her deep inside himself.

During the kiss they share in front of the police station, he lets loose of that submerged desire and tears run from his eyes. In her ear, he whispers, "Shorty, I hope you're not playing with me."

"No, baby, I'm through playing."

"Will you marry me?"

"Yes. Today if you want."

"Not today, but we can fly to Vegas next weekend."

"Yes, let's do that. You and I alone. We'll spend this week together and come back from Vegas man and wife. Shall we stay our pre-wedding week together at my place or yours?"

"Mine, because it used to be ours."

"Sounds good to me." Looking around, she asks, "Where are you parked?"

"It appears that my car has been stolen. We'll have to catch a cab."

"Stolen? But Daddy had it towed right here. It was parked here when we came to bail you out."

Wrapping his arms around her waist, he says, "But now it's not, so let's get a cab and go home."

"What is that I feel throbbing against my thigh?"

"If we don't get home soon, I will have to show you out here."

"Taxi!" she yells at the yellow cab across the street.

Chance isn't sure, but he thinks he sees Nadine sitting in the passenger seat of the U-haul truck that is pulling out of his building's driveway.

Nadine . . . he will have to talk to her. Telling her the truth will be best. He is back with his girl and getting married next Saturday. Chance can't help but smile from the thought. He is back with his girl.

They exit the cab at the same time the doorman exits the revolving door.

"Ms. Trent . . . and Mr. Bates?" He has a worried but curious look on his face. "I didn't expect to see you, sir. Your sister came and moved most of your belongings. I thought you were being held by the police."

"Yes, well, that's why some people get paid for thinking and others get paid for opening doors," Patrice answers snippily.

Knowing Patrice's moods, Chance suspects she is ready to tear into the doorman because of the statement he made to the police, but Derrick said something that caught Chance's ear.

"My sister moved my belongings? What are you talking about, man?"

"Your sister came about an hour after the incident in the street this morning. She said she was moving some of your belongings to her place. Her and the Mexican movers. One she was very friendly with. I think he is going to be your brother-in-law soon. Your nephew looks just like him."

"What sister?"

"Your sister, Mr. Bates, the one that drove your car yesterday to go get your nephew. She came and got your belongings. I held your nephew while they moved your stuff."

"What the fuck are you talking about, man? I don't have a sister." Chance pushes past him and runs to the elevator. When they get to the twenty-third floor, he sees his door wide open.

"Ugh, fuck!"

When he enters, the condo is almost as bare as it was when they moved in; African masks and art—gone, stereo system—gone, two Persian rugs—gone, microwave oven—gone, coffee maker—gone. He walks into his bedroom; plasma television—gone, hand carved headboard—gone, his two Jacob Lawrence prints—gone, his two-carat diamond pinkie ring—gone, his three Rolex watches—gone, his gold link bracelet and chain—gone. He walks to the closet, kicking aside one of Nadine's filled plastic bags. They left him one suit, one pair of shoes and one white shirt.

"I'll be damned!"

He reaches for the phone to call the police. It's gone—along with his alarm clock, bedside table and lamp. He looks to the corner for his portable bar; it's gone with all his cognac, including the 200-year-old bottle of Napoleon.

He grabs one of the green plastic bags and rips it open. It's stuffed with shredded newspapers and bed sheets.

"I've been had. That slick-ass little bitch!" He sits on his bed and laughs hard and loud.

Patrice sits next to him. "You know who did this?"

TONY LINDSAY

"Oh yeah, the woman you saw me leaving with this morning."

"The one with the baby? Doesn't she work at the Pancake House?"

"Not anymore, I'm sure."

"Do you think she got your BMW too?"

"Her, or one of her crew. They probably followed me this morning and waited for an opportunity to use the key she must have copied." Nadine is more from his world than he had guessed.

"Damn, Chance, what are you going to do?"

He's been to jail once today already being C. He isn't about to let C out again.

"What any other taxpaying citizen would do—call the police and my insurance company. But I'm going to have to use your phone because they stole mine," he says with a chuckle. "And, shorty, it looks like we're going to be spending our week together at your place." He leans toward her with a kiss.

*****

Patrice's mind is happily circling around one thought: marrying Chance in Vegas. The plan has her excited. Chance is talking about having to go to work and ordering computers, but she can't focus on his words for her own thoughts. She watches him grab his one remaining suit and shirt from the closet.

He pulls her from his bed and leads her next door to her apartment. When they enter her bedroom, they undress. He is saying something about going to Lincoln Park, but her eyes are on his erection. It's getting bigger with each throb. They will be Mr. and Mrs. Bates Saturday.

She's never really noticed how long and fat Chance's thing is before. Compared to the men she's been with since him, his is abnormally big. She didn't get a look at it this morning, but she felt it going deep. She attributed the deep sensation to the position. It wasn't the position; her man is packing.

Raymond had a half of a cucumber; Chance has a whole one. His even curves in the middle like a long, fat cucumber. It is hard and points up to the ceiling. Why didn't she remember how big he is? How could she have forgotten the way she cried the first time they were together over Big Time's house on that damn rug? She was sixteen years old and a virgin, acting like she wasn't.

"You're my man?" she'd asked him.

"Yeap, that be me," Chance told her, sliding his hand under her linen sundress to her thighs.

"And you want me to lie down on that rug and let you get some of my stuff?" She opened her thighs, letting his probing fingers rub on her coochie through her panties. She'd let boys touch her down there before with her panties on. She even let one boy lick it through her panties.

"Naw, shorty. I want us to lay down on dat rug and give each other some."

Somehow, one of his fingers had gotten past her panties. He was touching her stuff for real, rubbing his finger between her coochie lips, and it felt good. She was getting wet. She closed her thighs and pulled his hand out of her panties.

His hand went to her breasts. He didn't go under her dress. He was circling her nipple through the linen of the sundress and her bra. And to her surprise, her nipple was getting hard. He took her hand and put it in his lap. She felt the lump and rubbed it. She'd done that with boys before too.

A hand job, they called it. She even let one boy take his thing out. She wanted to see it all swollen up. Chance's lump was bigger than the other boys she'd given hand jobs. She grabbed it hard through his jeans. She heard him moan. He was sucking on her neck and his hand was back under her dress, gripping her thigh. His thumb was flicking around her coochie. Chance thought he was slick, but her mind was thinking.

"I tell you what. Since I'm your woman, I have the right to tell you what I think, correct?"

"What?"

"I'm your woman, right?"

"Yeah."

"And a good man at least listens to his woman, right?" His finger was back between her coochie lips. She opened her thighs for him. This time, his finger didn't slide up and down between her lips. It was pushing at her hole. He was trying to finger-fuck her. No boy had done that.

"I said a good man listens to his woman, right?"

"Yeah."

"Then this is my deal. I'll get down on the rug with you if you agree to tell Big Time in the morning that you want the weed connect by yourself."

His other hand had found its way under her brassiere.

"Shit, all right. Whatever, just come on."

He quickly moved the table and took two of the cushions off the sofa, leaving a sleeping Paco on one. She lay on one of the cushions. He flicked the light switch on the wall and the room became dark.

"Let's get naked," he breathed.

"Oh no, they might come out here. I'll take my panties off, but that's it. And you can pull your thing out, but you got to keep your jeans on." She wiggled out of her panties and heard Chance unzip his jeans. Her plan was to let him finger-fuck her and give him a hand job. No way was she going to lose her virginity on a rug in the projects.

When she reached over in the dark for his thing, she almost snatched her hand back because it felt so hot and alive she could feel his heart beating in it. She grabbed it tight and moved her hand up and down. She tried to see it, but it was too dark. She was going to roll over and put both her hands on it, but Chance started doing things to her coochie with his fingers that held her in place.

He was sliding between her lips and rubbing her tender thing at the top. She had never been that wet before. Instead of lying prone on his back while she rubbed his thing, he rolled on his side, and suddenly, one of his fingers was inside her. Something was going on down there, and it felt good to her. It felt so good that she let Chance pull one of her breasts out of her dress and brassiere and suck on it.

"Oohwee." She was feeling good. Chance knew how to do it. The best thing she'd done with boys before this was grinding. What they were doing was way better than grinding. Her whole body was tingling until Chance stuck too much of his finger in and hurt her.

"Ouch! Take it out." He must not have heard her because he kept his finger in and pushed even harder. "That hurts, Chance. Take it out. I'm not playing." She rolled away from him and his finger.

"Girl, you shoulda told me you was a virgin. I knew you was fresh, but I didn't think you was a virgin. You still got your cherry skin in there. Damn, and you want me to pop it. Damn, that's some love shit, girl." He sat up. "We got to go about dis all da way different. I ain't gonna pop your cherry skin with my finger. Hell naw. We fixin' to make love fo' real. We gonna have to get you to relax a little bit, though."

He was rubbing her thighs while he spoke to her. He reached into his jean pocket and pulled something out.

"You ever smoke weed befo'? Don't lie."

"No."

"Okay then. I want you to do dis like I tell you. Come over here. Let's sit against da couch."

He took her by the hand and she scooted across the rug with him, feeling little pieces of debris scratching her naked booty. Sitting next to him, she watched a small flame light a joint.

"It ain't hard to smoke weed. A lot of people try to make it all complicated, talkin' about you got to hold da smoke and all dat. You don't have to. When you breathe it in and feel it sting your throat, you can blow it out. Don't swallow it, though. Blow it out. Watch me." He held his lighter lit, so she could see him in the darkness.

She watched him inhale and exhale the smoke as easily as he took a breath.

"Do it just like dat." He handed her the joint.

She inhaled the smoke and blew it out quickly. The sting at the back of her throat was strong, but she held down the cough.

"Ouch!" Patrice figured the lighter must have burned his thumb because he let it go out, bringing back the darkness.

"Hit it again," he told her.

She hit the joint a couple more times. She didn't cough until she tried to hold the smoke in her lungs like she saw others at her school do. It wasn't until the third joint that she was able to hold the smoke in her lungs. She was a natural, Chance told her as they scooted back across the rug to the sofa pillows.

She was told that getting high would make her feel mellow. She wasn't sure what mellow meant, but getting high did make her feel. She felt her knees on the rug. She felt her hair hanging on her shoulders. She felt the tight strap of her sandal digging into her ankle. She felt the softness of the material on the sofa cushion, and she really felt Chance's fingers dancing on her thighs and up her stomach.

The dress, brassiere and shoes felt restraining, so she pulled them all off. After they smoked the joints, she found that she could see in the darkness. Chance was removing his clothes. Naked, he lay beside her on her cushion. Again, she felt his fingers. This time they weren't dancing, they were rubbing her and grabbing her all over. He squeezed her butt, her shoulders, and her thighs.

He kissed the tips of her toes and the backs of her knees while he was rubbing her hips. She'd never felt such thick wetness between her legs before. When he opened her thighs and started licking the insides of them, she felt her eyes cross and toes ball up. She hoped he wouldn't lick her coochie because she didn't want him to see the wetness, but once she felt his tongue down there, she didn't care what he saw or didn't see, as long he kept licking her like that. Chance knew how to do it.

He was lying on top of her and breathing hot breath into her ear. She felt him rubbing her down there. She thought he was rubbing her with the palm of his hand, until she felt his hands on her shoulders. Whatever he was rubbing her with covered her whole coochie, and it felt good to rub against. It was like grinding, except she was naked.

Then whatever he was rubbing her with changed. It didn't cover her whole coochie. It was sliding up and down between her soaked lips. Then it stopped sliding and positioned itself at the bottom of her coochie. It was rubbing against her hole, pressing against it. It wanted to go inside her. She wrapped her arms around Chance tightly and pushed toward what was trying to get into her until she felt as if her coochie was tearing or ripping.

Whatever was trying to go in her didn't push through. It stayed where it was and rubbed and rubbed and rubbed. It didn't hurt her, rubbing her like it was doing, but she cried. She cried because she wanted whatever was rubbing her, in her, but going in hurt. She wanted it in, but she didn't want to tear herself. She heard Chance say, "Hug me as tight as you can. Tighter."

When she hugged him with all the strength she had, he told her, "Now breathe in slow. If it hurts, blow your breath out fast and breathe in slow again."

As she took in her slow breath, she felt pushing, pushing, pushing then tearing. When she breathed out, it went into her and hurt so bad, she bit into Chance's shoulder to stop from screaming. She held onto Chance for dear life. She was certain it was ripping her apart. He didn't pull it out like she wanted him to. It stayed inside her, mixing up her two feelings, pain and pleasure. It hurt and felt good at the same time.

Chance was licking in her ear while he had it inside. He didn't pull it out; he kept it inside her. The pain was less but the pleasure wasn't increasing. If he hadn't been licking in her ear and kissing her neck, she might have stopped him.

Then he twisted his head down to one of her breasts and started sucking her nipple while still inside her. The pleasure was starting to grow with his sucking. He did more than suck her nipple. He was sucking the tips of her breasts and filling his mouth, and then he went back to sucking the nipple only.

As he was sucking her nipple, something was going on down there where it was, and something was happening with her toes and the inside of her thighs. She was starting to tingle again, and the tingling started where it was. But then he pulled it out and pushed it back in. The pain came back and pushed the tingling feeling away.

"It hurts when you take it out and put it back in. Leave it in or take it out, but don't go in and out, please," she cried. She was ready to stop.

"I'm sorry, baby. Just a little while longer. Let me stay inside you a little while longer," he whispered and moaned. The pain was greater than the pleasure, and he was doing nothing to increase the pleasure for her. He was moaning and groaning like something big was getting ready to happen to him. Then she felt it twitching inside her and heard him sigh. "Oh sweet, sweet Jesus. Please, Lord, never let me lose her."

If she believed in God, she would thank him for answering Chance's prayer from years ago. Since she doesn't, she leans back in her bed and opens her thighs, and thanks Chance for having a big, hard one, and deciding he has a little time before they have to go to Lincoln Park.

Chapter Sixteen

Sharon, who was standing in Linda's grandmother's kitchen, took the lid off the bucket and grabbed a breast from the pile of pieces. Linda was standing next to her, still looked spooked about the picture.

"Relax, girl. I think the hard part is over. You got past the picture."

"Oh, so you wasn't scared?"

"I didn't say that, but it's going to take more than a picture to send me back to the streets."

"You right."

After a quick dinner, they toured the house side by side, upstairs and down. From midway down the basement stairs, they noticed it was unfinished, but had been kept clean. Neither wanted to venture from the stairs.

The four bedrooms were all on the main level. Two of the four were large master bedrooms; one had a king-sized bed, the other a queen. Linda took the king and Sharon was happy with the queen. All the bedrooms had complete bedroom sets and a television with cable.

The friends were up until the early hours of the morning, filling their closets with the new clothes and watching cable. Neither said they were afraid, but they both were. Finally, exhaustion took over them both. They'd discussed sleeping in the same room, just in case, but Linda had gas—bad. And that sent Sharon to her own room.

They didn't share a room, but the next morning they discovered they'd shared a dream. It was 6 a.m., and neither woman was ready to get up, but they weren't given a choice. Linda's grandmother woke them up. They met in the kitchen, dressed in the matching yellow baby doll nightgowns they had bought during the shopping spree.

"Did she wake you up?"

"Yeah, and she was in my dream."

"Mine too. But you were also in mine."

"Yeah, girl, you was in mine too. Askin' all them damn questions." Linda moved to the stove, grabbed a hot water kettle, took it to the sink, filled it with water and carried it back to the cast iron eye of the stove, and cut on a jet.

Sharon rumbled through cabinets until she found the instant coffee. "Linda, it was hard trying to understand what she wanted us to do."

"I don't know what was so hard. She wants us to go to the bank. And when we get there, you are supposed to say something to the Mexican guard about getting some identification, and I'm supposed to open a checking account." Linda took two coffee mugs from the dish rack along with two teaspoons. Both women sat at the kitchen table waiting for the water to boil.

"But I have identification."

"Naw . . . wasn't you listening? You got to get new stuff. She said you have to be a new you." She put a spoon in each mug and slid one toward Sharon.

"And how is a bank guard going to do that for me?" Sharon took the sugar bowl and the creamer off the small spinner on the table.

"I don't know. I ain't never even heard of a Gainer Bank. What I do know is I don't like being frosted first thing in the morning." Linda hugged herself and rubbed her own arms.

Sharon shivered and said, "Me neither, and what was all that about the library?"

"Damn, girl, was you 'sleep in the dream? The library is where you have to go and take the GED classes."

"Oh. Well, I'll tell you, I might not have understood everything, but I saw that man she was pointing you toward."

"Mmm. Girl, wasn't he fine?" Their palms met for a high-five above the table. "And looked like he mighta had a little money. You noticed it wasn't until the end of the dream that she brought him in and hung him out there like a carrot. Grandma is a trip."

"Yes, she is, but I like her."

"Yeah, I do too."

Dressing to go to the bank took the friends almost three hours. Between talking, nervous expectation and their full closets, they were lucky to get out of the house. Linda finally decided that they should dress for errands instead of business, so they both dressed in new Levi's and cream silk blouses.

When they entered the bank, only Linda stood in line. Sharon sat in the chair next to the guard who smiled at her. She felt his smile was tight and forced. That didn't make her task of approaching him about the identification any easier. In the dream, she was only told he could get it for her.

She hadn't noticed the chair she was sitting in was for people opening new accounts until the guard said, "The manager that opens new accounts won't be in today. You'll have to go to another branch." Sharon liked his uniform. The creased, dark blue officer's dress complemented his tan color and black hair.

"Oh, I can't open an account. I would like to, but my identification isn't correct."

The tight smile returned as he bent down closer to her. "What's the problem?"

"The name is all wrong."

"You have the wrong name on your identification?"

"Well, not wrong, just old. The name matches the old me."

"I see." He leaned in even closer to her. "Then you need new identification for the new you?"

"Yes."

"And who told you to see me about this?" The guard's voice was barely a whisper.

"My friend's grandmother, Mrs. People. Did you know her?"

He stood erect. "Sweet Virgin Mother, I dreamed about you, Mrs. People, the priestess and a little burned girl last night." He was no longer whispering. "My wife said it was the pork roast I ate so late." He took two steps back from her. "But I know magic when I feel it. You are a witch, no? Never mind. I don't mean to offend one who travels with many spirits."

Sharon wasn't sure if it was pity or fear in the guard's black eyes. She looked from his eyes to the shiny badge on his shirt. It was easier to focus on the badge than his eyes.

"I was made aware of your need last night while I slept. The name Maxine Waters is now yours. You are a priestess, no? Never mind. The question was foolish from a simple man. Forgive me. Everything you need is across the street at the passport photo office. Tell the girl at the desk that you're going to Greece through the 'Waters.' Give her $1,800. No, don't give her money. Forgive me, priestess. I'll take care of it, photos and all."

He took another step back and said, "And, priestess, please spare me your magic. I am indeed a simple man. All you had to do was ask. No reason to work spells on me. I am a Christian, a good Catholic. Send no more spirits to my sleep, please. The little burned girl disturbed me greatly. Please, spare me." He bowed and hurriedly walked to the other side of the bank's lobby. When he got there, he looked at her and made the sign of the cross.

Sharon was sure what she saw in his eyes was both pity and fear. What did he mean the little burned girl disturbed him greatly? How could he know about her?

Linda interrupted her thoughts. "Girl, Grandma and Granddaddy banked here. They opened my account with no problem, and the manager made the funds from the insurance check available immediately. I got clout here," she whispered excitedly.

"That's good." Sharon's eyes were on the bank guard.

"Did you talk to him?" Linda asked.

"Yes. We have to go across the street to the passport photo office."

When they got across the street to the photo office, the bank guard had called ahead. And try as she might, Sharon couldn't pay for the new identification, which included a driver's license, a social security card, and a passport. Sharon Bates became Maxine Waters.

Back in the Chevy, Linda asked, "Why did those ladies keep callin' you priestess? I thought the new name was Maxine."

"It is, Maxine Waters. They think I'm some sort of priestess because Grandma went into the bank guard's dream last night and he must have told them I was a priestess."

"Girl, you got people thinkin' you do voodoo." She laughed and started the car.

"No, Grandma got people thinking I do voodoo. And something else was weird."

"What?" she asked while driving out of the bank's lot.

"The guard said one of the voices I hear was in his dream last night, and he called me 'one who travels with many spirits.' " Sharon's gaze was outside the Chevy window, but her mind was with the bank guard.

"What do you mean he saw one of your voices? Your voices got faces?"

"Yes and you've seen them." She turned from the window to see Linda's reaction. "Remember the little burned girl we found on the stairs?"

The happy expression dropped from Linda's face.

"Lord have mercy, you hear that baby? Oh, girl, seein' her is one of the worst things that happened to me as a kid. Oh, that little girl suffered. I dreamed about her for a couple of weeks, and every once in a while, I'll still dream about her. But you hear her in your head?"

Linda shivered from the memory and caused the car to swerve a little into the next lane. Sharon didn't comment on the swerve because she didn't notice it. She was in the stairwell of their childhood building. "I can close my eyes and still see her. I can smell her burnt flesh and hear her sobbing. After you ran from the stairwell, I went over to her. I held her in my arms, but she kept crying.

"I couldn't make it better for her. When the adults came, they took her out of my arms. She was alive and crying, but I couldn't help her. They took her from me.

"She was the first voice I heard in my head . . . and then came the mailman. You remember him, don't you? The one the men in our building beat to death because they said he was raping children. Well, it was true. He raped me when I was eleven." Sharon hadn't planned on revealing the rape. That was the first time she had said it out loud to anyone.

"He did that to the little girl in the stairwell too. She told me. He raped her and set her on fire."

Sharon's fists were in tight knots on her thighs, and the tightness was moving up her arms. She forced her fingers to extend, and took deep, slow breaths. Her head hung down as she breathed.

"He hurt so many kids."

Linda pulled over into a Mister Doughnut parking lot and parked. Sharon's body jerked in response to the abrupt stop.

"He raped me too."

Sharon found her head heavy, almost too heavy to turn and see Linda's tear-filled eyes.

"My daddy was one of the men who stomped the life out of him. My mama made me tell my daddy, and a couple days later . . . the mailman was dead. I wanted to be happy when they found him dead, but little girls don't know how to be happy about revenge. I was kinda happy, because I would never see him again. I understood that much about death." Linda made a sound that could have been mistaken for laughter, but there was no cheerfulness in it.

"I was happy he was dead. I saw them beat him into the sidewalk, and when they finished with him, I went down there and spit on him, and kicked him in his swollen, lifeless eye with my school shoes. I kicked him until his fat eyeball popped open.

"The first thing my mama taught us kids was to hit back. If somebody hit you or hurt you, damn it, you hit them back. So I kicked him in his fat eye.

"Damn, girl . . ." Linda couldn't finish her sentence for the tears.

The tears she felt fall on her own arm startled Sharon. She didn't know that she was crying.

"The mailman made me hate being a girl, Sharon. I figured if I wasn't a girl, he couldn't have done that bad thing to me. It wasn't until somebody told me that he did it to boys, too, that I started feelin' better. Ain't that some sick shit? When I heard that such a horrible thing could happen to boys, too, I began to get better.

"That shit he did to me warped my thinking. When somethin' bad happens to me, I always look to see if it happened to anyone else. When I see it happened to

215

somebody else, I feel better. But I'ma tell you, what he did to us, even now as a grown woman, I hate his ass for it. I'll go to my grave hatin' that bastard."

When Sharon saw how hard Linda was crying, she regretted taking her to such sad thoughts. She didn't want to share her misery.

"Linda, please don't cry." Sharon was trying to hold back her own tears. "It's okay . . . it's okay. The bastard got what he deserved. They killed him."

Sharon remembered when the police came to the building, questioning people about the mailman's death. They found no witnesses, and none of the residents had heard or seen a thing. There were no false arrests made. The mailman's murder was pinned on no one. He was dead, but not gone. At least not from her memory.

"How come you never told me he raped you, Sharon?"

"Probably for the same reasons you never told me. I didn't know how to talk about it and I wanted to forget it. I didn't tell anyone. I couldn't. He said it was a secret, our secret, but I wanted to tell because he hurt me. Do you remember Mrs. Loffit?"

"The fifth grade teacher?"

"Yes. I wanted to tell her what the mailman did because she always gave me hugs and told me I was a smart girl. And whenever I told her about boys hitting girls or being mean, she would believe me and discipline the boys. I was certain she would punish the mailman.

"I was going to tell her what he did, but the day I made up my mind to tell her, she had a heart attack right in front of the class. I watched her struggle to hold on to life. All the other kids started screaming and ran out of the classroom. It was just me and her alone in that room.

"I went over to her and shook her, but she didn't move. I shook her so hard her silver wig came off, but she was gone. I stood there, not crying, just looking, and then I saw the sparkle of her wedding rings: diamonds.

"I had asked her could I have them before, but she told me no. I took the rings off her finger and I kept them until I was thirteen years old. I gave them to my mother to pay the light bill one month. I hear Mrs. Loffit in my head too."

"Damn, girl . . . you have been through some tragedy. The little burned girl and the mailman had to happen all in the same week. You ever think about that, about how much bad stuff happened to you in such a short period of time? Girl, a grown person couldn't handle all that, let alone an eleven-year-old kid."

When Linda reached across the seat and held Sharon's hand, she no longer tried to hold back the tears.

"But it's going to get better for both of us now. We makin' it, girl. We doin' things. Makin' changes in our lives. I heard somewhere that tears clean the soul, so us sittin' here cryin' is good for us. We cleanin' our souls." Linda opened her purse and pulled out a small pack of tissues.

"We gonna sit here and have ourselves a good cry because we both need it." Linda blew her nose hard into the tissue and cried freely, as if she was child. Sharon wrapped her arms around her friend's shoulder and wept just as openly.

When the two friends got to the library, Sharon paused in front of the doors. She heard Linda a step behind, prodding her on with the new name.

"Let's go, Ms. Waters. Let's get in here and get it done."

The last two days of Sharon's life had moved at a fast pace, and she thought she needed a moment to catch up. She'd been released from the institution, moved in with and away from Elaine, made it to Gary, Indiana, met a ghost that gave her directions in her sleep, gotten a new name, shared secrets that she'd kept hidden for years and on top of all that, she was steps away from starting an education.

Sharon wanted to sit for a minute on the library steps and think, but Linda pulled the doors open and said, "The class is easy, girl. Don't be worried about it."

Inside the library, the air was cool and crisp. The wood floors had been polished to brilliance, and filled bookshelves covered every visible wall. Linda pointed to a posted notice behind the circulation desk. It read: GED CLASS REGISTRATION FROM 10 A.M. TO 2 P.M., MONDAY THROUGH SATURDAY. It was fifteen minutes after ten on a Saturday morning.

"Things are going your way too," she said with a grin. "I told you when we start doing right, good things will happen."

The best thing that happened to Sharon thus far was that she hadn't heard one peep out of the voices since she left Linda's apartment and rode to Gary. She'd listened for them, but heard nothing. The next best good thing was the new identification she handed the clerk at the library. Sharon could be a new person, and the reality of that sunk in when she signed the registration forms with the name Maxine Waters.

She didn't write her new name all together as she did when she signed Sharon Bates. She wrote a cursive capital M separate from the small letters of her first name. She did the same with the W of her new last name.

"Thank you, Ms. Waters. I'll see you Monday morning." The young male clerk returned her driver's license with a new library card, and Sharon gave him a smile.

"I'm in that class too," he said. "And you can check out the test preparation book from the reference desk. It will be a good idea to get it today, because after Monday, all ten copies will be gone."

Sharon was sitting in the passenger seat of the Chevy, happily looking through the pages of the test preparation book. A lot of the material would be review for her, and what was new didn't seem that difficult.

"You were right, Linda. I think I can pass this test."

When Sharon looked up from the book, Linda was parking in front of the house.

"I told you, girl, all I had to do was sit still, listen and really want it."

A different feeling fell over Sharon when she looked at the house. She felt cautious, like she should be careful. Walking up the walkway was as bad for her as climbing down a fire escape. By the time she got to the door, her heart was beating in her ears.

"Linda, something is wrong."

Linda opened the door and walked in first. Sharon timidly followed behind her.

"I must have left some bacon in the boiler. Something burnt good."

Sharon saw no smoke. "Linda, wait."

Linda was already past the foyer and in the living room when Sharon heard her scream.

It was the portrait.

The image wasn't Linda's grandmother. It was the little burned girl.

"That's the little girl! The little burned girl from the stairwell. Oh my God. This can't be real."

Sharon watched Linda take an unsteady step left, then another to the right. She moved closer when she saw Linda's knees bend. Linda collapsed into her arms. Sharon walked her over to the couch. Linda hadn't totally lost consciousness. She allowed Sharon to seat her on the couch.

The two friends sat on the couch and they looked again at the portrait. The child's image had been replaced with the mailman.

"Oh, hell naw!"

Linda stood and grabbed the candy dish from the end table. She slung it so hard at his image that she fell to the floor. The portrait wasn't damaged, and his image remained.

From the floor, Linda pleaded, "Grandma, get his ass out of here."

Sharon watched as Linda's eyes closed. She wanted to reach for her, but her own eyelids fell for sleep.

*****

They were in the stairwell where the little burned girl was found. Sharon was with Linda, Grandma, and a little girl, but the little girl wasn't burned and she wasn't crying. She walked over to Sharon and took her hand. "All I wanted to do was thank you. I felt you holding me. You stayed with me when I was hurting, so I stayed with you. Thank you."

The stairwell was flooded with a bright white light. That didn't bother Sharon at all. When the light faded, they were in her fifth grade classroom with Mrs. Loffit.

"I stayed with you, Sharon, because it was easier than going into the light. I was familiar with you and uncertain about the light. I hope I helped you some, dear."

The light flashed again and they were on the sidewalk of their childhood building.

"Fuck all you bitches! And old woman, you have no power over me. I stayed 'cause I wanted to stay, and I am not going anywhere," the mailman snarled.

Sharon and Linda stepped away from him. They watched Grandma twirl her hand until a small, black cloud was formed. She pointed her hand at the mailman. The black cloud went from Grandma's fingertips to the mailman's feet and began to cover him. When he opened his mouth to scream, the cloud went down his throat. It grew until it covered him totally, and then he and the cloud were gone.

The white flash of light returned and Sharon was sitting at the dining room table with Linda and Grandma.

"Only I am with you now. Wake up, girls. You have windows to wash."

*****

When Sharon woke, she was still on the couch, and Linda was still on the floor. It was Sunday morning.

"Oh, that was way too freaky for me. It was like I was only 'sleep for a couple of minutes, but, girl, it's morning outside. That means we slept through all of Saturday. Are you with me, Sharon?" Linda sat up from the floor.

"Yes. I'm right here."

"And the mailman had an attitude. He scared me, but Grandma set him straight. You know what all that means, don't you?" Sharon watched Linda get off the floor and come sit next to her on the couch. "It means you haven't been crazy all this time. It means the voices were real. Well . . . real as a ghost can be."

Chapter Seventeen

The police have come to the condo and left. Chance filed both reports, a stolen car and the home burglary. He told the police nothing about Nadine, and prevented Patrice from saying a word about her as well. She conned him clean, and a strong part of him respects that. He isn't about to turn trick on her. If the police catch her, it won't be because of information he gave.

He dresses in his last remaining suit, a gray pinstriped he has at Patrice's, and his mood is good despite his material loss. His insurance agent and Patrice are more upset than he is.

"You should have told the police her name."

"Why? I'm insured."

"She stole from you, Chance."

"Yes, but I can afford her theft. She might not be able to afford jail. If they catch her, they catch her. But I am not going to be the one to help the cops put another black person in jail."

"Chance, do you care about her? Romantically, I mean."

"No, shorty. I care about her as young black sister."

He feels it is an honest answer. Yes, Nadine rocked his world in the bed, but what he feels with Patrice is way better. She rocks his head, his heart and his meat, but there isn't any sense in telling her all that. He has already cried in her presence. Being any more exposed would be plain foolish.

Sitting in the passenger seat of Patrice's Bentley, which the repair shop delivered to her door, Chance's mind is on the responsibilities of his new job: ordering computers, furniture and whatever else Patrice will say is needed. He looks to her and smiles. She has a gray, light wool summer two-piece on. She dresses for business, and Chance appreciates it. He's back with his woman.

"Chance, that man is calling to us." Patrice points to a man walking up the driveway of their building.

Walking up is a clean shaven Magnum in a black suit, white shirt and gray tie. Chance suspects it's his funeral suit. As hustlers, they all had a funeral suit.

"Is that . . .?"

"Yeah, that's him." Chance quickly exits the car and embraces Magnum. "Good to see you, bro. Let's go do this." Chance opens the back door and Magnum climbs in.

"Hey, lady." He greets Patrice.

"Hello, Magnum. It's been a while."

Chance answers her questioning eyes when he gets back into the car. "When I was in jail this morning, I ran into Magnum. He needs a job and I need sales trainees. He's going to work for me." Chance speaks with finality in his voice. He is running this and wants Patrice to know it.

"Really? Well, isn't life full of surprises?"

When they enter the loft offices, Chance is full of pride when he sees how impressed Patrice and Magnum are.

"All this space is yours?" Patrice questions.

"Yes, and I need you to help me fill it." He puts his arm around her waist and they walk to the back table which holds the telephone, catalog and files. Chance hands Patrice the catalog.

"How many staff do you project hiring?"

"I'm thinking a secretary/receptionist, a sales assistant and three other salesmen besides myself. So, a total of six people."

"And will you need computers and desks for all?"

"Yes."

"Okay. Then you will have to have space partitions. I suggest the five-foot tall ones. Am I to order office supplies too?"

"Everything, Patrice. Anything you think we will need to be up and running Monday morning."

Magnum taps Chance on the shoulder and says, "My wife was a receptionist for a law firm until they merged and laid her off. She went to school for computers and stuff. Her and her girlfriend got laid off together. They're good workers, Chance. They worked at the firm for three years."

"Can they start Monday morning?"

"Yeah."

"Can you get them here this afternoon?"

"Hell, yeah!"

"Call them in for an interview. Patrice, you know what to ask them, right?"

"Oh, so I am to interview your staff as well, Mr. Bates?" She looks up from the catalog.

"Just a few software questions you know," he says, smiling.

"Yes . . . I know. All right, you are to about to get hit with consulting fees is what I know."

"Bill me."

He privately squeezes her left butt cheek, and touching her excites him quickly. He has to step away because of the way she looks down at his quick rise and smiles. He thinks she's excited too. It's the same way it was when they where kids. If he touched her, he got stimulated. He steps around the table away from Patrice, checking to make sure his sudden erection isn't showing.

"Magnum, when you get married man?"

"Two years ago. I married Juanita's little sister, Jasmine."

"No you didn't. Not that skinny little kid?"

"She's not skinny anymore, bro. She's filled out right nice."

"So you see Big Time and Juanita?"

"Every Sunday. We have dinner at their place on Jeffrey."

"So, he got the house."

"And they got married," Patrice adds. "What about their butterball of a son?"

"You got the right word for him, butterball. Paco is the biggest kid I ever seen, but he's a good kid, very respectful. And, Chance, Big Time got that house and three others. He's still big time. He's driving that CTA bus every day. And he's a deacon at his daddy's church."

"Big Time going to church?" Chance and Patrice ask.

"Man, Big Time has been saved for three years. Him and Juanita so deep in the church, they don't even allow liquor in their house; and it's been that way for a couple of years. Sometimes it's hard to remember the old Big Time. He goes by Edward now. Gets mad if you call him Big Time."

"No stuff. Maybe Patrice and I will go over with you one Sunday for dinner."

"Ain't no problem. We have a crowd every Sunday. Our family is big."

Chance immediately feels as if he missed out on an important part of his life when Magnum refers to Big Time and Juanita's family as "our family." There was a time he was part of the clan as well. He shakes his head hard. Just like he can't let touching Patrice's butt distract him, he couldn't afford to let thoughts of what could have happened slow him down today, either.

What is more pertinent to what is going on currently is Magnum's speech pattern. He isn't speaking in broken English and uses very little slang. Chance never knew Magnum had the ability to switch from street language to correct English. Magnum has obviously gone through some growth of his own over the years. Chance is pleased with his friend from the past.

"Don't tell *Edward* we coming, though. I want to surprise him. Big Time is a deacon." Chance hands Magnum his cell phone. "Call your wife and her friend. Then you and I have to go through these files."

Chance notices that Patrice doesn't ask how much she can spend on the office equipment. She simply opens the catalog and starts shopping. Rich girl attitude, he thinks. She's done in less than thirty minutes.

"They tried to give me some static about having everything here before five, but I told them the name of the company I order from, and told them that they would have what I need here within the hour. All of sudden it wasn't a problem, and they're sending a setup crew."

"That's my girl." Chance reaches into his wallet and pulls out a credit card. "Call your travel agent and get us first class roundtrip tickets to Vegas and a night stay at a hotel leaving next Saturday morning, returning Sunday evening," he says with a wink.

"Yes, sir," she says with a salute.

"You need to stop it. You know you like taking orders, woman."

"Only from my fiancé." She grabs his butt openly.

Within five hours, what was once an empty loft space now has partitions in place for five working areas, complete with desks, leather high-back chairs on rollers, computers, wastebaskets and office supplies. At the back of the space is a photo copier, fax machine, water cooler, vending machine with snacks and a coffee maker. The phone system is state of the art, and came with cell phones for each extension. Chance's computer came with a laptop, and has the ability to communicate with all the others in the office system.

"Yeah, I can work with this," he says, looking over the space while hugging Patrice from behind. Magnum and the two young women are leaving out of the door.

"I would hope you could."

The time he spent with Magnum went well. Magnum is smart and retains information quickly. Chance suspects his training won't take two weeks, and Patrice is equally impressed with his wife, Jasmine, and her friend, Mary. It was Jasmine who assisted the technicians in getting the computers online. Magnum was so proud of her. He grinned the whole time she was working with the techs. "Told you my baby had brains," he bragged.

Chance decided that Jasmine will have the duties of an office manager and sales assistant, whereas Mary will be the receptionist and secretary. Jasmine's computer knowledge is superior to his and Mary's. He offered her a salary of $28,000. The younger Mary accepted a salary of $22,000. Both salaries come with performance bonuses every six months.

The young women have clear diction and carry themselves professionally. As far as employees, things have gone well. He still needs two more salesmen, and he knows where to get one. He looks down at his only remaining watch. It is 5:30. The customers service reps at his old company work until seven on Saturdays. He can meet Peter, the college kid who was hit in the head with the water bottle, in the company's parking lot.

"Shorty, can you to run me over to my old job? I need to do a little recruiting."

As he is asking the question, Amy, Mr. Sharp's daughter, enters the office space. Chance notices her attire is more professional than earlier. Gone are the sweat pants and ponytail. She is dressed in black slacks and a pink button-down cotton shirt. In her hand is a slim leather attaché case.

"Holy cow! You don't waste any time, do you?" Amy says about the furnished loft space.

Chance and Patrice turn to completely face her. He wonders if he should release Patrice from the embrace, but doesn't. He's about to introduce her as his fiancée, but Patrice says, "Amy?" and walks free of him.

"Patrice! What are doing here?"

Chance sees the smile of recognition on Amy's pale face as she steps toward Patrice.

"Helping my fiancé setup his office. What are you doing here?"

"Fiancé? No, this isn't your Chance?" she says, pointing at Chance. "The one you were engaged to. You have to be kidding me."

The women hug and kiss each other on the cheek.

"I was driving by and saw people leaving the building, so I stopped in. I thought the white Bentley resembled yours, but I didn't think it was yours. Darling, you missed one hell of a party at the club last night, and after we all left there, we went over to Jamaican Bob's and played dominoes 'til daybreak. I called you, but your phone went straight to voicemail. I see why now. Having a reunion, were we?"

"Amy." Patrice turns to Chance and says, "Amy and I went to school together from kindergarten to college."

"Yes, and can you imagine after all that time, I am just now meeting you? I've been hearing about you for years."

Chance notices Patrice stiffening in discomfort when Amy holds her accountable for not meeting him. He's met few of Patrice's friends over the years and it doesn't bother him, because those he met had a tendency to talk down to him. He is comfortable with not meeting her friends.

"This is the building my father bought, Patrice. Remember?"

"Wait." Patrice turns to Chance. "You're working for Mr. Sharp? Amy's father?"

"Yes."

"That's right. You've never met him. You don't know who he is, do you?"

"My new boss is all I know." Chance wants to show Amy around the office and get her opinion on the computer network and phone system.

"Well, there are two houses on the golf course my parents live on, their house and the Sharp's."

Chance looks directly at Patrice. "Mr. Trent and Mr. Sharp are neighbors?"

"For twenty years."

"What are you saying, Patrice?" Chance sits on the new reception desk. He's not sure he likes where the conversation is heading. He's gotten this job on his own hasn't he?

"Amy, what did your father tell you about Chance?"

"Nothing, except that he was a hot shot salesman and I was to make sure he had whatever he needed. What I can tell you is that my father had a private detective look into something concerning you, Chance, but from my understanding through Maxine, you and father discussed whatever it was." Her brown eyes are on Chance. "Correct?"

"Yeah, I know about the detective." Chance feels a headache starting at the base of his neck. Is he being played again, and if so, to what end? What can Mr. Trent gain from having him work for Mr. Sharp?

"He's happy to have Chance aboard, Patrice. And I can tell you this, Chance; he's depending on you to hit the ground running. Purchasing Better Butter was not in the fiscal budget. He's taking a risk."

Chance sees Amy transform from a friend of Patrice's to a businesswoman while she's talking.

"I've been on the phone with him for forty-five minutes from his hospital bed. This is a big deal for the company. And what he's planning depends heavily on you, Chance. I doubt your father is involved, Patrice. Father is of the opinion that Chance is a superstar sales guy."

The tension in Chance's neck leaves as fast as it came. This job he got on his own merits.

"Is your father ill?" Patrice asks with concern.

"Yes and no. He's living with cancer, as you know. He was supposed to check into the hospital last week to have the test he's having tomorrow. He blew off the test last week and didn't tell mother he was scheduled for it.

"The doctor called her and she called an ambulance this morning. Forced them to take him to the hospital, but he's been on the phone like he was at the office, so he isn't that ill. I'm on my way to pick up Maxine and take her to him now. He's got something that has to be done, and supposedly, only she can do it.

"He'll be happy to hear you got the office set up, Chance. You can expect a call from him, probably at some ungodly hour in the morning.

"I've got to go. Maxine will be calling me any minute now, asking me my whereabouts. She's as much of a taskmaster as he is. Do you want me to ask father if your father had anything to do with him hiring Chance, Patrice?"

"No, let it lay for now. The truth will come out."

In his mind, Chance is happy with the truth. This job is his because he impressed Mr. Sharp. The fact that he and Mr. Trent are neighbors is a coincidence—nothing more.

*****

Dusk has claimed the city. Sitting alone in her Bentley, Patrice watches as Chance talks to a young white man. The kid is nodding his head yes, over and over. Chance must be telling him what he wants to hear, because everything appears to be on the affirmative to Patrice.

She really could care less what the kid and Chance are talking about. She wants him to hurry and come back to the car. The news her travel agent gave her has her giddy and excited. There is a flight out tonight and a return flight at 5 p.m. Sunday. They can get married tonight or in the morning. She is barely able to stop herself from honking the horn and calling him to the car.

Her cell phones rings. She thinks it's the travel agent, but it isn't; it's Amy.

"It wasn't your father."

"What?"

"It wasn't your father who had my father hire Chance."

"Okay."

"Don't you want to know who?"

"Sure."

"It was Maxine."

"Okay."

"You want to know why?"

Patrice's call waiting signal beeped. "Hold a minute, Amy."

She hears Chance's voice. "I have to walk inside with him for a minute. He needs help bringing out his belongings."

"He's quitting tonight?" Patrice asks.

"No, he's going to call them Monday, but he doesn't want to have to come back to the office. I'll be back in five minutes." He waves and walks into the building. Patrice flashes her cell phone back to Amy.

"Now, what are you talking about, girl?"

"She's his mother!"

"Whose mother?"

"Maxine is Chance's mother. That's why she had father hire him."

"Amy, have you been you drinking?"

"Not yet. I'm sober."

"Amy, Chance's mother is probably in an institution somewhere."

"Well, Maxine told father that Chance is her son and he doesn't know that she is his mother. Father made me swear not to say a word to him or Maxine, because she's waiting for the right moment to tell him. And you know what . . . after father told me, Maxine came back into the room and I really looked at her . . . and, Patrice . . . they favor a lot. Father says if you put a wig on Chance, you got Maxine, and it's true. She's his mother. What are you going to do?"

"Me? What can I do?"

"Tell him."

"No. No way, and don't you tell a soul you told me. Forget we talked."

Patrice flips her phone closed.

"We're going to Vegas tonight. He can deal with all that mess when we get back," she says to no one.

*****

Talking with Peter goes easier than Chance planned. The kid had been interviewing for three weeks with no employment prospects. Chance's offer makes his day, and he doesn't have a problem reporting to work Monday morning. The remaining sales position Chance plans to fill with Better Butter's present top salesman. He'll drive out to Michigan City Monday afternoon. He and his sales force.

"I'm going to have to rent a ca," he remembers.

He walks through the dark parking lot to Patrice's Bentley. When he slides into the car, she tells him, "I have good news and bad news. Which do you want first?"

She's smiling, so Chance figures the bad isn't that bad.

"The bad first," he says, adjusting the seat belt.

"No tickets to Vegas are available for next weekend."

"Damn. The good news?"

"We got tickets and a hotel for tonight!"

"Returning when?"

"Tomorrow night."

"Well, let's roll, shorty."

URBAN AFFAIR

Chapter Eighteen

Grandma came into their dreams less and less over the two years Sharon lived in Gary. Linda's last time seeing her was the day before she married the butcher Grandma pointed her to in their first visited dream.

Sharon's last visited dream was the night before she was to return to Chicago, which was also the day of Linda's wedding. That was pretty much how things worked out the whole two years. Everything happened in perfect sequence. Sharon didn't have to worry about living with Linda and her new husband, because she'd found a new job a week before the wedding. She'd interviewed successfully for a position as an executive assistant with East Lake Bakeries.

What Sharon was told in her last visited dream didn't occur until twenty years later. Grandma told her to keep an eye out for her son.

Sharon didn't think she was going to get the job at East Lake Bakeries because the résumé of Maxine Waters only had internship experience. She and Linda had both done a two-month internship in the bank president's office. It turned out, however, that the president of Gainer Bank and the owner of East Lake Bakeries were members of the same country club. When the bakery owner asked the bank president about the dark black girl who typed 170 words a minute, the bank president told him that if he wasn't retiring, he would have kept her as his executive assistant. Maxine Waters got hired.

Sharon no longer feared Chicago. She no longer thought the city could destroy her, because she had no plans on returning to the streets. She was more than what she was when she left. Maxine Waters earned her GED certificate, graduated from secretarial school number two in her class, became a secretary/executive assistant, had good money in the bank and no interest in the streets or street people.

Maxine Waters reported to work thirty minutes early every day and she was always available to stay an extra hour or two at the end of the day. After her first five years with East Lake, her official title was executive assistant to the owner. Her duties, however, included those of the human resource manager and executive assistant. After her first decade, every employee knew that if there had been a vice president position at East Lake Bakeries, it would have been held by Maxine Waters.

She was involved in the day to day operation of the bakery as much as Mr. Sharp, and if he wasn't available to answer a question, the same question could be asked of her and the answer would be just as informed. When Mr. Sharp was hospitalized for three weeks during his first bout with cancer, it was Maxine who held the reins in his absence.

When she'd taken the call from the aggressive salesman who insisted on talking to Mr. Sharp's personal assistant, her plan was to blow the call off, but while she pretended to take the message, he left his name: Chance Bates. And for her, time stopped.

She had the caller repeat the name, and he spelled it twice. She didn't reach for a pen to copy the information. Instead, she reached for a Newport and her lighter. She told the caller Mr. Sharp wasn't available, and to call back in an hour.

An hour later, she was talking to him again. East Lake Bakeries had no need for his products, but she arranged a time for him to drop off samples at the gate that afternoon.

Ten minutes before the scheduled time, she walked down to the guard booth. She watched a shining black BMW pull up to the gate. The driver couldn't see her in the back of the booth, but she saw him. She thought he would look like Cherry—he didn't. He looked like her. The guard took the samples, and the shiny BMW left with her son.

That afternoon, she went through the motions of work and smoked three packs of Newports. That day, she left the bakery at three in the afternoon, which was a rare event for her.

At forty-four years of age, she was single and had been happily dating the same man for fifteen years. Jasper Collins was a barber and contractor, and his two professions kept him busy. He told Maxine on their first date that the opportunity to marry and have a family had passed him by, due to the time he served in prison. He wasn't looking for a wife this late in life. He was forty-two when they met. He was looking for a nice female friend to share his time with. Their "friendship" has lasted fifteen years.

She drove her Lincoln Town Car to Jasper's Barber Shop on 63rd and Morgan. Jasper was alone in the shop and sitting in one of four barber chairs. He raised his slender frame from the chair and smiled at her. He didn't allow people to smoke in his shop, so there was no ashtray for her to extinguish her cigarette. She opened the door and flicked it out onto the street.

"What are you doing here, Maxy?"

During the second year of their friendship and after the first time they made love, Sharon told him all about her past. She expected him to run for the hills. Instead, he gave her a key to his home.

"I talked to my son today and I saw him. Jasper, I saw him."

Jasper walked to her and wrapped his arms around her. He said nothing.

"It was him. He looks like me. It was Chance, my son. He's a man."

She cried into Jasper's chest, uncertain as to why.

"He called into the bakery this morning. I took his call and had him come to the gate. I had to see him for myself, but I don't have a clue as to what to do next."

She stepped out of his comforting embrace and walked to the door.

"I have to go."

She left without another word to Jasper. She returned to the bakery and buried herself in paperwork. When she looked at her wristwatch, it was 9 o'clock. On her note pad she saw two messages from Chance Bates, calling to make sure she'd received the samples.

"You are persistent, son. I'll give you that."

Over the next three months, Chance continued to call the bakery. Maxine made sure his calls were directed to her. They exchanged pleasantries and she got to know a little about him over the phone. He was single and dated a lot. He even went so far as to ask her if she had any young, single friends. He enjoyed the blues and had vacationed in London. Her son was a college graduate and lived in his own condominium. Chance Bates was a successful young businessman, and a little bit of a charmer. She couldn't stop herself from blushing when his flowers arrived for her on Secretary's Day.

Over the years, she'd come to recognize the actions of a good "gate opener," a salesman who knew how to get past a secretary to the boss, and Chance displayed the qualities of the best she'd seen in the business. Even if he were not her son, when Better Butter became unable to complete several shipments, she would have put his calls through to Mr. Sharp. He'd earned it, but because he was her son, she told her boss that it was time to find a more dependable supplier, and she insisted that he at least meet with the young salesman. Her boss agreed.

Then, unexpectedly, the detective who was hired to look into Better Butter's tragedies provided her and Mr. Sharp with information about Chance. It was two days before he was to come to the bakery. The file showed her that her son had more street in him than she suspected. After reviewing the information, it was Mr. Sharp's plan to have Chance arrested when he arrived for the meeting. She had to work fast to protect her son.

Her high priority project for the past five years was planning the acquisition of Better Butter. Due to her research and investigation, it was decided that an offer would be made the next fiscal year. However, over the next two days, Maxine worked frantically on changing the proposal. She changed it to aid her son.

They were sitting in Mr. Sharp's office, reviewing the detective's file the evening before Chance's arrival.

"Sidney, he is creative. You have to give him that." She was sitting in the horribly uncomfortable chairs that she'd ordered twelve years ago. Mr. Sharp refused to part with them, insisting that being outdated was not a good enough reason to replace them.

"Maxine, he hijacked a truck. *Creative* isn't the word I would use."

"He creates opportunity. Isn't that what you said a good salesman does?"

Her plan was to paint Chance in a favorable light to Mr. Sharp, despite the detective's findings.

"Discovers opportunity is what I say a good salesman does." Mr. Sharp rocked back on the springs of his antiquated chair. Maxine hoped the springs would hold him.

"Well, he did create this opportunity. There is no arguing that, but I think this opportunity is one we can't afford to pass on."

"We? What opportunity has he created for us?"

"It's time to buy Better Butter."

"No, that's on the board for next year." He closed the detective's files.

"Next year their plant won't be closed by state inspectors. Sidney, this is the time to buy while they're getting the negative press. We are not the only company who has Better Butter in its sights, but I bet you we will be the only company giving them an offer at this time." She sat up prone in the chair and looked directly at Mr. Sharp.

"Sidney, let's offer them an out. They have to be looking for one. They were a step away from bankruptcy court before the inspectors. Not being able to make shipments for a month will certainly close their doors. If we make them a decent offer now, of course one considerably less than the one we were planning on making next year, they will see it as a lifeline. Believe me, Sidney."

Maxine saw the cigar rolling from side to side in his mouth. She knew his mind was churning.

"You got a point. A darn good point. This is the time, but we don't have the staff in place."

"All we need immediately is the sales force, and you and I both know the right person for that job."

"Who?"

"The creator of the opportunity."

"Maxine, I'm ready to send that boy to jail. I am not going to hire him." He picked up the detective's file and slapped it back down on his desk.

She recognized the finality in Mr. Sharp's voice. She'd heard the tone used with her, his daughter, his wife and hundreds of employees. She had no choice but to go for her big gun. The truth.

"He's my son, Sidney."

It was Mr. Sharp's turn to sit up prone.

"You mean like he's black and part of your whole black family type of son?"

"No. I mean I birthed him and he is my son."

"Whoa, that's news."

Maxine watched him scratch at his face in thought.

"He has no idea of our relationship, and I'm not sure if I'll ever be able to tell him."

Mr. Sharp took the half-cigar out of his mouth.

"I won't send your son to jail, but giving him the job is another matter altogether."

"The meeting is already set, Sidney. Meet with him. See if you think he has what it takes to do the job. I'm positive that you'll sense what I do."

"Meet him, huh?"

"Let him pitch you. If he's good, give him a shot. If he's not, he's my problem."

Mr. Sharp rocked back again on the creaking springs. He shook his head no, but he said, "Fair enough, I'll meet with him. Get my daughter on the line, will you? We need to go over some numbers for the Better Butter purchase. You have an offer number in mind, right?"

"Yes, I do."

Jasper had told her several times over the years that their friendship developed the patience of Job in him. He, as a reborn Christian, didn't understand her belief in spirits and her flat out refusal to go to church with him. Early in their dating, he tried to convert her to Christianity, but he had no answer to her rebuttal: "I have seen spirits, Jasper, with my own eyes. Have you seen your Jesus? I know where the spirit that guides me lives. She came to me in dreams. She has protected me and freed me from a lifetime affliction. All she asks is that I do what is best for me. There are no commandments to break."

They were dining at an Italian restaurant, and their friendship was a little over a year old. They had yet to consummate the relationship.

"Maxy, if it's not the Lord's commandments that is stopping you from spending the night with me, then what is it?"

"The commandments don't govern me, Jasper, but they do govern you," she said with a sly smile. "I wouldn't want you to think of me as an evil temptress."

"So, you are not sleeping with me for my soul?"

"No. I'm not sleeping with you because I'm not ready. Like you, I have things that I need to do, and chasing behind a man isn't one of them. You lost time to prison. I lost time to a mental institution and the streets. I am learning who I am, and I cannot confuse my mind with wanting you. I need to find me first."

Sharon was certain he would accept her quest for self as the reason for her refusal for that night. She didn't think it would hold for the next several months, but it did. It was Mother's Day of the following year when her needs, not his, brought them together.

When Sharon returned to Chicago, she reasoned that to truly be Maxine Waters, she could have no connection with her past life, and that included her family. For six years, living under those parameters wasn't a problem for her. The newness of the job and being Maxine occupied her time. Maxine enjoyed the theater, dining at ethnic restaurants, reading non-fiction and historical fiction, volunteering at museums and getting involved with the state's Republican Party.

Maxine rented a townhouse in Palatine, Illinois, and joined a health club. Her life was far removed from the projects on Western Avenue. One of her brothers had actually parked her car at a Republican rally and didn't recognize her in her bob-cut hairstyle. She took her keys from his hand and walked away, pleased.

What caused her to falter and reminisce that Mother's Day was a young man selling flowers on the corner. She was with Jasper and they were driving over to his mother's for dinner. The young man was selling both red and white carnations. Through her window, he asked was her mother alive or dead. When she realized she didn't know, she broke down in tears.

She was too upset to have dinner with Jasper's family, but she didn't want him not to, and driving her all the way back to Palatine would've caused him to miss the dinner. He suggested that she stay at his place until the dinner was over. She agreed.

Alone in his house, she couldn't stop herself from thinking of her mother. She had no idea if she lived on Western Avenue, or if she was even still alive. To solve the latter question, she called the hotel her mother worked for and found out she was, indeed, still employed there. A small portion of relief settled in her chest and grew into being enough.

She didn't think it necessary to visit her mother or have any contact with her. "Let sleeping dogs lie," she said to herself. Seeing her mother was what Sharon Bates needed to do. Maxine Waters needed something to stop her from thinking like Sharon Bates. She climbed the stairs up to Jasper's bedroom, stripped off her red Mother's Day dress, and lay across his bed and waited for him to return.

The passion she let loose on Jasper freed another need of hers. The need to talk. Sharing a pillow with him, she told him all about her life: the prostitution, the murders, the voices and her son. She told him that she had given birth to a child, and that was all she did. She didn't miss him, and she couldn't force herself to feel guilty about it. She had a good new life, and he was part of an old, bad life. Maxine Waters had a good job, good credit, a good male friend and no children. So there was no need for her to celebrate Mother's Day. She was not a mother.

And that was true until Chance Bates called into East Lake Bakeries and entered the life of Maxine Waters.

Chapter Nineteen

The flight to Vegas is almost four hours long and Chance has slept the entire flight. Patrice hasn't slept a wink. She's wondering if she should buy a wedding gown. Should she call her parents? Should they go to the chapel tonight? Should she help Chance buy the rings? Should they get gold or platinum settings? And is she doing the right thing?

She looks at Chance lying back in the first class seat. He is a handsome man. *Put a wig on him and you have Maxine.* Patrice can't remember what Maxine looks like. Should she have told him? Amy was probably drunk. Chance's mother was in a different world and besides, he doesn't care about his parents or any of his biological family. He'd told her that often enough.

"Patrice?" A familiar voice from across the aisle is calling. "I thought that was you!"

It's Nash, one of the options her parents wanted her to try. He is looking darn prosperous in his dark blue Ralph Lauren suit. He is an attorney who has worked with her father in the past.

"I was speaking with your father only this morning. We spoke of you and he suggested I give you a call myself. Imagine seeing you like this. It must be fate." His whitened teeth gleam at her. Her parents love Nash.

She and Nash had gone at it hot and heavy for a while. He was one of the men who was just as busy as she was, and their schedules wouldn't merge. He was definitely the best option she had experienced.

"I often think of you and the time we spent at your parents' cottage in Union Pier."

She decides to stop him now before Chance wakes.

"Nash, I'm traveling with my fiancé." She signals by putting her finger to her lips.

"Your fiancé? But just this morning your father assured me you were still single. Are you playing with me, Patrice? Come over here. The seat next to me is empty."

"No, thank you. And my father was mistaken. I am no longer single."

"An unknown fiancé . . . and on a flight to Vegas. My Lord, Patrice. You aren't eloping, are you? Certainly you wouldn't do that to your father?"

"Nash, my travels are not your concern."

"Not my concern? Patrice you cannot deny that if it weren't for us both being driven to succeed, we would be a couple. We connected in more ways than one. Have you forgotten the whipped cream and fishnets? I haven't. Oh, and the weekend in New York. You had me speaking French, Patrice." She sees his eyes close in memory. He opens them and says, "If you are running to Vegas to marry, I say it again; it's fate that I'm on this flight."

Patrice did remember their time at Union Pier, and it was very enjoyable. Nash has a gifted tongue, and he isn't afraid to explore with it, and he uses sex toys. Nash brought out a freaky side of her. In New York, he spent money on her like he was a rap star. The sex wasn't great, but the shopping made up for it.

The first class attendant announces the plane's descent, and they are told to buckle up. Chance wakes with the announcement. He leans over and kisses her. Patrice's eyes are on Nash.

*****

He heard it all. He woke up when her name was called. He pretended to be asleep to eavesdrop. He acted as if he was sleep because he wanted to hear her tell the snide bastard to fuck off, but she didn't. What he heard was she had spent time with him at her parents' cottage.

Chance helped Mr. Trent sell the cottage six months before they broke up, and they were still a couple when she went to New York. She took the trip a month before she told him that she couldn't marry him. She'd been with the snide bastard while they were engaged the first time.

Once they see he is awake, the across-aisle conversation ceases. He hopes she will introduce him as they disembark from the jet. She doesn't. The snide bastard walks right alongside them through the airport— no introduction.

Outside the airport at the cabstand, through the hot air and well lit Vegas backdrop, Chance catches the wink Nash sends Patrice.

She smiles.

Her teeth twinkle like the lights of the strip behind her.

The first blow Chance lands is a neck-snapping, straight right jab. Following it is a left hook. A split second later, the upper cut puts Nash on his snide ass. Patrice goes to her fallen suitor. Chance turns and walks back into the airport. There is a flight back to Chicago leaving in ten minutes. Standing at the gate, he looks to see if Patrice is coming through the crowd. She isn't. He boards the plane.

He flies back in business class, guzzles down three little bottles of gin, holds back his tears and falls back to sleep. When he lands, his thoughts are on selling his condo. He's been given several good offers in the past, but the time wasn't right. It's right now. The only key in his pocket that opens any place he wants to be is to the

Lincoln Park office. He catches the train and two buses because he is in no hurry.

He pushes the alarm numbers into the keypad and enters the loft office space. Over his shoulder he sees morning has come. His workspace is the largest of the five. On his desk are the files from Mr. Sharp. He sits in his new high back chair and begins going through them.

The cell phone Mr. Sharp's secretary gave him rings.

He pulls it from his suit coat. "Hello," he answers.

"Chance?"

"Yes, sir, it's me."

"Good. My daughter tells me you have the office set up?"

"Yes, sir, and I've recruited two salesmen. My plans are to go out to Better Butter on Monday afternoon and get the third. I've also hired two administrative staff."

"My, you have been the busy beaver. Have you had time to review the files I had shipped to you?"

"Yes, and I'm pleased to see that some are old clients."

"Do you foresee any problems with bringing them over?"

"None at all, sir."

"Good. Well, I'm out for the week, but Maxine will be in the Lincoln Park office Monday morning with you. She'll relay what's expected."

"Sir, my plans were to visit you today, if that's okay."

"Sure. Come on by in the afternoon and bring me a Starbucks Columbian roasted. The coffee here is shit."

"Will do, sir."

Chance pulls his own cell from his pocket and dials the number of the real estate broker who has been hounding him.

"Thomas Tyler," the voice on the other end answers.

"Thomas, Chance Bates. What's up, man?"

"You, my successful brother. What has you ringing my phone this early, disturbing my putt?"

"You're on the greens already, man?"

"It's not that early in Miami, my Nubian brother. I'm getting in a round before my flight back to the Chi. So, what's up?"

"What was the last offer for my condominium?"

"Four hundred and seventy-five, and she wanted to move in yesterday."

"Sell it."

"Don't play with me, blood!"

"I'm not playing, brother. Hit me up early Monday morning and we can get on with it." Mr. Trent sold Chance the unit for $375,000. He stands to make a hundred grand.

"You got an agent?"

"You. So, you'll get paid from both ends. Make it happen, African."

"It's done."

Chance flips his phone closed and Magnum's résumé catches his eye. He looks down at his watch: 7:15 a.m. It's kind of early, but he decides to call anyway.

Magnum answers on the first ring, and he sounds wide awake. "Man, Edward, I told you we were leaving out, man!"

"It's not Edward. It's me, Chance."

"Hey, what's up, C?"

"I was calling to get Big . . . excuse me, Edward's address."

"Eighty-six thirty-four Jeffery. We eat about two o'clock. You coming through?"

"Yeah, I think so."

"Hey, if you up, why don't you come past the church?"

"What's the address?"

"Forty-nine fifteen Cottage Grove. Service starts at nine."

"I'll see you there."

Chance goes into the office bathroom and checks his appearance: a little stubble. His shirt is a dark green, so it shows nothing. A few wrinkles in his jacket, but over all, he's presentable. He does undress his upper torso and bird bathes with the hand soap. Feeling a bit fresher, he heads out for the bus.

He is expecting a storefront church. That is not the case. The building is new and impressive. He walks up two flights of new concrete stairs to get to the massive oak doors. Two little girl ushers are outside, and one opens his door. The other hands him a church bulletin. Its 9:10. He's late.

When he enters the sanctuary, the first person in the pulpit to catch is eye is Big Time a.k.a. Edward. He's standing, stomping his feet and singing, and behind him is an all-male choir which includes Magnum. Chance sits and enjoys the service.

He finds the preacher long-winded, but the message hits his heart. He speaks of God's love being divine and not understood by Man. He says Man cannot say who God will bless, love, or forgive. God loves everything He created, he tells the congregation. Even the hoodlums that broke into the church and stole the hams. God's love is for all.

When the service ends, Big Time doesn't waste a second slicing through the congregation to get to him. The embrace lifts Chance from the floor.

"Oh, the Lord is good! My brother, you don't know how many prayers me and this church has sent up for you." When he puts Chance down, Juanita is standing next him.

"Come over here, C, and give me a hug! We have all been praying for you." She is pregnant and very large. Chance can't get his arms around her. He settles for hugging her neck and kissing her on the cheek.

"And Freddy told us you got him and my sister hired with your company."

"Freddy?"

"Magnum . . . we try not to call him by that name, but sometimes he won't answer to anything else. We praying for him too." She giggles.

Big Time is looking at him, grinning like a kid. "Come with me. I want you to meet the church elders."

He leads Chance to the first row of seats, where five older people are sitting.

"Dad, this is my friend, Chance Bates."

Chance extends his hand to an older version of Big Time.

"Good to meet you, son."

"And, Chance, this is Elder Collins."

Elder Collins appears gravely disturbed. He stands. "Chance Bates did you say?"

Chance still has his hand extended, but he's not sure that he shouldn't take a step back.

"Son, it is indeed a pleasure to meet you!" His embrace is tighter than Big Time's. "My Lord is unseen, but He works in mysterious ways. Praise Him!"

*****

Patrice is sitting on the edge of the bed in the honeymoon suite. Her father's words circle in her head. *Chance is violent.* There was no reason for him to beat Nash. And the way he looked at her, she felt certain that he was going to beat her next. She'd almost made a horrible mistake and "brought a mongrel to the show."

When Nash steps out of the bathroom, she gasps. His right eye is swollen shut, and the bruise on his chin is purple. Despite his obvious injuries, he has a can of whipped cream in his hand and is dressed in a pair of black fishnet pantyhose only.

Men are for fun, Patrice tells herself, and pushes Chance out of her mind.

*****

Big Time's home is full of people, and his dining room table is loaded with food. Family and friends are standing around the table, holding hands. Big Time has asked Elder Collins to lead them in prayer.

"This is a selfish payer, Lord. I am asking You to give me strength to do the task that is set before me. I ask that You guide my words in doing Your will and open closed hearts to Your divine purpose. What I think You want me to do, Lord, may cause me to lose my best friend, but I hear You, Lord, and I will obey. Amen."

Magnum whispers in Chance's ear, "He forgot to bless the food, but don't let that stop you from filling your gut. It's not gonna stop me." He snickers.

Chance eats so much, he is lulled into sleepiness. He is nodding on the couch in Big Time's den when Magnum taps him on the shoulder. "I know you're my boss and all, but around here, I'm the only one that takes a sip now and then. And I was wondering if you want to step outside and drink this half-pint of cognac with me."

When Chance looks up at Magnum, his mind goes back to the morning they had the shootout at Big Time's place. Patrice had butted in on the conversation between Big Time, Magnum and him. Magnum told him to control his "bitch" or he would. Patrice kept talking, Magnum slapped her, and it was on. If it wasn't for Big Time slapping the gun out of his hand, Magnum would have died right there in Big Time's apartment. Instead, they had a shootout that lasted thirty minutes, and resulted in a cop being shot twice in the buttocks.

"You picked the right man to ask, my brother." Chance slowly rises from the couch and stretches.

Elder Collins walks into the den and to Chance, he says, "Son, take a walk with me."

Magnum laughs and throws up his hands in surrender. "Next time, Chance."

Chance follows Elder Collins out of the front door of the house.

On the sidewalk, Elder Collins asks, "Do you have a church home, son?"

"No, sir."

"Well, when you're ready, think about our church. You've been in our hearts for years."

"I appreciate that, sir."

The old gentleman keeps a brisk pace and Chance, with a full stomach, is a half-step behind.

"The reason I asked you to join me in this walk has to do with your mother. You see, your mother and I have been dating for fifteen years, and I want you to know that I love her dearly."

"Excuse me, sir, but . . . I think you have me mistaken."

"No, son, it's no mistake I know you probably think your mother is locked up in some mental hospital, but she's not."

Chance stops walking. "Elder Collins, is that right?"

"Call me Jasper, son."

"Elder Collins . . . Believe me when I tell you that you are making a mistake."

The old gentleman hands Chance a photo. "Look at the face close, son."

"I know this woman," Chance says. "She works for Mr. Sharp. Her name is Maxine Waters."

"Yes, that is her name, but she was once Sharon Bates. Look at the face, son. See the family resemblance?"

"I see a dark woman with a narrow nose. Do you know how many dark women's faces I've looked into over the years searching for family resemblance? If Maxine Waters is my mother, then I hope she makes a much better friend to you than she did a mother to me." Chance hands him back the picture and walks down the block to the bus stop.

"What are people trying to do to me today?"

Chapter Twenty

Maxine spends her Sundays at the gym. This is her total body day. On Mondays, she works her legs and abs with heavy machine weights. Wednesdays, she works her upper body and abs with heavy machine weights. Fridays, she works her back and thighs with heavy free weights and Sundays are cardio days: rowing machine, treadmill and reps with light free weights on her whole body.

She's on the weight bench when she notices Jasper walking toward her in his church suit and hat. Something must be wrong for Jasper to drive out to Palatine on his day of worship. She quickly completes another set and sits up.

"Your son was in church," he says, handing her a towel.

"He was at your church?"

"Yes, he and our youngest deacon are friends."

"It's a small world." Looking into his eyes, she sees the worry. Intuition tells her that he told Chance. *Damn it,* she thinks.

"I spoke with him. I told him who you are."

"What gave you the right?" If she weren't in the middle of her workout, she would walk out of the gym and leave him standing where he is. But if they walk out alone, away from others, she might yell and say something she will regret later. "How did he react?"

"He responded with anger."

"I wish you wouldn't have done that. He is about to have quite a bit of pressure on him. He didn't need more." She wraps the towel around her neck and sighs.

"It was God's will, not mine."

"Jesus told him I was his mother?"

"Maxy, don't do that. Don't make small of my beliefs."

She lies back down on the bench. "Thanks for telling me, Jasper." She starts another set.

Jasper leaves.

*****

Chance sees a Starbucks coffee shop across the street from the hospital. He gets two large, Colombian roasted coffees. When he enters the room, he notices Mr. Sharp is watching the financial reports. That's what he usually does on Sunday afternoons after the gym.

Mr. Sharp is hooked up to no tubes or machines. He's sitting up in the bed.

"Mr. Bates, I've been waiting for that Starbucks. Did you get raw sugar?"

Chance laughs. "Yes, sir, I did."

"That's a good fellow."

Chance hands Mr. Sharp the coffee, a stirrer, and six packs of raw sugar. He opens all six packs and dumps them into the tall paper cup. "It's hot. There must be one close by."

"It's across the street."

"That's good to know. Have a seat, young salesman. You've just made your boss happy."

Chance takes the chair to side of the bed, allowing him to see the financial reports as well.

"We made the local news, Mr. Bates. Our purchase of Better Butter was reported at the top of the show. The cameras panned the bakery and the Better Butter plant. You're in the big time, kid," he says with a grin.

"Yes. It feels like it. What do you think about me going out there tomorrow and making an offer to their top salesman?"

"I wouldn't go for the number one. Get number two. He'll come through the door trying to prove something to you. Number one is going to be a primadonna and he'll think you need him."

"That makes sense."

"Take Maxine out there with you. She can read people. She'll help you make a good choice."

"This is probably inappropriate, Mr. Sharp, but I have a question."

"An inappropriate question? Already? I like the sound of that. Ask away."

"Did you hire me because I am the son of Maxine Waters?"

"Damn, you get right down to it, don't you? The answer is no. I met with you because you are Maxine's son. I hired you because you have steel in your balls. This is going to be an uphill battle, son, and the last thing I need is a proper, by-the-book sales guy.

"I need someone that won't have to be held by the hand. Now, don't misunderstand me. Your truck hijacking days are over, but your initiative and guts, that's what I need. I need orders, son, and you're the kid that can bring them in."

Chance stands. If he knew the gruff Mr. Sharp better, he would hug him.

"Thank you, sir. You made the right choice."

"Talk to you Monday afternoon, Mr. Bates. You and Maxine stop by after the trip out to Better Butter."

"Oh and, sir, I may need to rent a car for a couple of days."

"Why?"

"My BMW was stolen and the loaners aren't my style."

"I have a 600 Benz at the bakery. Use that until your car is replaced. Amy has the keys. Her cell number is 773-555-4321."

"Thank you, again, sir."

*****

Maxine is walking in the same hospital door Chance is leaving from. She stops in front of him. He has her brown eyes, thin lips and thick hair, and she figures he is only a few inches taller than her. Her three-inch heels have them eye to eye.

"Mother."

"Son."

"I'm not going to therapy over this," he says with a grin. "You are my mother. It is as plain as the noses on our faces. I can accept that, but I can't afford to think about it. Not now. I have a task before me and I need to handle it. I don't feel this is something that we can't work around. It shouldn't get in our way. At least it won't get in my way."

"Mine either."

"Good. I suggest maybe a couple of months down the line you and I sit down for dinner and talk. What do you think?"

"I think we can plan on it happening . . . a little sooner than that."

She walks through the door and waves goodbye over her shoulder.

As plain as the noses on our faces. She smiles at his back as her elevator door closes.

"You just missed your son," is Sidney's greeting.

"I saw the arrogant little shit."

"He knows about you, Maxine?"

"Yes, it appears the Lord told Jasper to tell him."

"The Lord? Never mind. Do you have the figures?"

"They're right here, sir."

*****

Amy is a block away from the hospital, on her way to see her father. She meets Chance on the corner. She's driving a silver Porsche 911.

"Father is letting you drive his S Class. My, my, you are the clever one."

"Not really. I told him I needed to rent a car because mine was stolen, and he offered it."

"Chance, my mother doesn't drive that car. Father parks it at the bakery to prevent us from driving it."

"He didn't act like it was a big deal."

"Where is Patrice?"

"In Vegas with Nash, I suppose."

"What? No. I thought it was you two."

"No. It's them two." The interior of the Porsche's cockpit is sleek. He likes it.

"Nash is a hunk."

"Whatever." He's not about to get pulled into talking about Patrice and Nash.

"You want to go get a drink?"

"Oh yeah. I could use a real big one."

"Good. I go to this place on Sundays that's not crowded at all. The Long Island Iced Teas are to die for. The owner is a blues aficionado. I love the blues, but through the week, the place is a gay disco club, so I had no idea.

"On Sundays, the owner and his buddies hang out. You would think the place was closed. I stumbled on it one Sunday when I ran out of gin. At first he wasn't going to let me in, right. He said it was a private club set, but when I told him I only wanted to come in and listen to the Bobby "Blue" Bland he was playing, he opened the door for me. I've been going every Sunday since. It's a group of old guys with no teeth, but I like it."

TONY LINDSAY

Standing outside at the door of the club, Chance feels the blues. Johnny Lee Hooker is coming through the door. Amy buzzes the button.

"It's a closed set. Come back tomorrow," a raspy voice yells.

"It's me, Charlie, Amy." She turns to Chance and says, "I told you. They don't let just anyone in on Sundays."

When the door opens, John Lee Hooker rides the airwaves and wraps his arms around Chance. The song is "One Bourbon, One Scotch, One Beer." The gospel music the choir sang moved him this morning, but the blues guitar of John Lee Hooker settles him down.

Sitting on the barstool, sipping a Long Island Ice Tea, he has finally unwound. The past 24 hours put him through a wringer, and during his third Long Island, he decides to share his experience with the friendly, blues loving Amy, who is on her fourth Long Island.

Junior Wells is blowing the harmonica. Buddy Guy is playing the guitar, and the song is "Hoodoo Man Blues". The lyric that sends Chance down chatter lane is "Somebody done hoodooed the hoodoo man."

"She must have hoodooed me a long time ago, because I been a fool for that woman since day one. Whatever she wanted me to do, I did. I thought she loved me. Two times I thought she loved me. Fool me once, shame on you. Fool me twice, shame on me.

"Yesterday morning, I stopped a man from killing her and we go to the Drake and fuck like long lost lovers. We were back together yesterday, got re-engaged . . . is that a word? Well, you know what I mean.

"Did I tell you my place got robbed? Yeap. And it was another woman I'd slept with, and she stole my BMW. You know it's a poor cowboy that doesn't have a horse. I have been riding buses all day. I rode an airplane too.

259

Patrice and I rode first class out to Vegas. Yeah, she thought I was 'sleep, but I heard her and Nash. I knocked his ass out. Damn. I beat up two men for her in two days.

"Did you know my mama works with us? Yeap. She's your daddy's secretary. My mama and your daddy work together. Ain't it a small world? And get this, she been with her boyfriend for fifteen years, but couldn't stay with me for a year. It must be something about me that drives women away.

"I went to church today, and I have to admit, there is something real good about that place: people praying for each other. I'm going back next Sunday." He drains the last of the Long Island Iced Tea.

"I was going to tell you to take me home, but the last person I want to see on earth, right now, is Patrice Trent. I'm selling that condo. I am never stepping another foot in there. The robbers cleaned me out. Nothing left in there but memories. I'm moving back out south, buying myself a nice two-room flat. Yeap. I'm moving back to the south side of the city and joining a church.

"Hey, that's Sonny Boy Williamson's 'Fattening Frogs For Snakes.' Love that song. Can I get you to take me to a hotel or should I call a couple of cabs for both of us?" When Chance stands, the room swings slightly to the left. It's not spinning, but he decides it's time to stop drinking.

"What, only you get to talk? I been sitting, listening, and holding my comments until I thought you were finished." Chance looks to Amy and laughs. She's right. He hasn't heard a word from her.

He sits back down. He hears himself say, "Bartender, two more Long Islands." He really didn't mean to say that. Well, ordering it doesn't mean he has to drink it.

"Amy, will you please forgive my rudeness and, please, feel free to talk?"

"First, I would like to address Patrice. You cannot blame yourself for her. Patrice has always been a flake. Not marrying her is a good thing. She has no loyalty. She doesn't give. She only takes. If she's not the star of the show, then there is no show in her mind. It's hard being her friend. I pity who she does marry.

"Now as far as the cab goes, I don't leave my Porsche anywhere. Yes, I'm drunk, but I'm five blocks from here. I've made this drive in this state many times. As far as you going to a hotel, I think it would be better for you to go to my place, because I can drive to the bakery early in the morning, then you can get the car and be back to the Lincoln Park office to meet with Maxine, who we will be there at no later than eight o'clock. That I promise. What do you think?"

Going to his white boss' daughter's house does not sound like the right thing for him to do, especially feeling as sociable as he does now. He decides to call the cab, but what comes out of his mouth is, "Sounds good. Do you have a washer, a dryer and an iron?"

"Yes."

"Okay."

Chance isn't sure how it happens. She is showing him the small closet where the washer and dryer are, and she takes off her jersey blouse to add to the small load of his shirt and socks.

"It has to balance," she says.

She has on no brassiere. Her small breasts require no support. Chance has never seen pink nipples in the flesh. While he stares, she says, "A lot smaller than Patrice's, right? I'm sure you'll find every part of me smaller than her."

She slips out of her jeans right in front of the washer. She has on a black lace thong. She pops it at her waist. "They don't make these in her size, do they?"

For the next hour and a half, Chance makes the most invigorating love of his life. His meat hasn't stayed this hard and this long since he was seventeen. He can't cum. No matter how hard he pounds into her, he cannot reach an orgasm. It is exhaustion and her complaints of dryness that finally stop them.

When she rolls out of her bed and goes into her nightstand, she retrieves a white tube. He watches her finger the contents of tube inside herself, then she squeezes some on the tip of his hard meat and rubs it over the length. She throws the tube to the floor and mounts him.

It sounds to Chance like she is having orgasm after orgasm, and he is getting a bit irritated because he felt he was nowhere near having one, until she stops her rapid thrusting and starts slow twisting. The slowing down, along with her moans, gets him where he wants to be. He releases his own overdue nut.

"Oh, you got to love that Viagra," she says, falling to the side of him.

That explains it. If he weren't so exhausted, he would argue with her, but all he wants to do is sleep.

Chance hears a loud, annoying chirping sound. He's been lying in Amy's bed awake for at least five minutes. From the bathroom, she yells, "Hit the teddy bear on the nightstand. Slap his head down."

Chance does and the chirping stops. The teddy bear has a clock in its stomach.

Amy comes out of the bathroom, nude and damp, with a towel around her hair.

"So, you've fucked the boss's daughter. What's next?" She lies on the pillow next to him.

"No. The boss's daughter fucked me. I was the one seduced last night."

"Perhaps, but did you like it?"

"Yes. I liked it a lot, but no more Viagra."

"Oh, that was a mistake on my part, one I will feel every time I sit today. You beat up my little kitty cat pretty bad. She's all puffy and tender. She's not used to such a big one, nor is she used to doing it for two hours and fifteen minutes. No more Viagra for your big buddy. He obviously doesn't need it."

Chance looks over at the teddy bear clock, because the way she is openly talking about her coochie is getting him hard.

"You excited and excite me, naturally."

"Little ol' me, excited you? I thought brothers liked 'the big booty.' I have a little booty. What about me excited you?"

"Honestly?"

"Yes, be honest."

"I have never seen pink nipples."

"What?"

"I have never seen pink nipples, straight pubic hair or thighs that didn't touch."

"So, it's purely physical."

"Yeah, right now it is."

"Chance, am I the first white girl you've slept with?"

"Yes."

"Was I any different than a black woman?"

"All women are different. Sleeping with two different black women yields two totally different experiences. So, I can't compare sleeping with you to sleeping with a black woman, but I can tell you I have never had an experience such as the one we shared."

"I like how you said that. If my kitty wasn't sore and tender, I would give you some more. Those words got to me."

"We don't have to use each other up right now, do we?"

"No, we don't, but if we continue to share experiences, we will have to keep it secret at least for a while."

"I agree."

*****

Nash was boring as hell. A whole can of whipped cream and nothing. No spark, no shimmer, no quiver, nothing. And he had the nerve to offer her a vibrator when he saw she was unsatisfied. He didn't even try to get hard again. He came and handed her a toy. Oh, hell no. And the fool even asked her to stay in Vegas for the rest of the week with him. Patrice couldn't get back to Chicago and Chance quick enough.

She needs a plan, a real good plan, a slick plan. A getting her man back plan. She needs a lie. A doctor's excuse. Anything to help her get her man back. Amy will be the only person who hasn't left for work yet that she knows. She needs to bounce her thoughts off of someone. She drives straight to Amy's house from the airport.

Patrice is standing on Amy's porch about to knock on the door, but what she sees doesn't register in her mind the right way. Behind Amy's glass panel doors, Patrice sees Chance and Amy locked in a hell of a kiss. The guy must just look like Chance. Patrice knocks, and when the guy that looks like Chance looks up, Patrice sees it is Chance, and she goes through the glass panels of the door.

Her large frame won't completely fit through the door panels, but she is able to get her arms in and her hands on Amy. She pulls her through the door panel onto the front porch. She throws her against the left wall, the right wall, and finally to the floor of the porch. She kicks her between her legs, in her stomach, in her neck, in her ears. Not satisfied with just kicking her, she drops down on her knees, onto her chest. She is trying to pull Amy's black hair out of her head when Chance pulls her off of Amy.

*****

Chance was kissing Amy, and suddenly, she was pulled from his arms. Patrice has snatched her through the door and is kicking her ass. He runs out onto the porch and tries to break the fight up, but Patrice's rage is too intense. He can't get through to her. There is nothing he can do to stop Patrice in this state. When she drops down on Amy's chest, Chance grabs her shoulders, stopping her from yanking Amy's hair out of her head.

Chance sees the police car pull up. They get out with weapons drawn, ordering him to let go of Patrice. Amy screams. The police fire upon him. Chance feels burning in his chest and shoulders. He has to let Patrice go.

A paramedic is asking him for the name of a family member. He closes his eyes.

A doctor is in his face, yelling about blood matching and a family member, and him losing too much blood. He closes his eyes.

"Maxine Waters," he hears a man shout.

Things are better when he closes his eyes; less noise, less frantic people, less bright lights.

*****

When Maxine gets the call from Jasper, all she understands is "hospital," "his mother," "Chance," and "blood." She drives non-stop from Palatine to the north side of Chicago. She parks in the emergency lot. In the emergency room, she spots Jasper pacing.

"Jasper."

"Maxy, come this way." He pulls her through double swinging, chrome-plated doors to Chance. He's on a stretcher. His shoulder and neck are covered in bandages. The bed next to him is empty. A doctor comes in and asks her if she's O positive. She says yes. She is instructed to get on the bed and lay back.

Jasper whispers in her ear, "I have to go check on my mother."

The nurse asks what her relationship is to the patient.

"Mother," she answers.

*****

When Chance wakes up, his throat hurts, and he can barely swallow. He is thirsty as hell.

"The damn police shot me. Oh, I got to sue them." He brings his right hand to his left shoulder. It is bandaged, and so is his neck. He has an IV in his hand, and he is hooked to at least two monitors. He looks under the sheet and sees a tube running into his meat, and his right knee is bandaged as well.

"I'll be damned."

A nurse enters the room. She is a round, older lady with rosy cheeks and grayish blond hair.

"It's good to see you awake, Chance. You gave us all quite a scare. Your poor mother has been here night and day." She checks his IV and goes under the sheet to check the catheter. "We can take that out today."

"How long have I been out?"

"Three days."

"How bad am I injured?"

"Well, you were shot five times. Three in the chest. Let's just say you won't be going out dancing for a while."

"I need a phone."

"Not yet. The doctor is on his way."

What the doctor tells him is that his right knee was replaced, his left lung has been punctured, his left shoulder was shattered and had to be rebuilt, and there are still bullet fragments in his chest, close to his heart. They will have to be removed when he is stronger.

He wasn't feeling too bad before talking with the doctor. After, he feels trounced. His knee and his shoulder ache.

His first visitor is Maxine. She walks into the room, freshly dressed and smiling at him. She has flowers in her arms and a *Black Enterprise* magazine in her hand.

"I bought you fresh flowers and something to read. Fresh flowers always make me feel better."

"The nurse said you been here night and day."

"She's exaggerating."

"I thought so."

Maxine is standing at the side of his bed. She adjusts his sheet and blanket. "Chance, ours is not going to be a normal mother and son relationship."

"What's happening at work?" He's trying to change the subject. He has enough aches. He doesn't need a headache.

"Sidney cancelled his test, got released from the hospital and met with your sales and administrative staff. He went out to Better Butter and recruited a salesman. He and Amy are filling in for you until you're released."

"How is Amy?"

"Not the best. She and Patrice Trent had been friends for years. Last I heard she's suing her. Patrice broke her ribs."

"Damn. How much does Mr. Sharp know?"

"Very little. Amy has been tight-lipped about whatever happened. He's not the prying type when it comes to Amy."

Chance pushes the button that administers the pain medicine.

"Is Patrice in jail?"

"Hardly. This will be handled in civil court."

"Was Elder Collins at the hospital when they brought me in?"

"Yes. His mother suffered a stroke. She's home now, but Jasper swears her having the stroke was God getting him here. It was Jasper that got me here to you."

"Oh, we have the same blood type. I was trying to understand what that doctor was yelling about. Our blood must match. Imagine that." He sleepily grins at her.

"Do you always have to be a smart ass?"

"Only with you, mother."

Chance feels the pain medicine taking over, and gives in to it.

*****

Three weeks pass before Patrice decides she is no longer angry with Chance, and decides to go to the hospital to give him the opportunity to make up with her. She wouldn't have gone this day, except she is curious about the sale of his condominium. Her father told her Chance sold the unit and made out quite well, and he's purchased a two-room flat on south Drexel Avenue. Why would Chance move so far away from her? He certainly can't expect her to spend nights on the South Side.

At the nurse's station, she learns that Chance has had to have another surgery to remove bullet fragments from his chest, and his visits are limited to five minutes.

When she walks into the room, she sees Chance propped up with pillows. He doesn't look that ill to her.

"Hello, Chance."

She doesn't understand the grimace on his face. He must be in pain from the surgery. She steps closer because she sees he's struggling to speak. She lowers her ear to his thin, dry lips and hears, "Get the fuck out of here."

Shocked, she stands erect. It must be the medicine, she thinks. She leaves and decides it will probably be better to talk to him when he is released. She will plan a big party for him. It will be the urban affair of the year.

*****

When Chance is released from the rehab five months after he was shot by the police, he has to walk with a cane. The physical therapist tells him and Maxine that the odds are that he will be required to use it for the rest of his life. He doubts it, and so does his mother. They tell the therapist that the strongest trait in their family is overcoming odds.

Chance is leaving the rehab a wealthy man. Maxine's lawyers settled out of court with the Chicago police department for $3.5 million. Chance's lawyers were talking $150,000. When he told Maxine, she asked him if her lawyers could get involved. He hesitated until she said, "Please."

Not only has she secured him a fortune, she insists on living with him in his new home until he has settled in, and she isn't taking no for an answer. Nor is she accepting a refusal from him about being Jasper's best man at their church wedding.

She joined the church after Chance's chest surgery, because she'd prayed with Jasper and promised his Jesus that if Chance pulled through the surgery and allowed her into his life, she would join the church. Both things happened, so she joined.

They are in the rehab parking lot, attempting to pull past a bright red BMW that is blocking their path. The woman driving the car obviously sees them. The door of the BMW opens and a pregnant woman gets out.

She walks to the passenger side of the car where Chance is sitting. Her hair remains short and her legs still pull his eyes to them. It's too cool for the short skirt she's wearing. Chance figures she's in it for him. He rolls down the window, smiling. He's happy to see the woman and the car. A cool breeze blows into the window.

"I heard you got all shot up. I was coming to see you."

She's speaking with what Chance thinks is honest concern. He accepts that. Yes, she stole from him, but her actions hurt way less than Patrice's. He thought about that often while he was stretched out in the hospital. He spent much less time in her company, but thoughts of her filled his mind as much as Patrice did. The fact is, he's happy to see her because he cares about her. He wants to get out and hug her, but he sits still.

"Nice car," he says.

"Yeah, I got it painted red. Looks better on me." She drops two Rolex watches into his lap and a crumbled $300 check.

He grins and looks over to Maxine and says, "Mother, this is Nadine, a friend of mine."

Nadine bends over to see into the car. "Good to meet you, ma'am."

"You too, dear," Maxine returns.

Nadine stands straight and Chance's eyes go to her swollen stomach.

"Whose baby you carrying in your stomach?" Chance asks.

"Whose you think?"

Chance sees no challenge in her eyes. He hopes it is his child. They'd made love good enough to create a life. Of that he is certain.

"We're going to have to take a blood test."

"Like I care." She reaches into the car and rubs the back of his neck.

Her hands are gentle and her touch makes him think back to their shared time. He's soft on her, but he hopes his eyes don't show it.

"Where are you staying?" He looks directly into her face. She looks tired and beaten. Something bad has happened to Nadine.

"With you. I went by the condo a week ago, but my key didn't fit."

Her hand is on his earlobe now.

"Yeah, I sold it . . . Where is your son?"

She stops playing with his ear and sighs. He sees her tears welling.

"His father took him and left for Mexico right after we robbed you. I been trying to find them, but I never knew the bastard's real last name. And the Mexican police won't help me because his father is Mexican. It's only so much I can do over the phone. Andrew is gone for good, unless his father decides to bring him back."

Nadine is hurting. Chance sees it and says, "Follow us on home. We'll talk more there".

"I need gas money."

Maxine hands him a twenty. He passes it to Nadine and she walks back to the red BMW.

Maxine says, "I like her."

Chance says, "Yeah, me too. And that's a problem."

OCTOBER 2005
1-893196-23-2

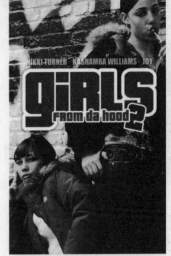

OCTOBER 2005
1-893196-28-3

NOVEMBER 2005
1-893196-25-9

DECEMBER 2005
0-9747025-9-5

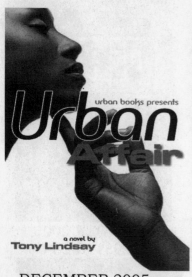

DECEMBER 2005
1-893196-27-5

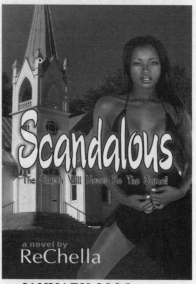

JANUARY 2006
1893196-30-5

JANUARY 2006
1893196-29-1

FEBRUARY 2006
1-893196-41-0

FEBRUARY 2006
1-893196-37-2

MARCH 2006
1-893196-32-1

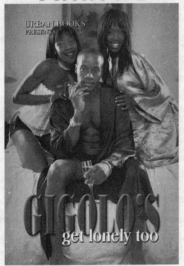

MARCH 2006
1-893196-33-X

APRIL 2006
1-893196-34-8

OTHER URBAN BOOKS TITLES

Title	Author	Quantity	Cost
Drama Queen	LaJill Hunt		$14.95
No More Drama	LaJill Hunt		$14.95
Shoulda Woulda Coulda	LaJill Hunt		$14.95
Is It A Crime	Roy Glenn		$14.95
MOB	Roy Glenn		$14.95
Drug Related	Roy Glenn		$14.95
Lovin' You Is Wrong	Alisha Yvonne		$14.95
Bulletproof Soul	Michelle Buckley		$14.95
You Wrong For That	Toschia		$14.95
A Gangster's girl	Chunichi		$14.95
Married To The Game	Chunichi		$14.95
Sex In The Hood	White Chocalate		$14.95
Little Black Girl Lost	Keith Lee Johnson		$14.95
Sister Girls	Angel M. Hunter		$14.95
Driven	KaShamba Williams		$14.95
Street Life	Jihad		$14.95
Baby Girl	Jihad		$14.95
A Thug's Life	Thomas Long		$14.95
Cash Rules	Thomas Long		$14.95
The Womanizers	Dwayne S. Joseph		$14.95
Never Say Never	Dwayne S. Joseph		$14.95
She's Got Issues	Stephanie Johnson		$14.95
Rockin' Robin	Stephanie Johnson		$14.95
Sins Of The Father	Felicia Madlock		$14.95
Back On The Block	Felicia Madlock		$14.95
Chasin' It	Tony Lindsay		$14.95
Street Possession	Tony Lindsay		$14.95
Around The Way Girls	LaJill Hunt		$14.95
Around The Way Girls 2	LaJill Hunt		$14.95

Girls From Da Hood	Nikki Turner		$14.95
Girls from Da Hood 2	Nikki Turner		$14.95
Dirty Money	Ashley JaQuavis		$14.95
Mixed Messages	LaTonya Y. Williams		$14.95
Don't Hate The Player	Brandie		$14.95
Payback	Roy Glenn		$14.95
Scandalous	ReChella		$14.95
Urban Affair	Tony Lindsey		$14.95
Harlem Confidential	Cole Riley		$14.95

Urban Books
74 Andrews Ave.
Wheatley Heights, NY 11798
Subtotal: _____
Postage:_____ Calculate postage and handling as follows: Add
$2.50 for the first item and $1.25 for each additional item
Total: _____
Name: _____
Address:_____
City: _____ State: _____ Zip: _____
Telephone: (   ) _____
Type of Payment (Check: ___   Money Order: ___)
All orders must be prepaid by check or money order drawn on an American
bank.
Books may sometimes be out of stock. In that instance, please select your
alternate choices below.
                              Alternate Choices:
                    1._____
                    2._____
          PLEASE ALLOW 4-6 WEEKS FOR SHIPPING